BOSTON TANGLE

Boston Tangle

Regency Comes to America

Judith Lown

eFrog Press

In memory of my parents, who fell in love in Boston.

Acknowledgments

With gratitude to Linda Scott, without whom *A Match for Lady Constance* would be an untitled partial chapter in the hard drive of a discarded computer, and *A Sensible Lady* and *Boston Tangle* would never have been written. Many thanks to Nancy Johnson, for unfailing encouragement and valuable input. And where would I be without Shelly Chung, an editor who really understands what I'm trying to do and does everything possible to make me look good. As always, my love and gratitude to my husband, John, for his support and unfaltering affirmation.

CONTENTS

Prologue

Hatton Court
England
July 1816

"Drusilla, darling, I can only hope that *someday* you will find the happiness I have found."

Lady Constance Hatton swept into my room, a pale peach dressing gown swirling about her, clutching her fluffy white dog, Medora. With golden curls held back by a matching peach ribbon, Lady Constance would have looked as young and fresh as a girl in her first season, were it not for the subject of her delight: a necklace—no, really a collar—of diamonds that twinkled brilliantly even in subdued candlelight, and matching earrings that looked like miniature chandeliers.

"Constance! I have never seen anything so magnificent! But you had better wear them only in the evening. In sunlight, they will blind anyone gazing on them!"

We both tried to muffle our laughter. Family and guests of Hatton Court were settling in for a good night's rest in preparation for the crowning celebration of a week of festivities. The wedding of Lady Constance Hatton to Blaise de Grenault, Marquis de Rochmont.

Lady Constance settled into one of a pair of winged chairs flanking the fireplace and adjusted the peach bow securing Medora's topknot.

"It has been quite the most delightful week, hasn't it, Drusilla? But, I must say, I am eager to have it over. I so long to go away with Rochmont. Strange, isn't it? Four months ago I hadn't as much as exchanged two sentences with him, and now, being with him is essential for my happiness.

"We'll be going to the Continent, of course. I really have no idea when we shall return. I shall miss you dreadfully, Drusilla. We must write to each other. I don't want to lose your friendship. And, of course, Rochmont and I will eventually make our way back to England." She giggled. "Cannot you picture Mama pursuing us if we don't?"

Lady Chase was perfectly named. And her involvement in her children's lives was well known.

Lady Constance sobered abruptly and began to pace, absently patting Medora. I recognized the familiar signs that my friend was trying to address a matter she considered to be serious.

I remained seated in the chair opposite the one she had just vacated and watched her pace back and forth across the room, earrings swinging, gown floating about her.

She stopped abruptly and fixed me with a stern look.

"The one concern I have, the only concern that I wish I could see resolved before Rochmont and I leave, is *you*, Drusilla. Your happiness."

Lady Constance had been an incorrigible matchmaker. I assumed she had given it up when she fell in love with Lord Rochmont. But, evidently, I was wrong.

She must have read my thoughts.

"Don't worry, Drusilla. I'm not hatching some scheme to match you with Ferdy Courlan or Alastair Plinkindon."

She settled herself once more in the chair opposite mine and studied Medora for a moment.

"It's Jack, of course."

Please! Don't let's talk about Jack.

But I saved my breath and my dignity. If Lady Constance wanted to talk about Jack and me, she would talk about Jack and me. And I would have to guard not just my words, but also my tone of voice, my facial expression, even my gestures. Lady Constance, having navigated five London seasons, was skilled at detecting what people did not want to say.

I rarely use the subterfuge of deliberate misunderstanding, but I needed time to collect my thoughts.

"Whatever is the matter with Captain Hatton, Constance? He seemed perfectly himself this evening."

"Good lord! It is worse than I thought." Lady Constance covered her eyes with slender hands. The diamond engagement ring she wore winked at me.

I was going to have to bluster this one out. "Don't talk nonsense!"

But Lady Constance persisted, answering in soft, sad tones.

"Drusilla, my dear, dear friend. I am not asking you to confide in me. I wouldn't presume. But I know my darling brother so very well. I confess that I used to be amused watching him enchant gullible females with his boyish charm and deceptively guileless blue eyes, until they believed that *this* time, his affections were truly engaged. *This* time, a declaration of undying love and an offer of matrimony were certain.

"I've hesitated to speak to you, because you really have conducted yourself impeccably in the face of Jack's marked attentions. Not once have I seen you gazing after him as he walked away from you. Nor have I seen you pause upon entering a room, searching for him. I have never heard you make reference to him in conversation with other ladies, a sure mark of infatuation.

"I hope with all my heart that the absence of these signs of your attachment to Jack are evidence of true indifference to his attentions. I pray that you are the one lady who can actually enjoy Jack's company on his own terms and not get your heart broken."

Lady Constance favored me with a tremulous smile. She had perfected the art of smiling through tears without actually crying.

My friend was asking for reassurance and I would reassure her, as much for my sake as for hers. This moment—if ever—I did not wish to examine my feelings for Captain Jack Hatton.

"Captain Hatton has provided me with hours of entertainment, not to mention the pleasure of being envied by every lady who sees him chatting or dancing with me. But I have never let myself dream dreams of true love where he is concerned, I promise you, Constance. Stop worrying, and get all the rest you need to look as radiant as you will feel tomorrow."

Lady Constance rose to take her leave. I followed her to the door. Turning, she gave me a parting smile, reassured that her glorious day would not have the tiniest cloud of worry.

"You have relieved my mind, my dear Drusilla. You are the best of friends," she said before closing the door behind her.

I walked to a window that overlooked the lawn sloping down to a tree-lined stream. A decorative bridge over the stream was visible in the moonlight.

Give yourself credit, Drusilla, for relieving your friend's mind. But what are you to do to relieve your own? Or to soothe the ache that is beginning to develop in the region of your heart?

Of course, I had always known that permitting myself to be the lady of the moment for Captain John Hatton, while flattering and even sometimes exhilarating, could only end in dullness and loneliness for me. If I were lucky. For most ladies, it ended in heartbreak. Jack Hatton never made promises he failed to fulfill.

With me, at least, he never made improper advances. He simply added fun and sparkle to ordinary life. And, with amazingly little effort, he made one feel as if one were the prettiest, wittiest female he had ever met. The intoxication that resulted was more potent than any champagne or brandy could induce.

Tonight, at the conclusion of our waltz, he had, as usual, bowed over my hand and said, "Thank you, Miss Fortesque."

Then he had looked into my eyes and simply said my Christian name for the very first time: "Drusilla."

Only my name. But his voice and his eyes implied so much more.

Then he turned, and walked away.

A lady of weaker constitution would have fainted.

Late the next afternoon, family and guests gathered on the front steps of Hatton Court to send off the newlyweds for their wedding trip.

An elegant landau awaited the couple.

A footman opened the massive doors of the mansion and the Marquis and Marquise de Rochmont emerged arm in arm. The Marquise, Lady Constance, was holding her little dog, Medora. She had decided to put the eyesight of those assembled in jeopardy by wearing the diamond necklace and earrings I had seen the night before. The couple stood for a moment, Constance smiling at friends and family and Lord Rochmont gazing fondly at her, his harsh features softened.

They descended the stairs slowly, Lady Constance floating in a cloud of *eau de nil* chiffon, diamonds dazzling in the sunlight. Across from where I stood on the first step, Lady Chase dabbed at her eyes with a tiny lace square. Lord Chase's face was stern and he swallowed hard.

Beside me, Jack Hatton murmured his approval. "I must hand it to Connie. She found the one man in the world who can indulge her whims without letting her shred his independent judgment."

Lady Constance paused as she reached the bottom step and kissed her mother and father. Then she turned and gave me Medora to hold. The former stray from the streets of London was wearing what appeared to be a diamond collar.

I glanced at Lord Rochmont, who raised an eyebrow and looked amused.

"Drusilla, darling, do be a dear and hold Medora for me whilst I get situated in the carriage and throw my bouquet," Lady Constance said.

She bent to kiss the air by my cheek and whispered, "I'll throw it in your direction. Please do try to catch it."

Constance was clearly too caught up in the excitement of the moment to realize that catching a bouquet while holding a dog might be beyond my skill.

Lord Rochmont assisted his bride into the landau. He bent to say something into her ear. We could all hear her silvery laugh in response, and see her slender arms reach around his neck—and her bouquet slip to the floor of the carriage. The driver gave the horses leave to start and the newlyweds were conveyed down the driveway wrapped in each other's arms, unaware of family and friends waving farewell from the steps.

I looked down at Medora.

If a bride throws you her bouquet, it means you will marry within a year. What does it mean if she gives you her dog?

When I looked up to share my amusement with Captain Hatton, he wasn't by my side.

Jack Hatton, who had been my constant companion throughout the week, simply disappeared for the balance of the afternoon and evening. I had prepared myself never again to see him or hear from him once I had returned to Bath from Hatton Court, but I was shattered by his early desertion. Would it have been all that difficult for him to play the gallant with me for one more afternoon? One more evening?

I threw myself into being charming to Ferdy Courlan, who never failed to be grateful for any attention from a lady. His enthusiastic, if somewhat disjointed, discussion of some of his newly acquired horses required no effort on my part to think of witty repartee. Which was fortunate. I had developed a headache and retired at the earliest possible moment, pleading fatigue from the excitement of the day.

Chilly drizzle greeted me the next morning when the chambermaid drew open the curtains. How fitting.

When I arrived in the breakfast room, it was empty of guests. I hoped be able to eat and escape without having to make conversation with anyone.

"Good morning, Miss Fortesque."

Unmistakably, *his* voice.

"Good morning, Captain Hatton."

He strolled over to the breakfront and hummed softly as he lifted silver covers off chafing dishes, helping himself to generous portions of poached eggs, ham, sausage, and four hot rolls. After pouring a cup of coffee—a taste he had acquired in his travels—he sat at the end of the table, just to my right.

"I'd imagined I would be the first to breakfast this morning, Miss Fortesque. But I see that, once more, I underestimated your common sense. Good idea to get an early start when traveling. You were planning to return to Bath today, were you not?"

His smile was guileless as always. Perhaps I was wrong in suspecting that he had deliberately planned to avoid speaking to me by having an early breakfast.

I confirmed my plans to return to Bath.

"Sorry to disappear so abruptly yesterday. Was summoned to a meeting by one of my father's minions. Seems I am going to be traveling soon, too. I'm off to Saint Petersburg. 'With all due dispatch,' I believe were my father's instructions."

Jack speared a bite of ham and chewed meditatively.

I sipped some cold tea.

"Constance believes that my association with the Foreign Office is just for my own amusement, Miss Fortesque. Dancing with bored diplomats' wives, keeping ambassadors' sons out of the worst gaming hells—that sort of thing. But Constance fails to see the sacrifices required."

He managed a look of saintly deprivation as he applied generous dollops of butter and raspberry jam to a roll.

"Take for example, my current assignment. Could it have been made in April when there was a chance of completing it and escaping a Russian winter before one is literally frozen in? One does not like to accuse one's own parent of lack of parental feeling, but ..."

Jack savored a mouthful of roll, butter, and jam.

I began to mentally compose a brief, casual farewell.

No doubt you will find no end of entertainments in Saint Petersburg, Captain Hatton, and I do wish you well.

I was eager to make my exit before I betrayed the sadness that threatened to overwhelm me, knowing that I would have no hope at all of seeing him for a year or more.

But, absorbed in his own thoughts, he continued his monologue without expecting any response on my part, oblivious to my distress over our imminent separation.

"My father's faith in my ability to decipher the arcane goings-on in the czar's court and survive the forbidding winter is flattering. But I could bear it if he chose to flatter someone else. From what I hear, my choice of diversions will be riding over endless frozen wastes in pursuit of bears and wolves or dancing attention on devious princesses in overheated palaces."

He stirred a teaspoon of sugar into his coffee.

"I have no doubt that, come December, I will be ready to *kill* for the sound of an ordinary English voice. Not one couched in diplomatic pomposities or silken promises. Just a normal English voice speaking normal English."

He continued to stir his coffee, frowning.

Suddenly, his face brightened. "By Jove!"

He smiled his most enchanting smile and took my hand.

"How fortunate that I should encounter you before you removed to Bath, Miss Fortesque. Otherwise, it might never have occurred to me. Just think, Miss Fortesque—*Drusilla. You* could accompany me to Saint Petersburg! What would be an ordeal for one could be an adventure for two!"

Whatever was my charming companion proposing? Had he taken leave of his senses? What had I ever done to give him the idea that I would abandon all propriety, and run off with him to my ruin? I would be a pariah if I agreed to his plan. Not even Lady Constance could reestablish me socially.

I was too appalled to speak, but removed my hand from his and stood to leave.

Jack stood, too and retrieved my hand.

"I am so very sorry, Miss Fortesque. What an idiot I was to frame things so poorly."

His smile invited my forgiveness.

"Of course I meant that we should wed, Miss Fortesque."

My first—and no doubt only—marriage proposal. Given in such an offhanded manner that the acceptance would seem overeager and the usual formula for rejection would seem presumptuous. I feared my hurt showed on my face. But Jack Hatton was too caught up in his scheme of brightening the dreaded Russian winter to notice.

"We'd have to get a special license, of course. But it should be no problem to find an obliging bishop."

Bishops were always eager to oblige any Hatton of Hatton Court.

He looked surprised when I snatched my hand from his grasp.

I needed to leave the breakfast room before I dissolved in tears.

"Tempting as it might be to go off on an adventurous lark with you, Captain Hatton, I shall have to decline your generous offer for any number of reasons. But principally, I cannot see your plan as a foundation for a reasonably happy marriage. Indeed, I suspect it would only lead to misery—well before the long Russian winter permits us to return to England."

Jack's face became grim.

"You will forgive me, Miss Fortesque, for so completely misjudging your character. I had thought you possessed more spine and independence of mind than the typical miss who inhabits the drawing rooms of the *ton*. But I see I flattered you. You talk a good game, but underneath the veneer of originality dwells a soul as prosaic as all the rest. I can only be grateful to have discovered my mistake before making it permanent."

With a curt nod, Captain Hatton left the breakfast room.

More spine and independence of mind. Jack Hatton's words echoed in my brain along with the crunch of the wheels of the carriage taking me back to Bath and the quiet life I shared with my aunts there before Lady Constance and Captain Jack Hatton opened an exciting new world to me.

In a sense, the recrimination had been correct. In spite of being treated like a convenient afterthought, if Captain Hatton had spoken one word of fondness for me, much less love, I would even now be writing a hasty note to my aunts asking for their best wishes, and waiting for word that Jack had found a bishop who would grant us a special license. Only hurt pride and the anger accompanying it had kept me from throwing caution to the winds and sailing off with Darling Jack Hatton for Saint Petersburg.

My mind told me that I had narrowly escaped misery. Dependent upon a gentleman who made a career of avoiding serious attachments. Trapped in a marriage that might not have the blessing of his aristocratic parents. Seeing boredom and resentment replace my husband's smiles and witty sallies. Or worse. Jack's fondness for opera dancers was no secret. And his sudden display of anger was instructive to any lady believing that the worst she could receive from him was neglect.

But my heart told me that I had missed my one chance to really live. My heart reminded me that the gloom I felt was not just a reaction to the rain that now pounded on the roof of the carriage. My heart warned me that without Jack Hatton's blue-eyed smiles, the sun might never truly shine for me again.

Stop being dramatic!

I must have spoken, because Medora looked up at me from where she had been sleeping in my lap. I patted her and she settled back to sleep. She was still wearing the *eau de nil* ribbon in her topknot from yesterday, but I had left her collar in my room along with a note. If those diamonds on the collar she had worn yesterday were as real as they looked, I couldn't risk being responsible for something I could not afford to replace.

I might never see Jack Hatton again. Who knew when I would see Lady Constance again? All I had left to remind me of that magical chapter in my life was the stray dog who had brought us together the day we joined forces to rescue her from a cruel London urchin.

I patted her topknot and realized that it was wet with my tears.

Chapter One

Boston

Late March 1818

In spite of the chill, I was happy to be outdoors. More than a week past Easter, and finally there was sufficient sunshine to signal the possibility that winter might finally be at an end. Surely daffodils would be blooming in England now. Here in Boston, I strained to imagine the faintest hint of green on the bare branches of trees that marched in a ring around Washington Place atop Fort Hill.

I had meant to paint a picture of the harbor—sparkling water, fishing boats in the foreground, billowing sails of an oceangoing ship or two in the background, fluffy clouds overhead. But a few blasts of icy wind off the bay made me turn my easel around, so I faced a grand townhouse that stood out as the most lavish amongst the handsome dwellings that circled the park. I had never before tackled an architectural subject, but the challenge was appealing. Furthermore, I needed something to occupy my time until Hez returned from running errands for Cook.

I set to work blocking out the main sections of the gray stone façade. Five shallow, crescent-shaped steps with wrought iron balustrades on either side led from the street to an imposing front door, which had been painted black. I could barely discern the wrought iron door knocker, which blended into the color of the door. Indeed, the house had an unwelcoming look. Shutters at every window of all four stories were closed. But centered at the top of the house was a partial fifth story—essentially a large room—with an unshuttered window looking over the harbor. In the middle of the window stood a telescope mounted on a tripod. Whoever used that telescope would be second only to those who manned signal towers in knowing which ships were approaching Boston Harbor.

As I painted, a gentleman stepped out of the front door and paused with a proprietary air to survey the panorama before him. He pulled on gloves, accepted a walking stick from a servant half hidden in the doorway, descended the stairs, crossed the street, and walked directly toward me. I concentrated on my work, hoping he would continue on his way without speaking.

"It really is perfectly correct for you to recognize my presence, Miss Fortesque, Miss Drusilla Fortesque, I believe. We *were* presented to each other at the Corrings', although with the crush, I can well understand if you have forgotten."

I certainly had not forgotten a gentleman who stood out for the perfection of his tailoring and the arrogance of his bearing among dozens of exquisitely tailored, arrogant gentlemen. Indeed, it was his tailoring and bearing that made him memorable—and his face, which at first glance appeared to be bland, but upon closer observation was closed, almost guarded.

"Sir Clive Brampton." Paintbrush in one hand, wiping rag in the other, extending my hand was not possible. I dipped a tiny curtsy.

Did I imagine a shadow cross his face, or had the sun dipped behind a cloud?

He replaced the finely crafted top hat he had doffed while greeting me, and moved to view my work, crossing his arms as he silently studied my painting for a full minute.

"One must admire your courage in attempting such a subject. I assume your training has been restricted to floral arrangements and gentle landscapes. If you are pleased with the finished product, let me know. I rather like the idea of hanging a portrait of my home in my home."

"Perhaps, then, it would be best if you sought out a *professional* who is *trained* in painting architectural subjects, Sir Clive. A gentleman of your discrimination would never be satisfied with the efforts of an amateur."

"False modesty does not become you, Miss Fortesque."

His straight mouth twitched a hint of a smile. Whether acknowledging an unintended rhyme or reluctantly acknowledging some worthiness in my efforts, I couldn't discern. I did not intend to ask for clarification.

"Your work shows promise, Miss Fortesque. And if the finished product lives up to that promise, I will make first claim to it. I wouldn't think of insulting you with an offer of money. But I am expecting some fine amber on the first ship out of the Baltic this spring. I imagine your aunt knows a jeweler who could use it to make up some stunning pieces for the two of you."

He tipped his hat, bid me farewell, and departed toward the harbor and the new Corring Wharf, where he maintained a suite of offices.

"Why you insisted on exposing your lovely complexion to this brutal wind is beyond my comprehension. You must protect it at all costs."

Aunt Camellia's tone was softly recriminating. She believed the maintenance of one's appearance is a lady's most important responsibility. And her pale, unlined face and glossy, fashionably arranged auburn hair were testimony to her devotion to that priority.

Medora looked up from where she was curled next to Aunt Camellia on the chaise lounge and licked a cake crumb off her black nose. The dog I had twice rescued showed no inclination to bestir herself to greet me.

"Now, Mama." Looking up from the notebook in which she was writing, my cousin, Ivy, remonstrated, "Cousin Drusilla is of a heartier constitution than you are and she is less preoccupied with feminine concerns of appearance. I find her independence of mind admirable."

Aunt Camellia gazed heavenward in silent petition before answering her daughter.

"Drusilla, bless her heart, is of an age where independence of mind is just as well. But you, my dear child, would be better off with that book on your head, practicing grace and elegance rather than scratching down lord knows what vacuous thoughts that float through your mind."

I feared Ivy might burst into tears, but she silently put down her pencil, closed the book, placed it on her head, and began to walk slowly across the room, trying to approximate Aunt Camellia's strict standards of proper posture for young ladies.

Ada brought me a cup of hot tea and one of the small iced cakes that Aunt Camellia favored. As I settled into a chair by the fire, Medora hopped off the chaise and made her way to where I sat, tail wagging.

Might as well let her have the entire cake. I had quite lost my appetite. In the short time since I entered her sitting room, Aunt Camellia had gently reminded me that she considered me to be lacking in feminine wiles and too advanced in age to be taught them.

But why should I be letting Aunt Camellia's assessment bother me now? I had known it almost from the moment of our meeting in Bath last July. A meeting that took place a year after my hasty refusal of Captain Jack Hatton's casual proposal of marriage.

Now *I* was the one I feared might burst into tears.

"However did you occupy all your time out in the elements?"

For once I was grateful for the distraction of Aunt Camellia's inquisitiveness. But I was unsure just how many details of my morning I wished to share.

"I did some painting."

"How lovely."

Aunt Camellia approved of ladies showing off aesthetic talents.

"What did you paint? I think you have real talent, Cousin Drusilla. Will you show us what you painted this morning?"

Ivy's book fell off her head. She didn't bother to replace it.

"It's not yet finished," I temporized.

"But the way you prepare the background and outline the subject fascinates me. I have tried and tried to get the knack of it, but Mama has declared me hopeless. Please, Cousin?" Ivy pleaded.

I leafed through my folder of paintings and extracted what I had begun that morning. Aunt Camellia and Ivy studied it in puzzlement.

"That's nothing like what you usually paint." Ivy didn't bother to hide her disappointment.

"A strange subject for certain, but it is a grand house," Aunt Camellia observed.

She had moved from her chaise and was studying the painting with narrowed eyes. A sign of genuine interest. She was forever reminding Ivy and me that frowning and squinting were to be avoided because they cause lines on a lady's face.

I was sure that Aunt Camellia was cataloguing all of Boston's most impressive residences. It wouldn't be long before she ferreted out the name of the owner of the house depicted in my picture.

"It's certainly not on Park Row, and I can't think of any house on Beacon Hill that looks like that."

"Hez was running errands for Cook along the wharf and dropped me off on the hill that overlooks the harbor. I fancied I could paint a picture of ships and water and clouds, that sort of thing. But the wind was so sharp off the bay, I was forced to turn my back to it. This house was what I was facing, so I decided to try a new challenge."

Aunt Camellia laughed her soft little laugh. "My dear Drusilla! Do you have *any* idea who lives in that house?"

I would have to tread carefully. I did not want to discuss an exchange of my painting for fine amber. Indeed, I was reluctant for Aunt Camellia to know much of anything of my encounter with Sir Clive Brampton. Truth be told, my aunt's favorite entertainment was social intrigue. And where it was not present, she would manufacture it. I didn't care if she wished to fabricate whatever she chose to about Sir Clive, but I preferred not to be included in her speculations.

Sir Clive, reputed to be of enormous wealth, had arrived in Boston shortly after the cessation of the recent war, taken possession of the mansion on Washington Place, and leased offices in the new Corring Wharf. It was thought that he had close business dealings with Josiah Corring and, quite possibly, marital prospects with Miss Beryl Corring, Josiah's daughter, who was universally recognized as the richest, most beautiful—and therefore most sought-after—young lady of Boston.

"Oh yes." I tried to sound as matter-of-fact as possible. "It belongs to Sir Clive Brampton. I believe he is in shipping."

Aunt Camellia was so amused that she permitted herself a series of little laughs as she settled back on her chaise.

"To say that Sir Clive Brampton is in shipping is to say that Bonaparte had political ambition. Sir Clive doesn't have a fleet of ships as does your uncle, my dear Derrick. Sir Clive has *fleets* of ships. He doesn't just trade in beaver from the Pacific. He is in the India trade, the China trade, and heaven only knows what other trade."

I could have added the Baltic trade, but I resisted.

Aunt Camellia sighed before continuing.

"Apparently, Sir Clive has some business dealings with Josiah Corring, apart from leasing offices and warehouses in the new wharf. If Derrick were here, he would have ferreted it all out. And did you notice Miss Beryl Corring's attentiveness to Sir Clive at the reception? Rumor is that the Corring-Brampton relationship might very well involve something much more permanent than shares in voyages and warehouse leases.

"I hear that Sir Clive has sent his man, Starnes, to New Bedford, to ferret out those Quakers' secrets, which means that he will soon have a whaling fleet, if he hasn't one already. Of course, the best families of Boston are not associated with whaling. I wonder what the Corrings think of *that* endeavor. Perhaps Sir Clive is of a more independent nature than they had reckoned with."

Aunt Camellia tapped a perfectly manicured index finger against her delicately rouged lower lip.

"I wouldn't wish to make a prediction about anything Sir Clive might be thinking or what he might do," I said, tiring of Aunt Camellia's embroidering on rumors. "I have never encountered a gentleman who could maintain a less readable countenance. And his arrogance and abruptness border on rudeness."

Aunt Camellia sat up straight.

"He *spoke* to you? He saw your little painting?"

"That is how I knew who lives in the house. He studied my work for a full minute without saying a word and declared it promising—for an amateur."

Aunt Camellia lifted a finely arched eyebrow.

"How very, very interesting," was all she said before turning the subject to Ivy's spring wardrobe.

That afternoon, as usual, while Aunt Camellia and Cousin Ivy napped, I set up my easel in the window of the front parlor, which looked across to the Mall and the Common beyond it. Before returning to England in August, I would have to decide what to do with the bulging portfolio of watercolors I had produced that recorded the cycle of the seasons in the trees lining the Mall. When I had arrived, it was still summer, and the trees were in full, green leaf. Then I had attempted to paint the glory of their fiery autumn colors. But all too soon, the branches stood bare, the only cheer was brought by a red bird, called a cardinal, I was informed. As winter days stretched on and spring came with no noticeable relief from frigid weather, I looked to the bright red bird for encouragement.

But today my cardinal was no place to be seen. Neither was his drab little mate. I gave up trying to resist the gloomy spirits that had been threatening my equanimity all day. It was homesickness, I told myself. I missed my family back in Bath. But I had accepted the invitation to spend a year in Boston because life with my mother's aunts and sisters in Bath had become stultifying and I had been quite desperate for a change of scene.

When Uncle Derrick Fortesque, his wife, Aunt Camellia, and their daughter, Ivy, appeared, the distraction was a godsend. Uncle Derrick, the black sheep of my father's family, had made a fortune during his years of wandering and had settled in Boston.

Aunt Camellia, noticeably younger than my uncle, was fashionable and amusing. And my cousin, Ivy, flattered me with her shy admiration.

After a week of exploring Bath and its environs, Aunt Camellia had invited me to return with her and Ivy to Boston, while Uncle Derrick continued on to the Mediterranean and parts East to explore new opportunities for commerce.

Ivy had just celebrated her seventeenth birthday, and Aunt Camellia thought that before Ivy turned eighteen, she needed to put her hair up and be introduced to society.

"I'm thinking of May," Aunt Camellia said. "Ivy's birthday won't be until July first, but if we wait until then, she'll miss all of the spring and early summer socializing. So I shall give a party earlier and call it her eighteenth birthday celebration. No need to bother with the precise detail of her actual birthday.

"It will be a small affair. I am from Baltimore, you know, so I have no family connections in Boston, which puts Ivy at something of a disadvantage. But England is generally looked to in matters of taste and manners, so it would help her confidence to have a cousin by her side, who has been out in London society and can give her pointers on how to go on."

"I must warn you that if I am not given the nod by the recognized leader of Boston society, I will have little chance of success," Ivy whispered to me softly while her mother was chatting with one of my aunts.

But Aunt Camellia's hearing was excellent.

"Don't be dramatic, Ivy," she told her daughter.

"It is true that the Corrings' only daughter is of an age with Ivy and they will be giving a ball for her this spring. And it is true that Mrs. Josiah Corring has appointed herself as the arbiter of Boston society. But there are some perfectly pleasant, civil—and I might add *prosperous* families—who manage to have active social lives, and even make advantageous matches, without Ione Corring's imprimatur." Aunt Camellia waved a delicate hand, dismissing both Mrs. Corring and her pretentions.

A change of scene was just what I had needed. I didn't bother to tell Aunt Camellia that I had had no formal coming-out in London. My introduction to the highest levels of London society was entirely the doing of my dear friend, Lady Constance Hatton—now the Marquise de Rochmont—who had dragged me willy-nilly into a London season and the acquaintanceship with her brother, the most handsome, charming—and heartbreaking—gentleman I could ever expect to meet.

And so, I had accepted the invitation to come to Boston for a year—to escape. But I discovered that there is no escape from oneself.

Don't let your thoughts become maudlin.

I picked up a paintbrush, intending to create another picture of bare branches. But without a conscious decision to do so, I began to paint a face that was quite familiar to me. The face that haunted my dreams and the quiet moments of my waking hours. The face that I inevitably compared with the faces of every gentleman I met. The square jaw, straight nose, firm but generous mouth, gold hair that fell carelessly over his forehead—and a pair of teasing blue eyes.

I don't know how long I stood looking at the portrait I had painted, permitting waves of longing and misery to wash over me, before I realized that miserable as I was, I would be inexpressibly more miserable if Aunt Camellia or Ivy—or even Ada—happened upon me and saw Jack's portrait.

I quickly took it down, put it in the bottom drawer of a nearby chest so I could retrieve it later, and hastily painted a few bare branches on a fresh sheet. Could I discern a hint of green on those branches?

"Cousin Drusilla?"

I dropped my paintbrush.

Ivy rushed to pick it up and handed it to me. Once more I was struck by the contrast in appearance between my cousin and her mother. Both ladies were finely boned, blessed—or cursed—with the palest, most delicate complexion, and extraordinary aqua-blue eyes. But where Aunt Camellia was shorter than average, Ivy was sufficiently tall to look the average gentleman in the eye—which, of course, she never did, because her gaze when meeting anyone was inevitably downcast. And where Aunt Camellia was blessed with luxuriant auburn hair, Ivy's hair was just sufficiently on the titian side of blonde to be called "ginger," and had the unfortunate habit of curling wildly in the humid Boston weather. It was so fine and soft that Ivy was forever losing the ribbons that she used to try to keep it off her face. Her other solution to this problem was to wear it in a thick plait down her back. Both options made her appear to be very young. Only her height kept her from looking four or even five years younger than her age.

"I am so very sorry to have startled you, Cousin Drusilla."

"Don't you think we know each other well enough to dispense with formalities? Either 'Cousin' or 'Drusilla' will do nicely." I had made the suggestion before without success.

"I am so sorry. I'll try to remember. I am not at all certain what Mama would think of that, though."

"If Aunt Camellia protests, I shall explain my preference."

Ivy sat in one of a pair of wing chairs by the hearth and began to write in her journal. I returned to my assessment of an illusive hint of green on the branches of the trees across the road.

"Did you actually have a conversation with him? What is he really like?"

Merciful heavens! Had Ivy entered the room before I managed to hide Jack's portrait?

"He?" My voice almost broke.

"I cannot believe your sophistication, Cou . . . Drusilla! You have spoken with the most intriguing man in Boston and you are concentrating on painting instead of thinking about your encounter!"

I gave up painting one more picture of bare—or even faintly greening tree branches—and tried to frame an impression of Sir Clive Brampton that would satisfy my impressionable cousin.

I wiped my brush and considered.

"Sir Clive is of . . . average height."

Perhaps an inch taller than Ivy, but I didn't want to draw attention to her own height, one of her greatest worries.

"And average build."

I placed paints and brushes in their case and sat in the wing chair opposite Ivy.

"His hair is brown, as are his eyes, I believe."

Ivy looked crestfallen.

"How terribly disappointing!"

What had she expected? More of the hint of the pirate that, even at his age, her father exuded?

"Surely there is *something* that distinguishes him? That makes him stand out from the ordinary gentleman?"

Arrogance for certain. But I chose not to mention that.

"He is, perhaps, the most exquisitely tailored gentleman I have ever met. And, even though Beau Brummel had departed for the Continent before my London season, I encountered many gentlemen who followed his example slavishly. But Sir Clive's attention to detail in his attire is without peer."

"But what is he like as a person?"

Ivy could be as dogged as Aunt Camellia in her questions and much less subtle.

"I am not sure what you mean," I temporized.

"They say that the eyes are the windows of the soul. Didn't you catch even a glimpse of his soul?"

Poor Aunt Camellia. How would she ever shepherd Ivy over the rocky slopes of society if she persisted in asking such gauche questions? I would be gone come August, but Aunt Camellia would have to cope until some gentleman decided that Ivy's fortune overbalanced her verbal *faux pas*.

"I can't say that I did."

How could I look into the soul of a gentleman whose eyes are shuttered?

Chapter Two

A week of dreary, rainy weather prevented my return to Fort Hill. But at last spring made its appearance, and I had no excuse to delay finishing the picture of Sir Clive Brampton's townhouse. I waited until afternoon to set up my easel, hoping to complete the project without an encounter with Sir Clive. Whether I wished to avoid his possible censure of my work or an interrogation by Aunt Camellia about an encounter with him, I couldn't say.

I was putting the final touches to my painting when a smart buggy drew up. Sir Clive tied the horse's reigns to a post and tipped his hat in greeting.

"Miss Fortesque."

"Sir Clive."

Again, he studied the picture silently.

"I quite like it. You have a certain style, Miss Fortesque."

"Thank you, Sir Clive."

Thank heavens for the lessons of a London season. Sir Clive was a master of the ambiguous compliment, carelessly thrown out to set a gullible lady's heart to fluttering.

"And I am not speaking only of your artistic talents, Miss Fortesque."

I raised an eyebrow.

Sir Clive granted me a full smile.

"Ah, London polish. You do not disappoint, Miss Fortesque.
I shall send someone from the framing shop for the picture."
He tipped his hat and strode off.

Aunt Camellia looked up from arranging some daffodils—which
had finally made their appearance.

"I am so relieved to see that you wore a broad brimmed hat,
my love. It's a delightfully sparkling day, but the sun will coarsen
your complexion if you do not take care. When one is very
young, a lapse or two is not quite as serious, but . . ." She smiled
sadly, acknowledging the inevitability of change and decay.
Mine, in particular.

She returned her attention to the daffodils and I prepared to go to
my room, thinking I had escaped questions about Sir Clive. Silly me.

"And did Sir Clive appear today?"

She added a tall-stemmed flower to the center of the bouquet.

"He did. Just as I was about to leave."

Aunt Camellia abandoned the pretense of flower arranging and
tapped her fingers on the mahogany table, signalling that I would
have to divulge more information about my encounter with Sir
Clive, or she would wrest it from me.

"He liked the painting and will send someone from the framer's
to pick it up."

Aunt Camellia smiled.

"Well, Ivy, my love, I would wager that within a week, your
fondest wish will be granted and we will receive a call from Mrs.
Josiah Corring. I daresay we might even be extended invitations
to the ball the Corrings are giving for Miss Beryl. Although,
I wouldn't count on being included in the most privileged invited
to dinner before the ball."

Ivy's book fell from her lap and bounced on the Persian carpet.

"Oh Mama! Do you really think so? But why should Sir Clive's approval of Drusilla's painting have anything to do with invitations to their ball?"

Aunt Camellia caught my eye and looked heavenward before addressing her daughter in the kind, soft tones that a nanny might use with a particularly slow charge.

"Ivy, my dear, if you wish not only to receive Mrs. Josiah Corring's initial acceptance, but also to remain in her good graces, you must pay attention to her preferences and prejudices. Which, for the most part, revolve around the tastes and manners of a limited number of families who are almost indistinguishable from her own. However, a greater Anglophile than Ione Corring never breathed. And a very rich Englishman with a *title*! What can I say? If Sir Clive Brampton has deigned to converse with our Drusilla, Mrs. Corring will have heard of it and she will decide that we are all worthy of further acquaintance."

"You make Mrs. Corring sound positively un-American, Mama! Anyway, Drusilla is English and she has been here for months without receiving the slightest notice of Mrs. Corring."

"I am neither rich nor titled, Ivy, my love," I reminded her as gently as possible.

"But Papa? He certainly is English." Ivy responded in halfhearted protest.

"Your papa is far too raffish to ever be fully accepted by the Ione Corrings of the world," Aunt Camellia gently informed her daughter.

How could a lady and gentlemen of the mental complexity of Derrick and Camellia Fortesque have produced a daughter as naïve as Ivy?

Within three days of Aunt Camellia's prediction, the ceremony of calling card exchanges had been completed. The moment that Ivy had longed for would soon arrive.

Aunt Camellia was embroidering tiny rosebuds on the neckline of a silk camisole. Ivy was writing in her journal. And I was, once more, painting the boughs of trees lining the Mall—at last budding green—when Ada brought in two visitor's cards, corners turned down, indicating that their owners were inquiring if we were home.

Aunt Camellia studied the cards and smiled her catlike smile.

"Please, show them up."

The visitors, Mrs. Josiah Corring and Miss Beryl Corring, soon appeared in the drawing room doorway.

Mrs. Josiah Corring possessed the elegance that can only be achieved by a lady who is slender to the point of gauntness. Her face was narrow and angular; her nose was thin, as was her mouth. She looked down on the world with piercing brown eyes under straight brows.

Miss Corring was as tall as her mother, but willowy rather than gaunt. Her dark blue eyes were soft under arched brows. Her raven hair contrasted dramatically with her creamy complexion, exceptional for anyone living in the harsh Boston weather. Her voice, when she greeted us, was as gentle as her mother's was strident. I thought for a moment that she reminded me of someone else, but I couldn't remember whom. Perhaps she resembled a model in a fashion plate.

Mrs. Corring settled herself on a sofa and gazed around the room.

"Your house is really quite commodious," she nodded to Aunt Camellia. "I have not had the opportunity of seeing any interiors of houses in the Colonnade. Although, I believe my cousin lives a few doors up from you."

Her cousin, Joseph Ridgeway, had taken his money from Corring & Thornton and invested in a mill, an act of disloyalty made worse by the fact that the mill was prospering.

"This is a handsome terrace, a great complement to Park Row," Mrs. Corring continued. "The work of our dear friend, Mr. Charles Bulfinch. However, we were concerned, because so many of these houses were built on *speculation*."

Although the Corrings also lived in a house designed by their dear friend, Mr. Bulfinch, it was on the *other* side of the Common, a *mansion*, built *to order*.

The contrast and its significance was unspoken, but understood by four of the five ladies present. Aunt Camellia would, no doubt, need to explain these important matters to Ivy.

"We feared, given the uncertain times brought about by the unconscionable foolishness of Mr. Madison and his cohorts, that there would be no one to buy the unspoken-for houses in the Colonnade. But I understand that there are several merchants from Cape Cod who have taken up residence here and the investment has proved to be sound. Of course, Hollis Jones, who, I believe is your neighbor, made that possible by buying up many of the houses in the Colonnade and holding them until times improved."

Mrs. Corring gave us a wintery smile, satisfied that she had conveyed the precarious social status of those who lived in proximity not only to her errant cousin, but also to newly arrived residents from less desirable ports south of Boston rather than those to the north from which *her* family hailed.

Although, as an Englishwoman, I had to think for a moment before I could understand that "the unconscionable foolishness of Mr. Madison and his cohorts" referred to the recent and regrettable war between our two countries, the rest of Mrs. Corring's recitation was clear to me: we had been found sufficiently respectable to merit her acquaintanceship, but she was being generous.

"I was delighted to learn that your Ivy, and our Beryl, are of an age," Mrs. Corring continued with a gracious nod toward Aunt Camellia. "Of course, we are planning a ball in honor of Beryl. We specifically instructed Mr. Bulfinch to include a commodious ballroom in the plans for our house, you know, in anticipation of this very occasion. And I understand that you are planning a little party in honor of Miss Ivy." Mrs. Corring glanced around the parlor.

It would have to be a very small *party in this quite restricted space.* The words weren't said, but we all heard them.

"So I thought it might be pleasant if Miss Ivy were included in a little group of young ladies who will be coming to our house for tea and dancing lessons next Tuesday afternoon." Ione Corring nodded regally in Ivy's direction, whose face shone with joy.

Aunt Camellia accepted the invitation promptly, not knowing when Ivy's ability to speak would be restored.

Ada arrived with cakes and tea. Mrs. Corring waved away the cakes. "I never eat sweets before luncheon."

Miss Corring helped herself to two of the confections and added sugar to her tea, studiously avoiding her mother's glare.

But before Miss Corring could bite into the second cake, Mrs. Corring had risen to her feet and announced that she would very much look forward to Ivy's presence Tuesday next.

Aunt Camellia, Ivy, and I rose to bid our guests farewell. Medora stirred herself from where she had been sleeping by the fireplace. She paid no attention to our guest of honor. Anyone who refused a sweet was of no interest to her. She hopped onto a chair so she could avail herself of Miss Corring's abandoned cake.

Mrs. Corring cast a baleful glance at the little dog. For a second I feared that Ivy's invitation to the realms of the most select young ladies in Boston might be withdrawn. But the moment passed. Perhaps Mrs. Corring was reminding herself that one could not expect better behavior from a dog living in a house built on *speculation.*

At luncheon, Ivy stated that she required new gloves and a new bonnet. Aunt Camellia, eager to encourage any flicker of interest in fashion shown by her daughter, and equally eager to form Ivy's taste, willingly sacrificed her afternoon nap.

Finally alone, I opened a letter from France that had arrived in the morning mail.

Chateau Rochmont
March 7, 1818

My Very Dearest Drusilla,

Your letter of this past August finally reached me. Blaise and I had departed Tuscany on a whim and we spent the balance of the warm months on the shores of lac de Genève. Pure Heaven! Then, to Provence for the winter. And now, just recently arrived in the Loire for spring. Your epistle was quite worn from its travels! But I was able to decipher your return address and the stunning news that you are ensconced in the city of Boston in America! I always knew you to be extraordinarily intrepid, but even I never dreamed you would brave such a journey. How lovely that you have been able to become acquainted with your father's long lost brother and his family. I only hope that you do not fall madly in love with some rough-hewn revolutionary. Blaise assures me that matters have settled down over there and everyone is really quite civilized. Actually, we have met a number of Americans in our travels and they are, on the whole, well-spoken and almost indistinguishable from the well-bred English.

Blaise and I plan to return to London for the season, but I shall miss you dreadfully! Your droll comments on the machinations of society and your unwavering understanding of what matters and what doesn't matter were always a tonic to my spirits.

You must promise to follow your plans to return this coming August. Perhaps you can visit us in London. Blaise tells me he has matters to attend to there in late September, early October.
Much love,
Constance

P.S. I assume that Medora is in your care. I do apologize for not throwing my bouquet and failing to retrieve her. Blaise can be so distracting!

As I read Constance's words, I could hear her voice—always full of zest and amusement. It took me back to the happiest time in my life, two years ago, when I met Constance at Hookham's Circulating Library, and later met her brother, Jack, the day we all rescued Medora.

No members of the *ton* sparkled with fun and laughter like Lady Constance and Captain Jack Hatton. No gentleman could waltz with the ease and grace of Jack Hatton. No wonder he was called Darling Jack.

And I might have married him.

All that remained of those happy days was Medora, who would attach herself to anyone who offered her treats, pats, and a pillow.

I picked her up and walked to the window overlooking the Mall and the Common. My cardinal and his lady had returned and were busy building a nest. How I longed for a nest of my own.

"Sir Clive Brampton wishes to know if Miss Drusilla Fortesque is at home."

Ada held a silver server on which rested a gentleman's calling card. But the gentleman in question had not waited for the niceties of etiquette and had followed her up the stairs. Ada shrugged and departed, leaving me to face Sir Clive.

"I hope you will excuse the abruptness, but I thought I spied you in the window and I wanted you to see the finished product of your work."

Ignoring my efforts to paint the greening trees lining the Mall, Sir Clive placed the matted and framed picture of his house on the easel.

"Oh!"

I had never before seen any of my pictures prepared for formal display and the finished effect startled me. Medora looked at me reproachfully for disturbing her repose.

I gave her topknot a little kiss and resumed patting her as my guest and I studied the picture in silence.

"You are pleased."

It was an observation, not a question.

"Quite. I have never before had one of my pictures matted and framed. I confess I quite like the results."

"No false modesty, please, Miss Fortesque. You are talented and you know it. I am looking forward to hanging your picture in my entrance hall and I wouldn't be at all surprised if other house-proud Bostonians begin to drop hints that you are welcome to use *their* abodes as subjects for your painting."

I was too surprised to think of an appropriate answer, or an answer that would not elicit Sir Clive's criticism of false modesty.

Ada came to my rescue by bringing in a tea tray. I poured out, and began to absently feed bites of cake to Medora.

"What a strange little dog, Miss Fortesque. At least she does not accost guests with excessive enthusiasm." I thought I detected a slight shudder. "What do you call her?"

"Medora."

"Strange name for a strange dog."

"It's from *The Corsair*. She was rescued from the cruel streets of London and her appearance made someone suggest that she be called 'Medusa.' I would have none of it. And since I was reading *The Corsair* at the time, 'Medora' came immediately to mind."

"Another Byron admirer, Miss Fortesque?"

I laughed and gave the remaining cake to Medora.

"Not a true admirer, Sir Clive, but it was amusing to hear gentlemen's objections to him when one was discovered to be reading him."

Sir Clive did not bother to disguise his look of approval, even admiration.

"An unsentimental lady. How rare. I regret that our paths did not cross in London." A somber look crossed his face that I suspected had nothing to do with regret for not meeting me two years earlier. "By the time you were in London, I had already been traveling the world for more than a year, developing my shipping business. But I do recall the name Fortesque."

"My great-aunt Louisa, I am sure."

"Ah yes. You will forgive me, I hope, for mentioning that several young ladies of my acquaintance walked in fear of the possibility of her censure."

"No forgiveness required, Sir Clive. I have great sympathy for those young ladies. She invited me to be her companion for a London season because I was the next niece in line for what she considered to be the great privilege of attending her while she tyrannized the *ton*. Had it not been for a chance encounter I had with Lady Constance Hatton while trying to rescue Medora, I fear that my time in London would have been bleak indeed. But even Great-aunt Louisa couldn't complain about my friendship with Lady Constance. So my time in London was quite enjoyable after all."

Sir Clive raised both eyebrows.

"No wonder you positively glow with London polish, Miss Fortesque! I well remember when Lady Constance first appeared. Of course, she was quite above my aspirations. Noble heirs surrounded her every move. I am amazed, though, that she was still unwed—when was it—two years ago? She must have been out at least four or five years."

"Actually, she married at the end of that season. I suppose it took her time to sort out all her suitors."

I found that I did not wish to pursue the topic of Lady Constance Hatton any further. Much more chatter about my time in London and the subject of another Hatton might inadvertently be broached. And I discovered that I definitely did not want to talk about Captain Jack Hatton with Sir Clive Brampton.

No one could accuse Sir Clive of insensitivity to subtle signals. He laid his cup and saucer on the tea tray and stood.

"It's been a pleasure, Miss Fortesque. Americans are the best of business acquaintances, however . . ."

"Perhaps it's just that you wanted to hear a normal English voice speaking normal English, Sir Clive."

"I believe you have the right of it, Miss Fortesque."

He retrieved the painting and I offered my hand in parting.

"I hope our paths will cross again soon, Miss Fortesque. Indeed, I am certain they shall."

Sir Clive Brampton thought me unsentimental. How wrong could someone be? Unsentimental? I, who for almost two years had spent hours, indeed days, reliving memories of that magical time in London, the time when *I* was the lady of the moment in the life of Jack Hatton. *I* was the one with whom he chose to banter, to exchange amused looks across a room when Great-aunt Louisa or Lady Redell said something outrageous. And most especially, *I* was the one with whom he chose to waltz.

But he had not been courting me. I was just the lady of the moment. The lady after Lady Antony Compton. The lady before . . . whom, I would never know. He had asked me to marry him in a casual, offhanded way—just because I was the lady of the moment when he realized he wanted companionship and amusement for what he thought would be a dreary journey. He had wanted to have the company of a lady who spoke normal English in a normal way.

Was I being courted now? Was this the way sophisticated gentlemen commenced a courtship? Certainly Sir Clive's cryptic compliments lifted my spirits and burnished my self-regard as nothing had since the fateful day I had rejected Captain Hatton's proposal.

Of course I had been singled out for attention by various gentlemen in Bath: widowers who were looking for a mama for their five children, aging squires who wanted a nurse for their waning years.

But I had never received the sort of attention that I was receiving from Sir Clive Brampton, an indisputably eligible gentleman. It was becoming increasingly difficult not to speculate what life as the wife of a rich and powerful gentleman might be like.

Oh dear! Drusilla! Whether you are being mercenary or romantic, you are losing your common sense!

I had always tried to be realistic in my assessment of my own attributes. On the negative side: shorter than average, figure a little too full to show off a dressmaker's skills to advantage, brown hair, hazel eyes, a slightly generous mouth. On the positive side: a perfectly oval face, finely arched brows, and clear, flawless complexion. And when I permitted myself the benefit of the doubt, I acknowledged that some gentlemen *prefer* a shorter lady, do not believe that a lady's figure must be a dressmaker's model, and are not admirers of the current fashion in rosebud mouths.

But even on my most confident days, I understood that I am not what is commonly called *pretty*, certainly not *beautiful*. I strove to be *attractive*, but I knew that *attractiveness* is a subjective attribute that must be helped along with careful wardrobe choices, thoughtful manners, and genuine interest in the interests of other people.

So, to be pursued—if, indeed I was being pursued—by a gentleman like Sir Clive—was as novel as it was unexpected.

I mentally shook myself. Time would reveal Sir Clive's intentions and motivations.

"Mama told me not to plague you, but honestly, Cousin, I cannot understand her admonition that I not mention Sir Clive Brampton's name to you when *she* rarely loses an opportunity to speculate about him—and his intentions toward you."

Ivy sat in the slipper chair by the window in my bedroom, bare toes curled over the edge of the seat, dimity nightgown tucked around her ankles, arms wrapped around her folded legs. Aunt Camellia would be appalled at such an unladylike pose, but I admired Ivy's supple grace.

I put down my hairbrush, having lost count of my strokes for the third time. The need to deflate my young cousin's romantic fantasies was more urgent than completing the one hundred brushes that would guarantee me lustrous locks for the next twenty-four hours.

"Ivy, my dear. I am certain that your mother meant nothing serious with her little teases about Sir Clive's interest in the painting of his house. And her caution to you, no doubt, was made to correct any misapprehensions you might have regarding what you referred to as 'intentions' on his part."

"So Mama was wrong then? He did not pay a call on you this afternoon? She pointed him out to me as we were walking home from the milliner's. He was making the turn from Common Street into Summer Street."

"He brought the picture I had painted for me to see after he had it framed and matted. Just a simple courtesy, I assure you, Ivy."

I was grateful that a single oil lamp provided the only light in the room. If my face was flushed, Ivy would not be able to detect it.

Ivy frowned.

"I must say, none of it makes much sense to me. For one thing, all I have heard in the few months since he arrived in Boston is that Sir Clive is elusive and distant socially, but he seems to seek you out."

"I'm sure that it all has to do with the painting. Sir Clive does not strike me as an impetuous, romantic gentleman."

Ivy nodded.

"That was the other thing that didn't make sense to me. I know you told me that he was quite unremarkable in appearance—but it was still hard for me to believe. One expects a gentleman who is the subject of so much speculation to be . . ."

"Handsome? Dashing?"

Ivy nodded again.

"Or outgoing and friendly—genuinely interested in other people."

As much as I disliked the role of cynic, I felt the need to emphasize one basic social reality to my young cousin.

"Ivy, my dear, when it comes to desirable attributes in a prospective husband, a sizable fortune will make an ill-favored man look passable. A taciturn man, engaging. Imagine what an enormous fortune can do for a self-contained, average-looking man!"

Ivy planted her feet together on the floor and crossed her arms over her chest.

"Well! That might be the way *this* society works, but it's not going to be the way society works in my novel!"

"Gracious! Your journal is a novel?"

"You won't tell Mama, will you? She'll tease me and ask to read it. And I'd rather die than have her laugh at it."

Ivy's pale complexion turned ashen in the dim light.

"I promise not to breathe a word to her about it," I assured her. "But have you thought of how you would keep it from her if it were published?"

The stricken look on Ivy's face gave me her answer. She chewed her lower lip for a moment and brightened.

"I'll just have to use a pen name. How do the French say it? A *nom de plume*! Let me think."

Ivy closed her eyes, meditating. I waited wondering what my fanciful cousin would choose for an assumed identity.

After a full minute, Ivy opened her eyes and clasped her hands to her bosom.

"Gwendolyn Honore!" She exclaimed, beaming. "My novel takes place in medieval times. Isn't that perfect?"

"It flows nicely," I said, "but why the medieval period?"

Ivy looked surprised at my question.

"Surely, there isn't another time when high ideals—chivalry, honor, all those sorts of virtues were valued as they were then? And the castles and the tournaments..."

And the cold, stone walls, and the stenches and the sieges and the arranged marriages...

"It sounds very romantic," I temporized.

"Doesn't it?" Ivy hugged herself. "And I intend to wait until I find a gentleman who can appreciate that. One who believes in beauty and truth and honor. One who would think nothing of giving his last morsel of bread to a hungry stranger."

You, on the other hand, dear Drusilla, have reached an age at which certain compromises with the ideal might have to be made.

The unspoken words lingered in my mind after Ivy left and I snuffed out the lamp.

Chapter Three

The next morning when I entered the breakfast room, I was astonished to see Uncle Derrick: immaculately groomed, but exuding the aura of a buccaneer. He stood and enveloped me in an embrace.

"You are a welcome sight for a weary sailor's eyes, my sweet."

"I'll wager you say that to all the ladies," I laughed.

"A wager you would win," Aunt Camellia's smile turned into a yawn. She sparkled with pale blue-green jewelry. A flawless aquamarine suspended on a heavy gold chain nestled in her décolletage; another jewel of impressive size was on her right ring finger, and large aqua drops hung from her ears. Uncle Derrick knew the importance of reunion gifts.

It was the first time Aunt Camellia had appeared for breakfast since my arrival in Boston, preferring to have tea and toast brought to her room while leisurely making her toilette.

"See what Papa has brought me!"

Ivy held up a necklace of multiple strands of coral beads from which hung an intricately carved pendant. In the morning sunlight, the coral picked up the reddish tones of her hair, burnishing her appearance with an ethereal glow.

"Oh, Mama! I want to wear them to the Corrings' ball!"

A fashion question roused Aunt Camellia from her drowsiness. She studied her daughter and the necklace for a moment.

"That would be such a waste, my darling. Save them for the time when all eyes are on *you*. Pearls will do well enough for the Corrings."

"Congratulations for attaining admission to the most exalted realms of Boston society, my sweet." Uncle Derrick patted Ivy's hand. "I pray my return will not spoil your success. Josiah Corring likes doing business with me well enough, but I believe Mrs. Josiah does not like the cut of my jib." He winked at Aunt Camellia. "Difficult to imagine why."

"That cannot be true!" Ivy exclaimed, dismayed. "But Mama doesn't believe that our invitations to the Corrings' ball have anything to do with Mrs. Corring's regard for me. Mama says that it's all because of Sir Clive Brampton's particular attention to Cousin Drusilla."

"Well, well, well," was all Uncle Derrick said before draining his coffee cup.

"Derrick! How cruel of you! Saying 'well, well, well' is worse than saying nothing at all!" Aunt Camellia protested.

"Sorry, m'dear," Uncle Derrick responded in tone lacking any contrition. "I really can't claim close acquaintance with the man. Let me think. Seems I ran into him in Cape Town—two, perhaps three years ago. Canny trader, for certain. Enough reserves to outbid anyone if he really wants a cargo. Other than that, I seem to remember that the Bramptons were an old Sussex family. But it's difficult to see the Clive Brampton I met living the life of a country baronet. It's just as difficult to see the Clive Brampton I met settling happily in Boston."

Aunt Camellia raised her eyebrow and smiled.

"Shouldn't you refer to Sir Clive by his title, Papa?" Ivy was a stickler for form.

"Don't see why, when he's not within hearing. But if he actually has the good sense to appreciate my exceptional niece, I might accidentally upgrade him to a baron. And, by the way, Drusilla, my dear, I did not forget you."

He reached into a jacket pocket and retrieved a large velvet pouch, which he handed to me. Its contents made me gasp. There was a double strand necklace of large, clear amber beads, with a pair of teardrop amber earrings to match.

I would definitely wear them to the Corrings' ball.

If Ivy was disappointed that our invitations were to the ball only and not to the more exclusive dinner before the ball, she showed no indication of it as we assembled in the foyer before departing for the Corring mansion. Aunt Camellia did not disappoint, wearing a deep décolleté gown of aqua silk, set off by her newly acquired jewelry. There wouldn't be a lady of any age at the ball that would attract more glances from the gentlemen.

Ivy's gown of palest yellow silk chiffon featured a bodice with exquisite tucks down the front, along with a modest neckline. With her hair plaited in a crown entwined with white silk flowers and her pearl jewelry, she was the embodiment of youthful innocence. Aunt Camellia had dictated every detail of Ivy's ensemble, so I assumed that the object was to eliminate any suspicion on the part of Mrs. Corring and other anxious mamas that Ivy was a threat to their darling's prospects.

My own gown was bronze watered silk with threads of green and gold, chosen to set off my amber beads and earrings. I had followed advice Lady Constance had given me during my London days and arranged my hair in a simple chignon.

Uncle Derrick, himself the picture of gentlemanly elegance, pronounced us a trio of perfection.

The scene at the Corring mansion was very like the scenes at any number of London balls, with guests slowly progressing up the grand staircase leading to the receiving line, which began with Mr. Ellsworth Corring. Reputed to be a brilliant student of philosophy at Harvard College, he was the tallest member of his exceptionally tall family—perhaps lofty thoughts came naturally to him.

Next in line were Mr. and Mrs. Edward Corring, the eldest child of the family and his wife. It was rumored that Edward Corring's commercial talents were social rather than financial. Perhaps that is why it was said he planned to offer himself as a candidate for Congress for the Federalist Party. His wife exuded a bland, self-satisfied air that would, no doubt, stand him in good stead in public life.

In spite of a certain frostiness in her greeting of Uncle Derrick, Aunt Camellia, and me, Ione Corring was full of smiles and graciousness for Ivy. Aunt Camellia had known what she was about in dictating Ivy's ensemble.

Mr. Josiah Corring, a tall man with gray hair and thick gray eyebrows over piercing, ice-blue eyes, greeted each of us heartily—the business side and the social side of the Corring family having different priorities.

But the centerpiece of the receiving line was Beryl Corring, a vision in periwinkle silk, with pearls at her throat, ears, and twined through her soft, dark curls, carefully arranged to look slightly disarranged.

Mrs. Bradford Thornton, mother of Beryl Corring's erstwhile swain, a short, buxom lady swathed in royal blue, had been deputized to encourage young gentlemen to see that no young lady was without a partner for the first dance.

Aunt Camellia's wisdom in her presentation of Ivy was confirmed when a steady parade of younger sons filled all the lines on her dance card. A message had been mysteriously sent regarding Ivy's suitability.

My partner for the first dance, a quadrille, was Mr. Douglas Robertson, a Scotsman by way of Barnstable, but deemed acceptable because of his reputation as a ship designer and the fortune that talent had earned. He was tall, dark, and sufficiently taciturn to affirm the stereotype of his nationality.

When we joined our set, I encountered Sir Clive for the first time in the evening—partnering a glowing Beryl Corring, who cast a triumphant glance at me as Mr. Robertson and I took our places. Sir Clive acknowledged us with a curt nod.

In spite of myself, I knew a moment of deflation. How could I, for a moment, have considered that a man of Sir Clive's eligibility would not choose youth, beauty, and fortune?

When the pattern of the dance brought us together, Sir Clive greeted me, "Miss Fortesque," stared pointedly at my amber jewelry, and raised an eyebrow.

After the quadrille, he sauntered around the ballroom with Miss Corring on his arm and disappeared in the direction of the card room when Miss Corring's next partner presented himself.

"It seems that Miss Corring has found a replacement for Mr. Benjamin Thornton," Miss Susan Jones, our neighbor from the Colonnade, observed, just before our own partners appeared for the next dance.

"I hope your evening wasn't spoiled by Sir Clive Brampton," Ivy offered, which let me know that along with Beryl Corring and Sir Clive, I also had been a topic of speculation during the previous night's ball.

I continued to brush Medora's coat without looking up.

"But there were so many other gentleman who seemed quite eager to seek you out as a dancing partner, I think that Beryl Corring is welcome to Sir Clive," Ivy declared, offering me unsolicited consolation with a newly acquired tone of *savoir faire*.

If one ball could produce that bit of sophistication in my cousin, how worldly-wise would she be by the end of the season?

"I did tell you that there was nothing romantic in Sir Clive's interest in my painting. Even at the reception at Corring Wharf, it was obvious to most observers that Miss Corring and Sir Clive were interested in each other," I reminded Ivy as I secured a pink bow in Medora's topknot.

Actually only Miss Corring's interest in Sir Clive had been obvious.

But I had no wish for further discussion on the topic of Beryl Corring and Sir Clive. "I am amazed that you had a moment to speculate about Sir Clive and Miss Corring. It seemed to me that you were a much sought after dance partner."

Ivy beamed and I knew I had successfully turned the conversation.

"It was the most wonderful evening of my life!" she exclaimed. "I must tell you. I met someone who might have stepped right out of my book. It would be difficult to imagine anyone of greater idealism and sincerity. I do hope . . ."

Ada appeared in the doorway. I resigned myself to waiting to learn the identity of Ivy's perfect prince.

The name on the card on the silver tray Ada held read *Miss Annette Ware*. Miss Ware was a young lady who had been a part of the group surrounding Ivy during the ball.

"Show her up, and bring some refreshments," I instructed the maid.

I would need sustenance to endure the eager reliving of last night's ball.

Miss Ware was short and slightly built, with brown hair, brown eyes, a small, pointed nose, and thin lips; attributes that, in another lady, might encourage diffidence—a quality quite lacking in our newly arrived guest. Dressed in an exquisitely tailored yellow gown that fought with her sallow complexion, she exuded an aura of confidence as she settled herself in one of the large wing chairs flanking the fireplace. Ivy hurried to fetch a footstool for her convenience, which Miss Ware acknowledged with a slight inclination of her feathered bonnet.

"I must congratulate you, Miss Fortesque," Miss Ware addressed Ivy, "I believe you made an excellent impression at the ball last night. And I am certain that you would enjoy becoming a part of a little group of us who are exploring the betterment of mankind through the elevation and refinement of the mind. We are meeting at my home tomorrow afternoon at half past two. I do hope you can come."

Ivy's joy at receiving such an invitation almost overwhelmed her powers of speech.

"I would be delighted to attend," she managed in a breathless whisper.

"Please try to be prompt," Miss Ware said as she stood.

She nodded to me and sailed out the doorway, almost colliding with Ada who was just bringing in tea and cakes.

Ada looked over her shoulder, somewhat confused, before placing the tray on the tea table.

"Oh, Drusilla!" Ivy had found her voice. "You must not be offended by Miss Ware's abruptness. She is simply brilliant and perhaps a little forgetful of social niceties. I realized last night that she is remarkably informed for a lady of her age—I believe she is only a year older than I. And she was able to converse with the young gentlemen from Harvard College on all sorts of elevated subjects. I really could not keep track of what they were saying, but the conversation was quite sparkling. Being included in their group is such an honor. I hope Mama will understand."

Of course Aunt Camellia had no objection to Ivy's accepting Miss Ware's invitation. Aunt Camellia would never have objected to Ivy's attendance at any function that included eligible gentlemen and was properly chaperoned. And Annette Ware's parents, rich and boring, were above any reproach. But Ivy's enthusiasm for an intellectual discussion group *was* beyond Aunt Camellia's understanding.

"Of course you may go, my love," Aunt Camellia assured Ivy. "But I fear it will be terribly dull. No dancing, no charades. Not even spillikins, I must warn you."

"Dancing and charades are all well and good, Mama," Ivy instructed patiently, "but the young ladies and gentlemen I met at last night's ball are also interested in matters of the mind. I find that quite admirable."

If I noticed Ivy blushing, I knew Aunt Camellia noticed, too. I suspected that Ivy's perfect prince was "interested in matters of the mind."

The following afternoon, after Ivy had departed for her intellectual adventure, accompanied by Ada, and Aunt Camellia retired for her afternoon nap, I decided to take Medora for a walk down the Mall.

As I was descending the front steps, I was hailed from next door.

"Miss Fortesque! What a delight! Do you mind terribly if I join you?"

I could honestly say that I was as happy to encounter Miss Susan Jones as she was to encounter me. Of all the young ladies who had attended the Corrings' ball, she was the most spontaneous and unaffected.

"I gather that you were able to escape the Meeting of Exalted Minds," Miss Jones laughed.

I struggled to assume a disappointed expression.

"I confess that I did not receive an invitation."

"Neither did I," my companion admitted. "I fear I have blotted my copybook with Miss Ware. She informed me that she had decided against inviting me because I am lacking in an appreciation for philosophical abstraction."

As an heiress, perhaps the richest heiress in Boston, Susan Jones had no reason to worry about the opinion of Miss Ware. Miss Jones's grandfather, Ellery Jones, had arrived in Boston from Scituate without pence in his pocket, and had amassed a fortune acquiring goods cheaply and selling them reasonably—never having to go to sea. Her father, Hollis Jones, had taken over his father's business and had extended his acquisitions to real estate. Indeed, he had made a tidy sum of purchasing houses in the Colonnade on speculation and reselling them. In fact, Uncle Derrick had purchased his house from Hollis Jones.

Miss Jones and I crossed Common Street and were walking down the Mall bordering the Common, when we noticed a large desk being moved into the house two doors down from the Joneses.

"Our neighbor is flourishing sufficiently to be acquiring all the accoutrements of success," my companion informed me. "I am certain you took note of him at the ball. Mr. Douglas Robertson: tall, dark, and rather rugged in appearance. A designer of ships from Barnstable. Said to be quite innovating and exacting. *I* found him to be quite taciturn. But he is single, so I am sure there is general agreement that his reticence is a sign of wisdom."

Miss Jones's blue eyes danced with good humor. I was reminded for a moment of Lady Constance. Not that any lady alive could hold a candle to her beauty and sparkling wit. But while Miss Jones was smaller and slighter of stature than Lady Constance and more likely to be called "pretty" than "beautiful," her sunny nature and ability to laugh at society's foibles without malice reminded me of my dearest friend—as did her composure when dealing with awkward social encounters, which was about to be put to the test.

Bearing down upon us was a tall, large-boned lady of advanced years and stately bearing. She was dressed in the fashion of the previous century, but had not powdered the gray wisps that peaked out from under her faded black bonnet.

"Miss Jones, how delightful to see you today."

I snatched up Medora, who had begun to sniff the camphor emanating from the skirts of the speaker.

"How kind of you to say so, Mrs. Thornton. May I present my friend and neighbor, Miss Drusilla Fortesque of Bath, England?"

I suppose you must.

The words weren't said aloud, but they were written on the old lady's face.

I barely caught myself from dipping a quick curtsy and acknowledged my presentation with a nod.

"How do you do, Mrs. Thornton. It is an honor to meet you."

She cast a glance in my direction, favoring me with a wince of a smile.

"A connection of Derrick Fortesque, I assume? It seems that we are experiencing another invasion of the English," she said, addressing the air above my head. "One trusts that it will be more pacific than the last."

Perhaps it was a whiff of revolutionary fervor—not camphor—that I had detected.

"Give my best to your mother," she said to Miss Jones. "I've sent her a note asking her to come to tea Thursday next."

With a nod, Mrs. Thornton was off.

Medora whimpered a protest. I realized that I had been clutching her tightly for fear she would jump down and offend the daunting old lady.

Wordlessly, Miss Jones and I sat down on a nearby park bench, both of us needing to recoup our energies after our encounter with one of Boston's legends.

"Dear Miss Fortesque, I hope you will not feel too offended by Mrs. Prudence's incivility. Just so you will know, we all call old Mrs. Thornton 'Mrs. Prudence' behind her back to distinguish her from her daughter-in-law, who is called 'Mrs. May' behind *her* back. And if it will make you feel any better, Mrs. Prudence can be even brusquer with those fellow Bostonians who, she believes, held traitorous sympathies with the British during our countries' recent conflict.

"There aren't too many of her generation left. And, from what I've been told, there never was anyone remotely like her, even in Colonial days. Rumor has it that she personally helped to apply face paint to disguise some of the men who destroyed three shiploads of tea—back before the war for independence. Gamaliel Thornton, her husband, is reputed to have been one of the participants, although it was never officially confirmed. As sympathetic with the cause as his family was, they were scandalized by the willful destruction of property. But the family fortune protected both Gamaliel and Prudence from any serious repercussion."

Miss Jones paused for a moment, contemplating Mrs. Prudence's slow, stately progress toward Summer Street.

"She has a long memory, and she thinks kindly of me because my Grandfather Jones was also a member of the Sons of Liberty, and might very well have thrown his share of tea into the harbor that night. Old Josiah Corring, who became Gamaliel's partner in Corring & Thornton, might have quietly supported the likes of Samuel Adams and Gamaliel Thornton, but was never politically involved. And his son, the current Josiah, became a dedicated Federalist and an implacable opponent of the recent war—something Mrs. Prudence will never forgive. Indeed, she has never liked the idea of her grandson, Mr. Benjamin Thornton, marrying Miss Beryl Corring.

"For her part, Beryl's mama has long encouraged the match of her daughter with Benjamin Thornton because *his* family has belonged to *her* family's closest circle of acquaintances for generations, and, of course, he possesses a sizable fortune, as does Beryl Corring. Mrs. Corring could not tolerate her daughter's fortune going to some unknown upstart. But I imagine that in Sir Clive, both mother and daughter see a perfect replacement for Benjamin. And I am certain that introducing her daughter as Lady Brampton would be a crowning achievement for Ione Corring. As for Beryl's papa, it's rumored that he would like to take on a new business partner, the war having frayed the trust between him and Mrs. Prudence's son, Bradford Thornton. And what better prospect for a dedicated Federalist than an Englishman?"

Miss Jones stopped her informative monologue abruptly.

"Am I boring you with local history and tales, Miss Fortesque?"

Miss Jones was giving me an opportunity to tell her that my sense of propriety overruled my curiosity, but I was incapable of telling that particular lie at that particular moment.

"No apology, please, Miss Jones. You know quite well that you have been both entertaining and informative. I live in fear of putting a foot wrong and spoiling poor Ivy's chances in Boston society. Just now, I had to remind myself not to dip a curtsy to Mrs. Thornton!"

Miss Jones's curls danced with laughter.

"Oh dear! That would have been a sight! Not that there aren't Boston ladies who would be quite pleased to receive a curtsy. Ione Corring, for example. A greater Anglophile never drew breath. During the war, the Corring mansion was the center of antiwar, pro-British sentiment."

"It sounds as if there are no warm feelings between old Mrs. Thornton and Mrs. Corring. Is that why I didn't see Mrs. Prudence Thornton at the ball?"

I had given up the slightest pretense of hiding my curiosity.

"Oh no! She rarely goes out in the evening these days. But she *does* attend all daytime occasions. Particularly Mrs. Corring's sewing circle. Ione Corring is obliged to invite Mrs. Prudence for appearances sake, and Mrs. Prudence always attends. She is dedicated to keeping up on all the news. So she walks from her place on Summer Street to the Corrings' mansion on what she persists in calling Olive Street. She refuses to use its new, elegant name: Mount Vernon Street. Quite a trek for a lady her age. But knowing that her presence is an irritant to her hostess makes it worth the effort."

"Certainly Mrs. Prudence keeps a carriage," I protested, laughing.

"She does. But she uses it only to convey guests to her house whom she wishes to insult by implying that they are too indolent or weak to walk."

"Oh dear!" I exclaimed. "And I thought the ways of London society were arcane! Perhaps we can work out a signal so you can warn me if I am about to commit a *faux pas*."

"I am not certain that would help you in the long run," Miss Jones mused. "If you navigate without hitting a shoal, Mrs. Corring, for one, might never forgive you. How then could she maintain her belief in her own superiority? Indeed, I believe it is my tendency toward social lapses that led her to encourage my friendship with her daughter. It requires contrast for a pattern card of deportment to be fully appreciated."

"Poor Miss Corring," I said, surprised at my feelings of sympathy for her. "How dreadful to be expected to be a model of perfection. No wonder she says so little."

"Your sympathy is well founded. I cannot imagine anything more trying than living up to Mrs. Corring's expectations. But Beryl Corring has a mind of her own, as she has shown by turning her back on Benjamin Thornton."

"Which must please his grandmother," I suggested. "I wonder if she knows."

Miss Jones laughed.

"You mean, because Mrs. Prudence didn't attend the ball? I assure you that she already has a more complete account of the happenings at the Corrings' ball than most of the attendees. Her first report will have been from her daughter-in-law, Mrs. May, Benjamin's mother. And my mother's invitation to tea on Thursday? Mrs. Prudence will be confirming what she has already learned and gleaning whatever new tidbits Mama can offer."

Evidently, sharing tidbits of social information was a talent that ran in the Jones family.

"Ivy, dear, I hope you weren't hopelessly bored with that meeting you attended this afternoon," Aunt Camellia inquired while buttering a roll.

Ivy had disappeared into her room upon returning from Miss Ware's gathering and had said nothing other than greeting her parents and me as she took her place at the dinner table.

"Oh, no, Mama!"

Ivy put down the fork she had just picked up.

"I don't believe I have ever been so inspired. Mr. Ellsworth Corring—he is in his last year at Harvard College, you know—read a most brilliant essay. He doesn't look at people as the rest of us do. He sees us as we might be, if only we all concentrate very hard on sublime thoughts. At least, that's what I understood him to say. His vocabulary is so advanced, I didn't quite catch everything, but I am certain that Annette—Miss Ware and I have agreed to call each other by our first names—can explain what I didn't quite comprehend."

So the perfect prince was Mr. Ellsworth Corring. I never would have guessed from having observed his performance on the dance floor.

"How lovely." Aunt Camellia looked a little puzzled, then brightened as she changed the subject to something she *did* understand. "I do hope you haven't made any plans for tomorrow afternoon, though. You really must have the first fitting for your gown for your party. I want it to be flawless. Actually, in the more intimate setting of *our* party, what you wear will stand out even more than Miss Corring's dress did at her ball."

"I remember our appointment with Mademoiselle," Ivy reassured her mother. "And the next lecture isn't for another week. You really ought to go with me, Drusilla. There will be some distinguished scholars in attendance. I am sure you would find their conversation more enlightening than Sir Clive Brampton's ever was."

Uncle Derrick caught my eye and winked.

"Not every lady shares your preference for the world of rarified intellect, Ivy, my dear," he told his daughter.

Chapter Four

I was happy to have time to myself the following afternoon when Aunt Camellia and Ivy departed for Mademoiselle's shop. Ivy's innocent concern for my marital prospects was depressing. Thank heavens for Uncle Derrick's understanding wink. The picture of life with a bookworm absorbed in arcane texts and erudite speculation with which Ivy was enamored was almost sufficient to make me think of Bath as a refuge of frivolity.

Rather than attempting another painting of the trees lining the Mall, I decided to paint a vase of pink and red tulips Aunt Camellia had placed on a small table beside one of the fireside chairs.

But when I set up my easel, tulips in a vase, regardless of how exquisite the vase, seemed too dull and restrictive a subject. Medora was sleeping in the chair next to the table on which the vase sat. I moved the easel back sufficiently so that my painting would have a wider perspective, including part of the fireplace and mantel. I hushed the voice of my governess who nattered in my mind about "appropriateness of subject and focus." If I wished to paint a vase of tulips *and* a dog sleeping on a chair *and* a portion of a fireplace and mantel, it was *my* paint and *my* picture.

I worked with two brushes, lapsing into an old habit of spearing the brush I wasn't using into the front of my hair. In deep concentration, with my back to the door, I was startled when Ada announced: "Sir Clive Brampton."

I turned, causing the brush from my hair to fall, leaving a streak of wet paint on my cheek.

Sir Clive retrieved the brush from the floor, and presented it to me with a bow before wiping the streak from my face with his handkerchief.

"As a rule, I have no objection to ladies painting their faces, but it's most effective if it's done subtly."

He tossed the soiled handkerchief in the easel tray next to a filthy wipe rag, and then took his familiar stance of silently studying my work in progress. I had barely finished blocking out the major portions of the painting, but when he spoke, it was clear that he understood the structure of my picture.

"Of course, the quality of the execution of your concept has yet to be revealed, but I applaud you for at least attempting something out of the ordinary."

Speechless, I silently motioned him to one of the fireside chairs. I picked up Medora and sat in the other, patting her as much to distract myself and collect my thoughts as to soothe her. Why ever was Sir Clive paying this unexpected call?

"You do not disappoint, Miss Fortesque. Forgive me if I have said that before. But I find your unique combination of presenting a most unexceptionable appearance cloaking a decidedly unconventional mind to be most refreshing. I can't think of another lady who would not paint either the vase of tulips or the sleeping dog. Perhaps the *most* adventurous would paint the tulips and the dog. But you have sketched out an *interior*, which at least has the potential of being absorbing rather than boring."

"You make boredom sound like something to be avoided at all costs, Sir Clive."

He favored me with a faint smile and lifted eyebrow.

"'At all costs' is perhaps a little strong, but surely, boredom is something to be avoided if at all possible."

"Is that why you travel and pursue commerce so avidly, Sir Clive? To avoid boredom?"

"Hmm" was the only answer I received.

Sir Clive took a snuffbox out of his waistcoat pocket, opened it with a fluid motion, applied snuff to his nostrils, sneezed into a fresh handkerchief, replaced snuffbox and handkerchief, and drummed his fingers on the chair arm.

"Actually, boredom was only one of many things I was escaping when I began my travels and commercial ventures, Miss Fortesque."

How had this conversation acquired such a serious tone? If only Medora would hear some noise outside and begin to bark, distracting Sir Clive from his somber reverie. But the self-centered little dog stayed fast asleep in my lap.

When Sir Clive resumed speaking, his voice was low and intense.

"I wonder if you have any idea, Miss Fortesque, what it is like to never find one's place in the social order. To never quite fit in? I suspect you know a little of it. But I also suspect that you are more temperamentally suited to accommodating that plight than I am.

"My family was—what is called in more exalted circles—the cadet branch. True, we had wealth, more wealth than our titled cousins, but our wealth didn't come from land. It came from trade and manufacturing. You know what that means in England."

He paused and studied the empty fireplace.

Why is this proud, reticent man telling me things that must be quite painful for him to even think about?

I searched for a distraction, some way to change to a less personal topic of conversation, but he seemed oblivious to my discomfort and continued his story.

"My wild, harum-scarum cousin did not have to concern himself for a moment about whether or not he would be included in any circle to which he aspired. He did not have to explain his claim to his identity as a gentleman, even though his behavior was frequently in direct contradiction to any claim of gentility.

"Then he hared off to Spain and managed to get himself killed, passing the baronetcy to me. And I foolishly, stupidly, thought that my place in the social order of our beloved country was finally assured. But I discovered that the stuffy old dictum is actually true. One must be *born* to the land. I was born a tradesman's son—grandson, actually. But it makes no difference. Oak End, the Brampton estate, might belong to me, but I will never belong to Oak End—much less to the world of Drayford Vale where Oak End is situated. So I left. You might say I ran away."

I prayed to make my face and tone impassive. Whatever the purpose of his telling me his story, I knew this was a gentleman who could not tolerate my sympathy.

"Surely it is not shocking to find oneself feeling stifled by English country life. I certainly felt a lack of stimulation, sometimes to the point of feeling stifled, by life in Bath."

Sir Clive laughed ruefully.

"I am certain that Bath is most confining for a lady of your intelligence and wit, Miss Fortesque. And I suspect I would find it amusing to witness how you negotiated life amongst the relics of the Pump Room. However, no one would deny that you have a place there—that you belong there—whether or not you ever choose to return."

"But I do think you have found a solution to your dilemma, Sir Clive. Boston is the perfect setting for you. In Boston, *everyone* who is *anyone* has roots in commerce. In fact, success in commerce is the *sine qua non* of acceptance here. And I trust you will not think me impertinent to mention that the level of *your* success is particularly appreciated."

"Fear of being impertinent makes a lady boring, Miss Fortesque. And we have already discussed my feelings on that subject." He paused for a moment. "You are partially correct about Boston. It is both a convenient and comfortable place to center my commercial and financial interests. But I really cannot see settling here forever. I cannot see becoming part of Boston society, establishing myself among all these very interrelated, very *American* families."

What was Sir Clive saying? Had everyone at the Corrings' ball come away with the wrong impression about the degree of his interest in Beryl Corring?

I really needed a cup of tea, but Ada had inexplicably failed to appear with the expected tea tray.

"In fact, Miss Fortesque, I believe that you have a dilemma similar to mine."

For a moment, I thought Sir Clive was referring to the missing tea tray. But his tone was sufficiently serious that I realized he was speaking of something else entirely. I focused my attention, still trying to discern the purpose of his surprise call.

"You have a place in Bath. But you really don't relish returning to it, do you? I have a place in Boston, but I do not wish to settle here permanently."

I reminded myself to breathe. Certainly Sir Clive was not . . .

"And it seems to me that our respective dilemmas could be resolved quite nicely if we were to marry."

In spite of my momentary premonition that Sir Clive was about to propose, I found myself to be incapable of speech. Only Medora's soft snores broke the silence.

Finally, Sir Clive cleared his throat.

"Surely you cannot be completely surprised, Miss Fortesque. I believe I have bordered on fulsome in my compliments of your intelligence and character. I had not taken you for a lady who believes in—much less insists upon—raptured protestations of undying love."

One does not have to insist upon something in order to dearly wish for it.

"Perhaps I misjudged. Are your affections engaged, Miss Fortesque?"

To tell you the truth, Sir Clive, I am not at all the clearheaded, practical lady you take me for. I am a hopelessly sentimental lady who cannot seem to recover from a one-sided attachment.

I realized that I would rather walk barefoot over hot coals than admit such a thing to Sir Clive.

"No, Sir Clive, I have no understanding with any gentleman."

The truth, but not the whole truth. I hoped my voice sounded firm.

Once more, my companion gazed into the empty fireplace.

"Ah, Miss Fortesque. I suspect that we have one more experience in common. The loss of someone for whom we cared—or for whom we believed we cared. I won't ask you about your romantic disappointment, Miss Fortesque. And I doubt that you will want to hear about mine. But surely, having lost our first loves does not mean that we are each to go through life alone? Surely mutual respect and even admiration can be as good a foundation, if not better, for a satisfactory marriage, as that affliction called romantic love?"

That affliction called romantic love? Yes, Sir Clive, you have the right of it. All I have known of romantic love has been an affliction.

"I really would have been surprised if you had given my proposal an acceptance straightaway, Miss Fortesque. Indeed, I am encouraged that you have not rejected it outright. Can I hope that you will take it under serious consideration?"

"Yes," I answered, with a clarity that surprised myself. "Yes, I will take your proposal under serious consideration."

He smiled, nodded, and stood to take his leave. I walked with him to the open parlor door. At least Ada had remembered that bit of her duties.

"I believe we could be quite happy together," Sir Clive said, and lifted my hand and kissed it. A courtly gesture that I found pleasing.

Fortune was with me, because Aunt Camellia and Ivy did not return for at least three quarters of an hour, sufficient time for me to compose myself. Even more fortunately, neither was interested in how I had spent the afternoon. They were too engrossed in serious questions of tucks or ruches, ruffles or flounces, ribbons or flowers. Ivy might have had aspirations of living a life of pure intellectual inquiry, but yards of pale green silk chiffon draped about her person by a modiste of Mademoiselle's skill had redirected her thoughts to more worldly matters.

Grateful as I was for the distraction of their conversation, that evening when I closed my bedroom door, the serious question about my future faced me.

Why had Sir Clive proposed? Why had he proposed at this time? Had everyone been mistaken about his interest in Beryl Corring? Had Miss Corring refused his suit?

Could I live in reasonable contentment married to a man who admired and respected me—and evidently would depend upon me to keep the demon boredom at bay—but didn't claim to love me?

Could I give up Jack?

That is a silly question, my girl. You never had Jack, so there really is no issue of "giving him up."

If I turned down Sir Clive's proposal and returned to Bath, would I live with a second big regret?

Was I being a fool, hesitating for even a moment? For not having accepted his proposal immediately?

What I needed was a good night's sleep so that I could consider all these questions calmly. Of course, a good night's sleep was impossible because of these very questions. I rose with the first light, hoping to get a cup of tea and a piece of toast in solitude.

But Uncle Derrick had already settled himself in the breakfast room when I arrived. He set aside the correspondence he had been reading and studied my face.

"Drusilla, my dear, you look as if you had received news of a death rather than an offer of marriage."

The shock on my face as I grabbed the back of a chair brought him to his feet. He gently settled me in the chair, patted my hand, poured me a cup of tea, and resumed his seat.

"I do apologize a thousand times, my dear. Camellia has repeatedly told me that I am an unfeeling scoundrel."

"How … how did you …" my raspy voice trailed off.

"Brampton paid me a visit at the wharf—when was it—two, three days ago, I believe. Can't say that he actually asked permission to pay his addresses. Not in his nature, really. But he was quite courteous, very concerned that I understand his profound admiration and respect for you, and, of course, his unquestioned ability to maintain you in a life of ease and comfort. He asked that I not mention his visit before he had the opportunity to speak with you. Last night, when you were so quiet at dinner, I guessed that he had made his offer."

"Have you told Aunt Camellia?"

"Don't worry, my dear. I am not enough of a dullard to inflict that piece of stupidity on you. Of course, Camellia loves you like a daughter, but the elements of intrigue in Brampton's proposal would send her off into ecstasies of speculation. Couldn't have that."

Relieved, I took a deep breath and sipped my tea.

"I take it that you did not give him an answer."

"No. In fact I was almost incapable of speech. It is true that he had shown me a little attention over that painting of his house. But, after the Corrings' ball, it seemed clear that he had serious intentions of offering for Miss Corring. I heard that he had been her dinner partner before the ball, he danced only with her, and he took her into supper. People assumed that an announcement was forthcoming."

Uncle Derrick smiled his fox-like smile.

"Oh yes. This is where things get delicious—as Camellia would say. Indeed, when the news reaches her ears, she will declare it to be beyond delicious—delectable, in fact." He raised an eyebrow. "It's been known for quite a while that Josiah Corring and Brampton have some sort of joint business ventures. Corring and Thornton still exists, but neither Josiah Corring nor Bradford Thornton has much enthusiasm left for the partnership. Both are looking elsewhere for new opportunities. Old Josiah and Gamaliel Thornton were friends first, before they were business partners. The present Josiah and Bradford Thornton were never close friends, and Josiah's intrigues during the recent war strained Thornton's patience. So it was no secret that Josiah was quite favorably disposed toward an even closer business relationship with Brampton."

As Uncle Derrick warmed to his story, I began to feel like a small player in a large drama.

"Enter Josiah's ambitious wife and beautiful daughter. Was Brampton ever truly interested in Miss Corring as a potential wife? I doubt we'll ever know. Although I don't doubt Camellia would move heaven and earth if she could find out. But if I had to make a wager, I would guess matters played out this way. Corring and Brampton were in discussion about some project that Corring was more enthusiastic about than was Brampton. During that time, Brampton was invited to several social functions—dinners, musicales, what have you—at the Corring mansion and Beryl and her mother decided that he would do quite nicely as a replacement for Benjamin Thornton, Beryl's recently rejected swain. But they must have rushed their fences at the ball, placing Brampton in the de facto position of Miss Corring's intended. And just yesterday, rumor on the wharves said that Brampton is exploring new business connections in New York."

But I really cannot see settling here forever. I cannot see becoming part of Boston society, establishing myself among all these very interrelated, very American families.

It all fit together perfectly. But where, if anyplace, did *I* fit in this story?

"What you say makes perfect sense, Uncle Derrick. Sir Clive told me that he doesn't see himself settling in Boston. But I still do not understand why he offered for me at this time. Just because he doesn't wish to be co-opted by the Corring family doesn't mean that he must marry someone else."

Uncle Derrick leaned back in his chair and crossed his arms over his chest.

"Don't sell yourself short, Drusilla, my dear. You are intelligent, tolerant, and polished in speech and manners. And for a gentleman of Sir Clive's sophistication, a lady with those attributes *and* exquisite taste can very well have more appeal than a certified beauty without them. Never, sweetheart, underestimate your attractiveness."

"At least when I have had a decent night's sleep? You put me to the blush, Uncle Derrick."

"No false modesty, Drusilla!"

I choked on my tea.

"That is what Sir Clive says to me!"

"So. Are you going to accept his offer?"

Had Uncle Derrick thrown a cup of cold water in my face, he couldn't have stunned me more. I supposed this was the way gentlemen conduct business.

"I don't know. Marriage is such a huge decision. And marrying someone who makes no claim to love me—nor I him, I hasten to add is—"

"And if you don't marry him, what will you do, Drusilla? You are perfectly welcome to remain here with us for as long as you like. I am sure Camellia would be grateful for help in caring for me in my dotage. Ivy has a good heart, but she's not the most practical of creatures. And if her infatuation with that head-in-the-clouds philosopher blossoms into matrimony, I suspect she will have her hands full looking after him. Or, you can always return to Bath. It's your home after all. I daresay you might come across a widower who wants a mama for his five children."

"I have already and have turned him down," I admitted, crumbling my toast.

"How old are you? Twenty and five?"

"Twenty and seven come September," I whispered.

"I'll not tell you what to do, my dear. However, I will say that few marriages are founded on the sort of breathless, passionate love that poets celebrate. But Camellia's and mine was, so I know a thing or two about the subject. Camellia was just shy of her eighteenth birthday when we met. Had just put up her hair. Never had I beheld such a ravishing creature. I was twenty years her senior and should have known better, but I pursued her with all my wit and guile. She tossed everything away to elope with me—family, fortune. Nothing more romantic. I have spent the rest of my life trying to make sure that she was compensated adequately for her impetuosity. And I believe—I hope—she doesn't regret it. But I would be deceiving myself if I did not admit that our intense, romantic beginnings extracted a cost for Camellia. Never so much as a note from her mother. Not to mention the loss of the fortune she would have inherited had she married the scion of the good Baltimore family her parents had selected for her.

"I suppose what I'm trying to say is that marriage always involves some trade-off. But I don't think it's necessarily a bad thing to be able to assess that trade-off right from the beginning. I can't tell you what choice to make, Drusilla, my dear. But I think you have the spine to face the alternatives squarely."

Uncle Derrick pushed back his chair, gathered his glasses and papers, and kissed me gently on the forehead as he left me to my thoughts.

I went in search of Ada to ask her to let Aunt Camellia know that I had retired to my room with a headache—not a total fabrication. The maid had not looked me in the eye since her failure to bring a tea tray to the parlor the previous afternoon. I should have discussed the matter with her, but I was depending upon her to keep Sir Clive's visit to herself. I did not need to contend with Aunt Camellia's speculations while I was weighing my future. Ada mumbled that she would relay my message to the mistress, and I felt like a coward for tolerating her insolence as I made my way back to my bedroom and closed the door.

I lay down with a lavender water compress on my brow, more able to relax after my conversation with Uncle Derrick.

How did I wish to spend the rest of my life? It was kind of my uncle to reassure me of a welcome in his home, but both he and I knew that I had never contemplated becoming a permanent part of his household. A year's visit is what I had planned. I had enjoyed the change of scene. It was fascinating to witness Ivy's emergence from her girlish cocoon and try out various enthusiasms. What would she become? An imaginative writer? An idealistic thinker—or more likely the wife who would make an idealistic thinker's life possible? Or something else? A lady who shared her mother's preoccupation with society and fashion? I sincerely wished her well, but I did not want to be part of her circle.

And, although Aunt Camellia had been a charming hostess and a fascinating lady to know, I had no desire to spend the rest of my life listening to her speculations about the intrigues of Boston society or poring over fashion plates and fretting about subtle signs of aging.

I was a welcome guest in Uncle Derrick's household, but guests eventually leave, and I would be perfectly happy to leave in August, as I had planned.

And my plan was to return to Bath. Bath was my home. My aunts would welcome me and life would return to the routine I had always known—except for my time in London. If it hadn't been for London, I would be looking forward to returning to Bath. If it hadn't been for London, I never would have considered coming to Boston. London had spoiled me for Bath. Jack Hatton had broken my heart. But it had been life in London that had turned life in Bath from being reassuringly predictable to being unbearably stultifying.

Miss Fortesque, I believe that you have a dilemma similar to mine. . . . You have a place in Bath. But you really don't relish returning to it, do you?

No. I did *not* wish to return to Bath. I did *not* wish to remain in Boston with Uncle Derrick and Aunt Camellia. There was really only one other option.

I think you have made your decision, Drusilla, my dear.

Chapter Five

I spent the next four days feeling as if an invisible cloud surrounded me. I had made the most momentous decision of my life. But only two people knew that the decision was mine to make. One of them, Sir Clive, made no effort to contact me. The other, Uncle Derrick, did not reveal by so much as a flicker of the eyelash that he was aware of what I was contemplating.

Then, as I was walking Medora down the Mall early in the morning, a young man I took to be a servant approached me.

"Miss Fortesque?"

He handed me a note.

"I am to wait for your answer."

> *Dear Miss Fortesque,*
>
> *May I have the pleasure of your company for a short drive tomorrow afternoon at half past two?*
> *CB*

"Tell him yes."

My time in the invisible cloud was about to come to an end.

As I dithered over what gown, what jewelry to wear, I was grateful that at half past two on the following afternoon, Aunt Camellia would, in all likelihood, be napping, and Ivy and Annette Ware were planning to attend yet another edifying lecture.

When Sir Clive handed me into his finely sprung curricle, I was content with the peach gown I had selected and knew that the choice of pearls rather than amber was wise.

As Sir Clive silently guided a pair of elegant chestnuts down the Mall, I assumed that our destination was the bridge to South Boston. But instead, he turned left on a narrow road running down toward the bay. We stopped in front of a small shipbuilding wharf with the name "Robertson" over the front door.

Sir Clive guided me down a pier stretching out from the building. A seagoing vessel, the sleekest I had ever seen, was lying in the shallows alongside the pier. *Flame Goddess* was emblazoned on the side of her bow.

"How absolutely lovely!" I exclaimed.

"I am happy you approve, Miss Fortesque," Sir Clive replied with a self-satisfied smile that told me he had assumed I would express unqualified approval of what was clearly a great source of pride for him.

"I have never seen so elegant a ship. But she doesn't appear to be of sufficient size to carry much of a cargo," I observed.

"She's not designed to carry cargo—unless wine and delicacies for her passengers are considered cargo. The Dutch call ships like her yachts. She'll take me down Maine, or to New York or any port south, in considerably more comfort than even the best sprung carriage. And I won't have to risk poor service in an inn. She'll have a crew on standby for departure at my convenience."

He turned to me then and took both my hands in his.

"And I do hope that you will be a frequent passenger on her for years to come."

"I think I would like that, very much."

The words tumbled out with no effort.

He took my left hand, deftly removed my glove, and placed a ring on my fourth finger. The ring—a large, deep crimson ruby—was, in its way, as stunning as the yacht. When I lifted my face to thank him, he kissed me briefly.

"You won't regret your decision, Drusilla. I swear it."

Sir Clive declined my invitation to share our news with Aunt Camellia.

"I will stop by your uncle's office and let him know. I'll leave informing the distaff side to you," he said with a knowing smile.

I didn't thank him for this thoughtfulness, but I know my relief showed on my face. Aunt Camellia's raptures over the engagement of a niece who was all but on the shelf would be better left with as few witnesses as possible.

She was standing in the front window as I entered the parlor and spun round when she heard my footsteps.

"Drusilla, darling, I just saw Sir Clive Brampton driving his curricle up the street. Don't tell me that you were out with him! It would be just too delicious, after all the talk of his making a match with Beryl Corring!"

I sat in the nearest chair and Medora hopped onto my lap. As I stroked her, I considered whether I should let Aunt Camellia ask a series of questions that would eventually lead to the news of my engagement or if I should just simply announce it. Either way, her reaction would be dramatic. I decided there was no point in delay.

"Delicious or not, Aunt Camellia, I did indeed go for a drive with Sir Clive Brampton. And, I agreed to marry him. We are engaged."

For a moment, Aunt Camellia was bereft of speech. She paused silently, one hand on her brow, the other on her heart.

Then she laughed a full-throated, earthy laugh, shook her head, and dabbed at her eyes with a wisp of lace.

"Oh my darling, darling girl. I am *so* proud of you!"

She walked over to me slowly, took my face in her hands and kissed me on each cheek.

Then she straightened suddenly.

"Certainly there is a ring!"

And the exclamations resumed.

We were sipping tea—champagne being postponed for dinner—when Ivy returned.

I scarcely had time to notice the glow on Ivy's face when Aunt Camellia burst forth with her announcement.

"The most wonderful news, my love," Aunt Camellia told her. "Drusilla and Sir Clive Brampton are engaged to be married! And you must see her ring! I vow, she will be the envy of every young lady in Boston."

"Oh! M . . . my very best wishes, Cousin," a startled Ivy managed as she dutifully examined the ring. "I don't believe I have ever seen such a beautiful garnet."

A look of despair covered Aunt Camellia's face.

"Ivy, my dear," Aunt Camellia said in her soft, patient voice, "a gentleman of Sir Clive's standing does not give his intended a garnet. Drusilla's ring is a *ruby*, a *pigeon's blood ruby*. I suppose your mistake is understandable." Her tone became reverent. "Rubies of that size and quality are rare."

Although I was longing for an early night after such an eventful day, I wasn't surprised to hear the soft knock on my door. Aunt Camellia had evidently assigned Ivy's distraction during dinner to her amazement at my good fortune. But I remembered the glow on Ivy's face when she first returned from the lecture, and guessed that something quite apart from my engagement was on her mind.

I put aside my hairbrush—seventy-five strokes would have to do—and told Ivy to come in.

"Oh, Drusilla, I know this was a wonderful day for you, and I am very happy for you. But I just have to tell someone. Today is a day I shall always remember. When I am very old, I will treasure the memory of today."

Ivy sat primly in the slipper chair, feet together on the floor, her nightgown covering her toes. She clasped her hands under her chin, almost in an attitude of prayer, or perhaps one of a saint receiving a heavenly vision.

I searched for an appropriate response, but it wasn't necessary. Ivy was eager to tell her story.

"Annette and I arrived early for the lecture—it was at the Federal Street Church. As courtesy to later arrivals, we sat in the middle of our pew."

Ivy relaxed her saintly pose, leaned forward, and grasped the edge of the chair.

"And you will never guess what happened then."

I could have made a very good guess, but I restrained myself.

"Mr. Ellsworth Corring came and sat by *me*."

Ivy paused for a moment to permit the full impact of this revelation to penetrate my brain. But just in case the importance of Mr. Ellsworth Corring's choosing to sit by her had eluded me, she explained further.

"He had clearly seen and recognized both Annette and me when he entered the church. And at that moment, he had to choose which aisle to walk down. If he had walked down the center aisle, he would have sat next to Annette. But he chose to walk down the side aisle—*which meant he wished to sit by me!*"

Ivy jumped to her feet and hugged me impulsively.

"Here I thought he had an attachment for Annette and my feelings for him were not reciprocated."

She executed a little twirl toward the door and leaned against it, hugging herself.

"So today, I believe both our futures have been set, although mine is still unspoken. I know that you have made a wise decision to marry without romantic love. But I am so happy that I will not have to make that choice."

Ivy's party—celebrating her eighteenth birthday in May, a birthday that only our family knew would not take place until July—was three days away. The doors to the front and back parlors had been removed and carried to the cellar for temporary storage. Aunt Camellia's talent for organizing fine details was on display. Pencil and notebook in hand, she swept around the double parlors indicating where a small dance floor would be located, where the string quartet would be seated, where the buffet would be set up. Ivy was sitting on the edge of her chair, following her mother's explanations with frequent nods of her head. I was brushing Medora—for want of anything else to do.

"And champagne . . ."

But we were not to learn Aunt Camellia's plans for the champagne.

Medora jumped from my lap, barking, and ran through the door leading to the landing at the top of the front staircase.

We heard a small screech from Ada, and then a masculine voice.

"Well, well, you fluffy bit of presumption, a fellow is always grateful for an enthusiastic welcome, but it would have been thoughtful of you to have spared my boot."

"Oh dear me!" Ada wailed. "Here, sir, use my apron. I'll get another from the kitchen."

Then, before I could remind myself to breathe, Captain Jack Hatton entered the parlor. He was holding Medora, barely keeping her from lavishing his jaw with doggy kisses.

He set Medora down on the rug and grasped my hands. "Miss Fortesque, how delightful to see you again."

I reminded myself that any lady Jack Hatton addressed always believed she was the most important lady in his life, and the boyish smile was the same, regardless of who received it.

"And you, Captain Hatton. I had no idea that you were planning a trip to Boston."

A brief frown crossed his face and he looked down at my left hand and moved his thumb, which had covered my engagement ring. He raised an eyebrow, but asked no question.

"It was a spur-of-the-moment decision, so I had no time to let you know."

I became aware of two pairs of curious eyes and recovered my manners.

"Aunt Camellia, may I present Captain, the Honourable John Hatton?"

"Mrs. Fortesque." Captain Hatton bowed to Aunt Camellia. "Captain Hatton is quite sufficient," he murmured.

"A military gentleman is always welcome in my home," Aunt Camellia declared.

"I fear it's the wrong military to be welcome in most Boston homes, Mrs. Fortesque."

"You will find that most Bostonians are happy to let bygones be bygones, Captain Hatton."

"You relieve my mind, Mrs. Fortesque."

Aunt Camellia cast Jack a radiant smile before remembering her duties as hostess.

"May I present my daughter, Miss Ivy Fortesque."

Ivy, eyes wide in wonder, bobbed a curtsy.

"A pleasure to meet still another charming Fortesque lady," Jack said, turning the full force of his gallantry on my tender, young cousin.

Ada arrived promptly with the tea tray. Jack was offered and graciously declined "something stronger."

"How is Lady Constance?" I was finally able to ask after tea was poured, sugar and cream dispensed, and cake passed.

"Ebullient, as always," her brother declared. "She sends her very best love."

The next item of protocol was confirming his parents' well-being. One couldn't imagine either Lord or Lady Chase being anything but thriving.

As the formalities concluded, I knew a moment close to panic as the full force of Captain Hatton's presence in the very room where I had often daydreamed about him hit me. His blue eyes were as guileless, his smile as ready and charming. But there were subtle changes. Was the wavy golden hair just a shade paler, or was that a hint of gray? Were there a few more creases around his eyes? What had happened in the intervening years—just two years—since I had last seen him? I couldn't very well ask, so I searched for something neutral to say because I wasn't yet ready to answer an inquiry from him about my ring. He might work for the regent's Foreign Office, but he wouldn't let diplomacy keep him from asking me direct questions.

Aunt Camellia came to my rescue.

"What brings you to Boston, Captain?"

"Truth be told, my father has become bereft of serious concerns since peace has broken out and has turned his interests to commerce. He asked me to try to discover what makes American traders so successful. Of course, Boston was the obvious place to come. Most in the government are complacent about England's primacy on the seas and in trade, but my father has always looked at matters through a different lens. He has hopes of more cooperation between our two countries. Whether or not he can convince the rest of the House of Lords to go along with his wishes remains a question. And it seems to me, your husband, Mrs. Fortesque, is in a unique position to appreciate American-English cooperation."

Aunt Camellia beamed.

"True, Captain Hatton. And may I add that our family appears to be making such cooperation a tradition. Drusilla has just become engaged to Sir Clive Brampton, an English gentleman with extensive interests in American commerce."

"My sincere best wishes, Miss Fortesque," Captain Hatton said. "When I saw your ring, I feared you might have foresworn your country for an American."

The moment I had dreaded had been negotiated. But I felt no relief. How long would I have to carry a weight in my chest?

Eventually, the ordeal of Jack Hatton's visit ended. Aunt Camellia was able to determine that he had let a house in the Tontine Crescent, that he would be delighted to attend Ivy's party, and that he intended to pay a visit to Uncle Derrick's office in the near future.

After his departure, Aunt Camellia collapsed gracefully into her chair and held a delicate hand to her forehead.

"I am trying as best I can to puzzle out why, Drusilla, my love, you have not, to the best of my memory, ever mentioned your acquaintance with Captain Hatton. Having once met him, could any female ever have forgotten him?"

If you only knew, Aunt Camellia, how I have wished to forget him, you would not ask why I never mentioned his name.

I was going to have to brazen this out. It was really too bad of my governess to have given me lessons in music and painting rather than in acting.

I laughed—and I think it was convincing.

"Of course I hadn't forgotten Captain Hatton, although I had forgotten his initial impact on feminine sensibilities. But I promise you, he means nothing beyond pleasant courtesy. I imagine that his sister, Lady Constance, has a similar impact on gentleman."

"Why is his sister called 'Lady' and he's not a 'Sir' or a 'Lord'? It seems so unfair," Ivy protested.

"He is a younger son. Actually the fourth of four sons, if I remember correctly. And since his father is an earl and not a marquess or a duke, he must content himself with 'the Honourable' and that only in formal introductions and correspondence," I explained.

"I trust his eldest brother is lacking his looks and charm. It would really be quite unfair for any gentleman with Captain Hatton's gifts to also possess a title," Aunt Camellia declared.

I agreed with her, but kept my counsel.

During the next two days, Aunt Camellia and Ivy's preoccupation with the coming party was a godsend. All that was required of me was to give my opinion about the placement of flowers, arrangement of chairs, selection of music. It took no effort to give my unqualified approval of decisions Aunt Camellia had already made.

How could Captain Jack Hatton waltz—don't use that word, Drusilla, it reminds you of what you had best forget—very well, stride back into my life, just when I had finally closed the door on my memories of him?

What was the *real* reason he had come to Boston? Had the assignments he received from his father, Lord Chase, *truly* turned from matters too sensitive for the Foreign Office to dispatch to matters of trade and commerce?

He knew you were here, Drusilla. Perhaps that is why he is in Boston.

No. That didn't make sense. He knew I was in Boston because Constance told him. And she would have also told him that I planned to return to England in August. If seeing me again was important to him, there was no reason for him to come to Boston in May. All he had to do was wait for me to return to England in August.

So, Jack had told the truth—or at least a part truth—when he said he had come to Boston at his father's behest. And whatever that purpose, Lord Chase considered it to be in the best interest of England. As an Englishwoman, I ought to be happy that Captain Hatton was looking out for my country's best interests. But why, oh why, did my country's best interests have to shatter my peace of mind?

Chapter Six

If the ball given for Beryl Corring was the grandest social event of the season, the party given for Ivy was the most exquisite. Aunt Camellia's planning genius provided the perfect frame for the newly polished Ivy, presented, not as a timid miss, but as a young lady of rare and stunning beauty. When he first saw her, even Uncle Derrick, no impressionable youth, drew in a breath of wonder.

"Ivy?"

"Of course, Papa!"

But instead of throwing her arms about him in delight, Ivy took his hands, brushed his cheek with her softly rouged lips, and permitted him a gentle kiss on her petal-white cheek.

Ivy was a vision, and she knew it. Her gown of pale green silk chiffon caressed her graceful curves and featured discrete décolletage in which nestled the intricately carved pendant of the coral necklace Uncle Derrick had given her. But what made Ivy's appearance truly extraordinary was her hair. Heretofore, dressed plainly to avoid calling attention to its flaming color, it was permitted to curl and fall carelessly from a Psyche knot, drawing attention to Ivy's porcelain complexion and blue-green eyes. The coral necklace, echoing her titian curls, drew eyes to the elegant proportions of her figure.

Aunt Camellia, in robin's egg blue and diamonds, smiled her cat-ate-the-crème smile.

"I know that pearls are expected for young ladies in their first season, but why wear pearls when you are the only young lady in Boston who can wear coral to such effect?"

Why, indeed. Aunt Camellia had transformed what conventional opinion considered to be Ivy's most unfortunate feature into a unique gift that would be silently envied by ladies and frankly admired by gentlemen.

I had chosen a gown of golden silk, which I knew suited me and set off my amber jewelry. But I did not begrudge Ivy her shining perfection.

From my place in the receiving line on the landing at the top of the front staircase, I was entertained by watching the first and therefore unguarded reactions of guests upon seeing the transformed Ivy for the first time. Mamas replaced initial looks of horror and dismay with strained smiles. Older gentleman reached for eyeglasses. Their sons, more often than not, stood transfixed at the foot of the stairs before remembering that they could approach the Vision. Even my usually implacable fiancé paused for a moment when he first saw Ivy, narrowed his eyes, and smiled appreciatively before acknowledging me with a nod and proceeding to climb the stairs.

"Your aunt has certainly set the cat among the pigeons," he chuckled as he greeted me.

I could not share his amusement and I suppose it showed on my face. It was true that I had relished Aunt Camellia's triumph when I first laid eyes on Ivy. And I had been as entertained as Sir Clive apparently was when I watched our guests' unguarded reactions to her transformation. But Sir Clive's choice of image—"cat among the pigeons"—disturbed me. Aunt Camellia had seen that Ivy, imaginatively groomed and gowned, possessed an exotic attractiveness that might even challenge the acknowledged perfection of Beryl Corring's more classic beauty. But was Ivy prepared for the flirtations of potential suitors, the petty jealousies of less sought-after young ladies, not to mention the thinly veiled hostility of their mamas? "Cat among the pigeons?" I feared that Ivy was more like a vixen cornered by a pack of hounds.

But if Beryl Corring felt the slightest twinge of jealousy, she soon discovered a satisfactory antidote—Captain Jack Hatton. Dressed in pale lavender accented with amethyst and pearl jewelry, her dark curls framing pansy eyes and rosebud mouth, Miss Corring was a foil for Jack's blond handsomeness. Seeing them together, I was transported back to London—surely, I had not seen Miss Corring in London. Then I realized it was not Miss Corring I was recalling, but Lady Antony Compton, whom Captain Hatton was squiring the day I met him. No wonder Miss Corring had seemed familiar to me. Her resemblance to Lady Antony was remarkable. And it seemed that Jack still appreciated brunette beauty. He might have lost Lady Antony to Major Howells, but it looked as if he had no competition for Miss Corring.

I fingered my ruby ring beneath my glove, reminding myself that I had made my choice and set about finding Sir Clive in order to introduce him to Captain Hatton—a task I was inexplicably dreading.

"Congratulations on capturing a lady of exceptional wit and insight, Sir Clive. My sister, Constance, will be eager to make your acquaintance. I must warn you, she will hold you accountable for Miss Fortesque's happiness. Constance can be quite exacting in her requirements before granting her approval of members of our sex."

Sir Clive gave me a sidelong smile.

"I shall do my best to earn Lady Constance's approbation, Captain Hatton."

Apparently, Sir Clive decided to put his resolve into immediate action. Not only did he delay his departure for the whist tables to partner me in a dance, he engaged Ivy in the next set. I was gratified to observe his ability to transform her guarded reaction to him into shy smiles.

"That was quite thoughtful of you," I told him as he was leaving the dancing for his more preferred entertainment.

"No need to flatter me, my dear. Ivy has a rare beauty that any gentleman can appreciate. Your Aunt Camellia is to be congratulated on recognizing her daughter's unique charms and knowing how they should be best presented."

Since Aunt Camellia had also created a setting in which guests relaxed and enjoyed themselves, my task as assistant hostess was not demanding. I did see Mr. Douglas Robertson, leaning against the wall, apparently studying a set of dancers with disapproval. Or was it just Miss Susan Jones and Mr. Benjamin Thornton of whom he disapproved? I didn't ask. There was an empty place in the set and a young lady without a partner. Apparently the elegance of his ship designs was not matched by equally elegant manners. But when I suggested to him that Miss Ware might enjoy dancing, he flushed, apologized, and went about his gentlemanly duty.

As the evening progressed I chastened myself for my fears for Ivy. What possible harm could there be in Ivy's being the star of a soiree given in her honor? Outwardly, she might look like a sophisticated heartbreaker; however, nothing in her deportment had changed. She still glowed when Mr. Ellsworth Corring deigned to converse with her. But she treated all of the young gentlemen who flocked about her with unaffected consideration. No vigilant mama could have found fault in her behavior.

Shortly before supper, Sir Clive reappeared.

"What would you say to a breath of fresh air?"

He nodded toward the doors that opened onto the balcony overlooking the Mall.

The night had turned chilly. Sir Clive silently removed his jacket and draped it around my shoulders. But there was nothing lover-like in his demeanor. His arms crossed, he studied the row of trees lining the Common, just visible as clouds drifted across a half moon.

"It has occurred to me that there is a matter I should have spoken to you about before asking you to marry me."

He grasped the railing of the balcony balustrade, apparently bracing himself for what he planned to say.

Oh dear God! Please don't let there be some first wife stashed away in a distant land.

"I mentioned to you that I inherited my title from my cousin Richard—actually, he was my second cousin—who was killed fighting in Spain. What I did not tell you is that some time after his death, a trooper's widow appeared in Sussex with a Spanish orphan, no doubt fathered by a British soldier, whom she claimed to be Richard's son. His sister, Katherine, prostrate with grief over the loss of both her father and brother within a short time, took in the waif and claimed him as her nephew, insisting that she saw some family resemblance in him that eluded me. The boy—he must have been about three years of age—was mute, never said a word. Since Katherine already had the care of her aging and eccentric great-aunt, it seemed to me to be a lapse of judgment on her part to also take on the care of a young child, especially a child who might never grow up to be able to earn any kind of living. I told her as much. But my advice was not welcomed."

Sir Clive let go of the balustrade rail, leaned against it, once more crossing his arms across his chest, his face obscured in shadows.

"If Katherine wanted to rear her brother's natural child, there really was nothing I could do or say to change her mind. And it did seem to relieve the worst of her grief, even though she persisted in wearing mourning long after the usual time for mourning had passed."

He paused for a moment in his recitation, and then resumed, his voice low and without inflection, as if he were delivering news of the death of a minor royal.

"But everything changed when a friend of Richard's returned from Spain, claiming that Richard had married a Spanish woman—actually, a Spanish lady of high birth. Suddenly, Katherine became convinced that the strange child she had taken in was the legitimate son—and heir—of her brother. Katherine's subsequent marriage to the local baron, Lord Dracott, enabled her to launch a full investigation into the possibility of her brother's marriage. She was determined to also establish that the child she had taken in was, indeed, her brother's legitimate heir."

The moon emerged from behind a cloud, revealing Sir Clive's face as a mask of pain. Instinctively, I reached out and grasped his hands, which felt icy, even through my gloves. For a moment, he held on as if I were pulling him from certain death. Then he gave a bitter laugh, dropped my hands and patted my cheek.

"You can well understand that I did not wish to remain in a small community where I would be seen as a bully fighting a pitiful orphan for my inheritance. So I left, stopping briefly in London to hire the best legal representation available before departing England to make my way in commerce."

I felt the need to reassure this proud man who had been placed in an untenable situation.

"I think you acted admirably, under the circumstances."

His face relaxed, and he smiled fleetingly.

"You are fair as well as sensible, my dear Drusilla. But, have you considered the implications of my circumstances? It is four years now, and certain facts have been established. Richard *did* marry a Spanish lady. That much has been proven beyond doubt. The question now is, will the authorities certify the legitimacy of the orphan? Will they recognize him as the son of Richard and his Spanish wife? If they do, I will lose my inheritance. Not that I will miss the rents of an estate as modest as Oak End. But I will lose my title. I will be *Mr.* Clive Brampton. And you would be *Mrs.* Clive Brampton, not *Lady* Brampton. I should have warned you earlier. If you feel that I misled you on this matter, you are fully within your rights to break our engagement."

What sort of person would I be to break a promise over the matter of a title? How dishonorable to even consider such a thing!

"Don't be silly!" I said, eager to reassure him, and perhaps also to affirm my own good character.

His smile did not completely relieve the strain on his face.

"I believe I said this before, but I promise you, you won't regret your decision."

He retrieved his jacket and we quietly reentered the parlor. No one seemed to have marked our absence, except for Captain Hatton, whose eyes narrowed as he nodded to me from across the room.

As supper was served and the evening came to an end, with Aunt Camellia receiving sincere accolades from her guests, I became increasingly aware that I had crossed a new threshold in my relationship to Sir Clive—or perhaps I had better teach myself to call him Mr. Brampton, just in case.

How a man of his pride must have agonized living through the events he had described. It was fortunate that he had the means to escape such an intolerable predicament. But how on earth could a three-year-old Spanish orphan conclusively be proven to be the son of a dead English soldier and a dead Spanish mother? There must be missing pieces to the story that Sir Clive either did not know, or did not include in what he told me.

Regardless, somehow, my commitment to him was more profound and irrevocable than it had been before our fateful conversation on the balcony. I did not love Clive Brampton. I had no illusion about that. He was a proud, arrogant man, who, I was certain, was capable of biting criticism and acid sarcasm. But he also had endured a twist of fate perfectly designed to demean a man of his character and temperament. Indeed, it was possible that the title giving him unique cachet in egalitarian America might be stripped from him in the not-too-distant future.

In spite of his wealth and dominance in commerce, I knew him to be vulnerable. Strangely, I felt compelled to protect his pride. If he did lose his title, it would be my role to assure him—and society—that it mattered not at all. And I knew it was vital that he never discover my feelings for Captain Jack Hatton.

"Miss Jones sent a message that you would be welcome to stop by for a cup of tea and a chat this morning," Ada informed me as I entered the empty breakfast room. Susan Jones and I had discovered that, with the exceptions of Uncle Derrick and her father, we were the only early risers in our respective households.

I cut through the opening in the tall hedge that separated our gardens and was shown into the Joneses' breakfast room.

"I wish I could be more fashionable and sleep in late after retiring so late," Miss Jones laughed as she poured out.

"The beauty of it is, that the fashionables aren't awake to see us being so unfashionable," I reassured her.

"You ease my mind, Miss Fortesque."

"Please, do call me Drusilla. If I am to carry the secret of your lack of sophistication, you really must treat me with less formality."

"And, do call me Susan. With a family name as ordinary as 'Jones,' one would think that my dear parents could balance it with a less ordinary name. However, this morning is no occasion for complaints, but for congratulations. Last evening was a triumph for your aunt and your cousin. Mama could not stop exclaiming. Miss Ivy must be in heaven."

"The nicest aspect of her success is that she remains so natural and unaffected. Sometimes I suspect that Aunt Camellia would like her to be a little more practical and worldly wise, but I could detect no change in Ivy's behavior, even though she was the focus of attention of most of the young men in attendance."

"Of course, Beryl Corring was perfectly happy to have all the *young* men pay attention to Miss Fortesque, because Miss Corring cared only about the attentions of Captain Jack Hatton. Captain Hatton is quite extraordinary, is he not?"

Be careful, Drusilla, my girl. The lighthearted touch is probably best. I laughed.

"Extraordinary is an apt description of Captain Hatton. Ladies find him charming. Gentlemen find him admirable. And, although he was born to privilege, he doesn't seem to be overly impressed by his family connections."

"You were well acquainted with him in London?"

"I am not certain that I would say 'well acquainted,' but our paths did cross from time to time," I temporized. "He is the next-eldest brother of my friend Lady Constance."

Susan looked puzzled.

"His sister is 'Lady,' but he isn't 'Lord'?"

I braced myself to instruct another American in the arcane uses of British titles.

"As the fourth son of an earl, he has no honorary title. But in formal introductions and in correspondence, he is addressed as 'the Honourable.' *Daughters* of earls, however, are given the honorary title 'Lady.' But if they do not marry a gentleman with a title, they are expected to revert to plain 'Mrs.'"

"So, when you marry Sir Clive, you will be called 'Lady'?"

Perhaps. Perhaps not.

"I will be given the honorary title of Lady Brampton—not Lady Drusilla. A 'Lady' before a Christian name is given only to daughters of earls, marquesses, and dukes."

"Perhaps it was worth a revolution to dispense with such confusing usages and the social distinctions they represent," Susan laughed, and then shrugged. "Not that we lack our own very clear, if unspoken, social distinctions. Which, by the way, added a *soupçon* to the pleasure of last night, observing the denizens of Beacon Hill appreciating the elegance of hospitality in a Colonnade home."

"Speaking of Beacon Hill appreciating the Colonnade, am I mistaken in my impression that Mr. Benjamin Thornton was particularly solicitous of you last evening?"

Susan wrinkled her brow momentarily, considering my question.

"I am not quite sure what to make of Benjamin Thornton. I've always had the impression that his parents, the Bradford Thorntons—in contrast with Mrs. Prudence—felt ever so slightly superior to our family. Not with the blatant snobbery of Ione Corring, but noticeable. I wonder if, perhaps, I have become the least objectionable young lady for Mr. Thornton, now that Beryl Corring appears to be well and truly out of his reach. Frankly, I wouldn't put it beyond Mrs. Prudence—with Mama's blessing—to have made a subtle suggestion to him."

"No false modesty, please!" I protested.

Good heavens! Was I beginning to talk like my fiancé?

"I am certain that if Benjamin Thornton is seeking out your company, it is because he finds you charming and attractive."

Susan smiled at me with a raised eyebrow.

"Your confidence in me is much appreciated, Drusilla. But I have never known the heir to the Thornton fortune to act without deliberation. He hides it with a 'hail fellow' demeanor, and can even make one believe that he is modest and unsure of himself, if he thinks one is sufficiently gullible to swallow his pose. I do confess, he is quite charming when he sets his mind to it, and being the center of his attention can make a lady feel every bit as beautiful as she wishes she were in her dreams. But I wonder," she added, stirring a half cup of tea and setting the spoon in the saucer without taking a sip. "I wonder if Benjamin Thornton's interest in me is actually more for someone else's notice."

"You fear Mr. Thornton's attentions to you might actually be his effort to let Miss Corring know that he doesn't care that she rejected him?"

"Precisely." Susan said, stirring her tea some more.

"Well, at least you are clever enough to be able to detect his game, if, indeed, he is playing a game."

I hoped to conjure the happy, gossipy Susan Jones, whom I preferred to the sober introspective lady she had become.

She rewarded me with a smile.

"You are right, of course, my dear Drusilla. And one evening's attentiveness does not mean that Mr. Thornton will do more than nod and tip his hat the next time we encounter each other."

She paused for a moment, chewing her lower lip.

"But, if Benjamin Thornton hopes that he can arouse jealousy in Beryl Corring's heart, I think he has an impossible task before him."

Of course, Susan was referring to Jack Hatton. I searched for a distraction.

"Benjamin Thornton might have been hoping that Beryl Corring would notice him paying you attention last night. But, from my observation, someone *else* was noticing his attentions to you. I could swear that Mr. Robertson did not look at all happy while you were dancing with Mr. Thornton."

Susan harrumphed.

"You are imaging things. He didn't utter a single word to me all evening long. And he did manage to ask Miss Ware to dance," she protested.

"At my suggestion. While he was glowering at Mr. Benjamin Thornton's marked attentions to you, Miss Ware was observing Mr. Ellsworth Corring's attentions to Ivy. *Voila!* A perfect match! I have known such pairing to end at the altar."

"Miss Fortesque! Sorry, Drusilla. Mr. Robertson might not be the most charming gentleman, but surely you don't mean to condemn him to life with Annette Ware!"

"If Mr. Robertson succumbs to Miss Ware, it is his own responsibility. But why should you spare a thought for his fate?"

"You are right, of course." Susan took a sip of tea. "The man is brusque to the point of rudeness."

"I wonder. Perhaps he is just reserved."

Susan shook her head.

"A gentleman who can be successful in designing ships is certainly capable of asking any lady to dance with him if he wishes to."

It seemed to me that she had given the matter considerable thought.

"Sir Clive Brampton is waiting to speak to you," Ada informed me upon my return. "I put him in the front parlor."

Sir Clive appeared to be contemplating the ashes in the fireplace as I entered the almost empty room, which had not yet been restored to its usual function after having served as a modest ballroom the night before.

"I am sorry, Sir Clive, but we still seem to be at sixes and sevens this morning. Uncle Derrick promised to send some lads up from the wharf to help move furniture back, but they haven't arrived."

"Don't apologize." Sir Clive took my hands and brushed my forehead with a kiss. "I told the maid I would be brief. I've decided to take *Flame Goddess* on a trial run down to New York, where I want to look at some investments. I don't expect to be too long there, a week, two at the most."

He took me by the shoulders and lowered his lips.

He means to kiss me, really kiss me.

But before our lips met, we both heard a rustle at the parlor door. We straightened in unison. In the doorway stood Ivy, gowned in white muslin sprigged with green, her blushing face framed by curls tumbling from a precarious Psyche knot, blue-green eyes wide open, pink mouth forming an "O" of surprise.

"Why, Miss Ivy! How charming you look this morning," Sir Clive bowed to her.

"I . . . I am so very sorry for . . . for . . ." Unable to name the cause of her regret, Ivy's voice trailed off.

"Nonsense. No need to apologize, Miss Ivy. I was just telling your cousin that I am taking a quick run to New York. Trying out my new yacht, *Flame Goddess*. If she is as seaworthy as I hope, perhaps she will have a true flame-haired goddess as a passenger before too long."

With a nod to each of us, he was gone.

"Let's wave him good-bye from the balcony." Ivy was opening the French doors by the time she finished the sentence.

I arrived at the balustrade just in time to see a startled Sir Clive return Ivy's farewell wave before his carriage rolled down the Mall.

Ivy watched as the carriage faded from sight. She sighed and turned to me. "I must beg your pardon, Drusilla. I have been intemperate, and quite mistaken in my judgment of Sir Clive and your engagement to him." She smiled a sad smile of contrition. "Please do forgive me. At the very least, I should have trusted your ability to assess and value a gentleman of true character. Sir Clive is as considerate as any gentleman I have met, and he is clearly in love with you."

She blushed and turned to study the balustrade. "I am sorry to have interrupted his bidding you farewell—it seemed as if my feet were glued to the floor. But I am truly grateful for the way he was able to gloss over my embarrassment and put me at ease. You are fortunate to have engaged his affections, Cousin."

I patted Ivy's hand.

"I am so happy, my dear, that you admire my fiancé. I do believe the feeling is mutual."

Chapter Seven

Aunt Camellia did not try to hide her dismay.

"Not another improving lecture!"

Although Ivy had resumed her less fashionable mode of dressing, her newly acquired self-confidence gave her appearance the aura of singular beauty. A few tendrils escaped the tight knot to frame her face and the contrast of her untrimmed bonnet drew one's attention to her porcelain complexion and aqua eyes. The heavy tome she was carrying revealed her destination.

"It is most important to live a balanced life, Mama. I think I would be mistaken to abandon the life of the mind just because I enjoyed some social success. And quite wrong to abandon old friends for new."

I suspected that Ivy's little homily was a quote from one of her "old friends"—Ellsworth Corring or Annette Ware—which, I could not decide.

Aunt Camellia watched silently as Ivy departed the drawing room, Ada trailing in her wake.

"I suppose it's all to the good for Ada to get some exercise and fresh air. But I had so hoped that Ivy's party would open her eyes to the attractions of gentlemen with more promising expectations than those of Mr. Ellsworth Corring."

"It is my understanding that primogeniture is not the law here, so he might very well stand to have a generous inheritance," I replied.

She dismissed my reassurance with a wave of the hand.

"I have no doubt that the Corrings will guarantee him sufficient income so that he can pursue castles in the air indefinitely. That is just the point. What a positively stultifying life for my daughter, whose unique beauty could gain her a truly splendid match."

Perhaps a life pursuing castles in the air is what Ivy wants.

"It's not quite time to give up hope, Aunt Camellia. You can be certain that if Mr. Ellsworth Corring is present at the lecture, Miss Annette Ware will also be there. Forgive me if I sound cynical, but I suspect that Miss Ware's cultivation of friendship with Ivy is related to Mr. Corring's being attracted to Ivy."

Aunt Camellia smiled.

"Thank you for reminding me of Miss Ware's machinations. I wonder if hoping for her success makes me a disloyal mother." She laughed and shrugged. "Never did I dream that my interests would coincide so perfectly with the interests of the dreadful Annette Ware. Now, if you will excuse me, I believe I shall take a nap. One must not let these little worries etch their dreadful mark on one's face."

Medora trailed off behind Aunt Camellia, apparently remembering that Aunt Camellia kept a box of bonbons on her dressing table.

I studied the view of the Colonnade from where I had set up my easel on the Common. In the foreground, trunks of trees lining the Mall partially obscured facades of the terraced houses, while leafy tree branches provided framing for upper stories and roofs. Not the usual perspective to paint, and therefore one I found appealing. In my mind's eye I saw Clive Brampton smiling his approval. Who else would appreciate my idiosyncrasies?

Jack Hatton.

I willed away the image of the laughing face that had eclipsed my fiancé's.

You had better become accustomed to the idea of Jack Hatton marrying Beryl Corring and settling down to a respectable, prosperous life here in Boston.

As stultifying a life for Jack as Ivy's would be with Ellsworth Corring. Oh dear! If Ivy married Ellsworth Corring and if Jack married Beryl, I will be connected to Jack by marriage. I tried to repress visions of endless social encounters with Mr. and Mrs. Jack Hatton.

I wiped off the brush and concentrated on blocking out the terrace of houses.

You are borrowing trouble, Drusilla. Ivy is very young. She is rich and beautiful. Why, indeed, should she settle for an otherworldly philosopher, when she turned the heads of every single gentleman at her party?

Even Sir Clive was obviously struck by her beauty and had responded to her with a gallantry he rarely chose to display.

When he returned to Boston, I intended to do what I could to encourage his friendship with Ivy. It would do her good to have a point of contrast with Ellsworth Corring's patronizing, absentminded attention.

I returned to my painting with renewed concentration.

"Novel perspective, Miss Fortesque."

Startled, I dropped my paintbrush. Mr. Douglas Robertson retrieved it and handed it to me. Why is it that gentlemen think nothing of startling a lady who is absorbed in her work?

At that moment, Susan Jones and her mother emerged from a carriage across the street and climbed the stairs to their home. As the door closed behind them, Mr. Robertson sighed.

So my suspicion was true. Douglas Robertson harbored tender feelings for my friend Susan. Why, then, did he act like such a dolt around her?

"I'm so sorry that Miss Jones did not see us. She might have joined us and given her opinion of my picture. I do value her judgment in things artistic."

Actually, I had no idea about whether or not Susan had any artistic judgment, but I couldn't think of another way of probing Mr. Robertson's reluctance to pursue his clear interest in her.

"Beauty is inevitably attracted to beauty," my companion mused, still gazing at the door of the Joneses' house.

"Then I am certain she would admire your work, Mr. Robertson."

I was rewarded with a frown.

"Much good it would do me. An oceangoing vessel isn't something one can produce in a ballroom or a drawing room to elicit the admiration of young ladies. And I believe you have noticed—and reproved me—for my lack of address in social situations."

Aren't you the stubborn, blockheaded, ungrateful numbskull?

"Would it be so difficult for you to ask Miss Jones for a dance? Or, perhaps, offer to fetch her a cup of punch? Ladies do notice those gestures, you know."

And I know for a fact that Miss Jones has noticed their absence from you.

Mr. Robertson put his hands on his hips and shook his head.

"You really do not understand Boston, do you, Miss Fortesque? In England, you have all those titles that tell you who's who and where you belong. And anyway, if you don't mind my speaking plainly, you have nothing to worry about it. You've gotten yourself a fiancé who is rich *and* titled. Well, here in Boston," he gestured toward Beacon Hill, on the opposite side of the Common, "we have very much the same system, but without the titles. And, since you seem oblivious to it, the fact is that Mr. Benjamin Thornton is as good as a lord around here, and he has clearly shown an interest in Miss Jones. I'm not such a fool as to entertain the notion that a lady of Miss Jones's standing would care if I brought her the entire punch bowl, what with her prospects of Mr. Benjamin Thornton."

It took all my restraint to keep from emptying the water jug I was using to clean my brushes over his white shirt.

"Never have I heard such silly snobbery and the assignment of the basest motivation on the part of a lady of great integrity, Mr. Robertson! Forgive me for having entertained, even for a moment, the idea that you might be worthy of her notice!"

Without another word, Mr. Robertson stalked away toward his house at the end of the Colonnade.

Dear Lord, what have I done?

How had I managed to interject myself into the private life of my friend? Certainly she, better than I, could judge whether Mr. Robertson's hesitation to pursue his interest in her was based on excessive humility or snobbery. Furthermore, I knew that she had hesitation about Benjamin Thornton's interests and she *had* at least noticed Mr. Robertson, if just to criticize him.

I silently pledged to refrain from meddling in my friend's romantic life. Then immediately broke my pledge, resolving to drop a word of encouragement to Mr. Robertson if the occasion presented itself.

Once more, I addressed my painting, but it wasn't long before a whiff of camphor alerted me to the approach of Mrs. Prudence.

"Where is that irritating bit of fluff you had with you the other day, Miss Fortesque?"

"Good afternoon, Mrs. Thornton," I temporized, wondering, for a moment, if she was speaking ill of Miss Jones before I remembered her encounter with Medora. "My little dog preferred an afternoon nap to an outing."

"Following the example of her hostess, no doubt," Mrs. Prudence replied with a sniff before attending to my picture. "Quite good, actually, Miss Fortesque. Of course, one had heard of your depiction of Brampton's town house, and suspected that his fond feelings, so to speak, had influenced his appreciation of it."

She dipped her head and pursed her lips. "But I should have known better. Not even the *fondest* of feelings would make your fiancé act against his better judgment, from what I understand. Not that I have had or ever will have the occasion to view the painting in question, nor, indeed, have extended conversation with Brampton. My days in commerce are over, Miss Fortesque. Their end was hastened by the recent hostilities between our respective countries, which *some* of us supported in the spirit of true patriotism."

As opposed to those who were lacking in patriotism?

"I do hope that England has learned her lesson and will refrain from taking up arms against your country again, Mrs. Thornton. Being soundly routed twice should have taught even the dullest of our rulers that it is foolish to question your independence and fortitude."

Mrs. Prudence favored me with a faint smile.

"I see that Brampton's reputation for requiring value extends to his choice of bride. Well said, Miss Fortesque."

She gestured to my painting.

"I quite like what you have done." She cast a glance up Park Row and down the Colonnade.

"Charles—Mr. Bulfinch, that is—cared passionately about bringing beauty and order to our city. I do appreciate his efforts, and it is quite fitting that he has been rewarded by being summoned to finish the work on the Capitol. But there is a part of my soul that cringes at our aping the ways—even the architecture—of the Old World. I know I am almost alone in my love for the Boston

I once knew, the narrow lanes and timbered houses. My own home on Summer Street is of a bygone day, Miss Fortesque: wood framed, surrounded by gardens—and not the formal sort, I promise you. When I am gone, I wonder who, if any, will appreciate it. Not my son or daughter-in-law, I fear. They chose to build a grand pile on Beacon Street. And certainly not my grandson, Benjamin, who prides himself on seeing the latest enthusiasm and finding a way to profit from it."

Mrs. Prudence stopped speaking and cleared her throat, once more directing her attention to my painting.

"Please excuse my outburst, Miss Fortesque. I am not in the habit of confiding personal matters to acquaintances."

I had to restrain myself from reaching out and grasping her hand, the bones of which stood out in relief from under her worn, black glove. I felt compelled to offer what solace I could.

"Your home sounds delightful, Mrs. Thornton, and well worth its own portrait. If you would permit me, I should be delighted to see if I can do it justice with my modest talents. What I paint would be yours, if, indeed, it meets with your approval."

"How extraordinarily thoughtful of you, my dear. Of course, you are welcome to set up your easel on my grounds anytime. At least there will be a record of what has now gone out of fashion, even if there aren't many left who might appreciate its appeal. Although, if my grandson Benjamin has the good sense and good fortune to gain the hand of Miss Susan Jones, *she* might very well see its worth."

The following morning, Aunt Camellia declared that Ivy's wardrobe required new additions for the warmer weather and spirited her off to the dressmaker.

Taking advantage of the solitude and fine weather, I retired to a bench in the back garden with my much-read volume of *Sense and Sensibility.* Lilac bushes on each side of the bench where I sat were in bud, with pale lavender barely showing through pale green clusters of nascent blossoms. I drew in a deep breath and thought I detected a hint of the fragrance to come.

Medora, who had followed me outside, curled up and fell asleep at my feet.

Usually, the tale of Elinor and Marianne Dashwood, Edward Ferrars, John Willoughby, and Colonel Brandon served to set my world in balance and affirmed my convictions about proper behavior and human happiness. But on my current rereading of their story, the familiar sense of wellbeing it had previously given eluded me. In particular, I was finding Edward Ferrars too weak to be admirable and Elinor not particularly sensible in her devotion to him.

I closed the book. It seemed to me that if Elinor *truly* had common sense, she would not have lost too much time mourning the defection of Edward. Who could admire a man who got himself entangled with a creature like Lucy Steele?

Clive Brampton, for one, would never be so foolish.

I didn't love Clive Brampton, but I admired him.

But *Sense and Sensibility* was a *romance.* In *romances* people fall in love, no matter *how* sensible they are.

"Miss Fortesque?"

Captain Hatton.

How long had he been standing there?

Medora ran to him, circling his boots and yipping a greeting. He scooped her up and deposited her in my lap before sitting beside me on the bench. Only the slim volume I had been reading separated us.

"The maid said you were out here and I told her not to worry about announcing me." Jack had long since perfected the art of encouraging servants to forget their most basic duties.

The all too familiar fluttering of my heart and shortness of breath occasioned by Jack Hatton's proximity made it difficult for me to form a normal greeting. To give myself time to collect my thoughts, I placed Medora back on the lawn and immediately regretted not having the distraction of having her on my lap to pat.

"I'm afraid you've missed Aunt Camellia and Ivy, Captain. They are out running errands."

"That is precisely why I'm here, Miss Fortesque. I saw them entering a dressmaker's shop not a half hour ago. I needed to speak to you in private."

He is going to tell me that he plans to propose marriage to Miss Corring and ask me if I think Lady Constance would approve.

Although I thought I had prepared myself for that question, I realized I very much wanted to postpone its asking for as long as possible.

"Oh dear, where are my manners! Would you like some refreshment, Captain? A cup of tea? Some biscuits?"

A decanter of brandy, perhaps? I could use some myself.

"Thank you, no. I . . . I just stopped by to ask you a favor. And it must be kept in strictest confidence, although I know I can trust your discretion."

Jack stood and paced back and forth in front of the bench. I took the opportunity to retrieve Medora, and patted her as I awaited the dreaded announcement.

He paused, plucked a cluster of lavender and green buds, and twirled them between his fingers.

"I suppose, first of all, I must tell you why I *really* came to Boston."

I was almost overcome with relief.

At least the dreaded announcement isn't being made today.

He sat on the bench, studying the sprig of lilac buds he still held. I placed Medora back on the lawn, no longer needing nor wanting a distraction.

"I suppose, then, that you are still working for Lord Chase?"

Jack harrumphed, and when he spoke there was an undertone of bitterness I had never before heard from him.

"I need *something* to occupy my time. Not much call for soldiering these days."

He stretched out his legs and studied his boot tips.

"Actually, in this instance, I am working more personally for my father than for England. Not that he perceives any real difference between himself and the kingdom."

He handed me the lilac sprig and resumed pacing.

"You must be aware that we were at war with America not that long ago."

I laughed. "I've hardly been permitted to forget that fact since my arrival. Indeed, no less a personage than Mrs. Gamaliel Thornton reminded me of it just yesterday."

Jack shook his head.

"It was a sad, pathetic war, I must say. But my father was content to see it come, because he was confident that we would win and restore these rebellious colonies to England."

"It seems so unlike him, to favor such an obviously foolish adventure," I mused.

"The only subject I've ever known to compromise my father's clear thinking was the loss of the American colonies. It's said that their loss was the cause of our monarch's madness, so I suppose I should be grateful that Father's reaction was limited to a loss of good judgment. Given his sentiments, it's not surprising that the prospect of reclaiming them presented an irresistible temptation for him. And, to be fair, he was not without encouragement—from this side of the Atlantic."

Jack sat down again and crossed his arms over his chest.

"I had heard that the war was unpopular among some Americans—particularly here in Boston," I mused, "but that seems to be a weak foundation on which to build hope for restoring colonies that have successfully established their independence.

"'Unpopular' doesn't begin to describe the extent of the opposition that formed here in Massachusetts and in some neighboring states. And a leader of that opposition was an old acquaintance of my father—none other than Josiah Corring."

"Acquaintance? When did they meet?"

"Shortly after America's independence, Corring was part of a delegation that came to London to negotiate a sea commerce treaty. As the most junior members of their respective delegations, Corring and my father struck up a friendship, and corresponded from time to time over the years. All perfectly benign until Madison was elected president, and took a rather hostile attitude toward England."

"But surely, once war was declared, their correspondence would have to have stopped."

Jack raised an eyebrow.

"It should have. But it didn't."

He stretched his legs and studied his boot tips again.

"We blockaded the American coast. Oceangoing commerce from Boston, for all practical purposes, ceased. But there were plenty of small fishing boats and vessels plying coastal towns—offering many opportunities to transfer a letter from Boston to a British man-o'-war and thence to England. Which is precisely what Josiah Corring did."

"Why in the world would he wish to do something like that when his country was at war with us?"

Jack looked at me with narrowed eyes and lowered his voice to almost a whisper.

"Because he wanted his country, the United States of America, to lose the war, and, once more, become a colony of England.

And he was not alone. The conspiracy was made up of men of sufficient standing that Father felt confident of their success—and England's."

"That sounds shockingly close to treasonous to me," I whispered back and caught myself looking about for potential eavesdroppers.

Jack shrugged.

"One man's treason is another man's true loyalty. I am certain that is how Father saw it. But then, when the correspondence ended abruptly, he assumed it was because Corring and his associates had changed their minds and had abandoned the project. Furthermore, what with Boney's defeat in Spain, his exile, his return to France, and the Vienna negotiations, Father's attention was focused elsewhere. He never gave the matter another thought until a few months ago, when Corring sent him an urgent letter telling him that Corring had received an unsigned note that read:

Not all the cargo of HMS Brindle was auctioned.

"Why would Corring write Lord Chase about such an innocuous, unsigned note?"

"Sorry," Jack ran his hand through his unruly locks. "I forgot to explain that during the war, Americans outfitted privateers—merchant ships with guns—to run the British blockade, and, if possible, capture British ships, tow them into American ports, and auction the ship and cargo off for profit. Corring discovered that shortly after he had dispatched a letter to my father, HMS *Brindle* had been captured by the privateer *Bon Esprit*. Evidently, when HMS *Brindle* was captured, Corring's letter fell into the hands of someone who wished him ill. Perhaps a business rival, or perhaps someone with very different political opinions. Unfortunately, the letter in question was particularly damning. It contained specific plans for an interim government for Massachusetts pending the reestablishment of the king's authority."

"How could Corring have been so foolish?" I wondered.

Jack stood and resumed pacing.

"He must have been quite as confident of the outcome of the war as was Father." Jack smiled fleetingly. "Now my father feels honor bound to rescue his old friend. And I have been sent to effect that rescue. If only Father had sent me to organize a small landing party to seize a fort. *That's* something I could manage. The thing is, time is of the essence. Corring's eldest, Edward, wishes to stand for election to Congress. But Corring fears that if Edward declares his intentions, the contents of the letter will be made public."

"Heaven forbid!" I could feel the blood drain from my face. "Surely, that might lead to charges of treason against Josiah Corring!"

Jack sat, and took my small, cold hand in his large, warm hand.

"I really don't think you need to worry about *that*. Corring has sufficient influence with important people, so he is safe on that score."

He restored my hand to my lap and I felt bereft.

"But his reputation for good judgment would be shattered along with Edward's political ambitions. Even his business acumen would be questioned, and although he would not stand to lose all of his fortune, his finances would suffer."

Jack's face looked grim.

"Father is loath to see that happen. Not just out of personal loyalty, but also because one of England's staunchest friends in America would lose influence that could be used to England's advantage. So, if it is at all possible, that letter must be found and destroyed."

There was no doubt that Lord Chase had given his youngest son a formidable assignment, and I was beginning to fear that Captain Hatton meant to involve me in his attempt to complete it. It was a task for which I felt totally unsuited. If that was the favor he wished to ask me, it was almost as difficult for me to grant as giving him my opinion of the suitability of Beryl Corring as a bride.

"I am certain that you will find some way to ferret out the letter," I said lightly.

Jack regarded me with narrowed eyes and smiled.

"If you have that much confidence in my investigative prowess, then you will not refuse to join my efforts."

So much for Jack Hatton *requesting* a favor of me. He had, instead, managed to use my own words to *trap* me into helping him.

"I cannot imagine how I could be of any assistance in this matter."

I knew my objection was futile, even as I spoke.

"Then you are more lacking in imagination and self-knowledge that I thought you to be, Miss Fortesque."

Jack sounded as stern as his sire, Lord Chase.

"You have been in Boston for months, and it is clear that you have established yourself in a circle of friends and acquaintances. If memory of your role in London society serves me, you are more likely the recipient of gossip and confidences, rather than the source of them. Put your mind to the question. Who might like to see Josiah Corring embarrassed? Who might wish to end Edward Corring's political career before it begins? Has Corring crossed someone in business? Your uncle might have some ideas, if approached discretely."

He looked off in the distance, just above my head.

"And there is also Sir Clive."

Jack picked up my book, thumbing the edges.

"I have no idea, of course, just what you and Sir Clive discuss in private, but in the short time I have been here, I have heard that he is a silent partner in a number of business arrangements and partnerships. It is said that one secret to his success is that he knows all the skeletons in everyone's closets."

I concentrated on the lilac sprig as I twirled it between my fingers. Jack Hatton had said nothing about my fiancé that I did not already believe. But hearing it stated so baldly made me feel as if I should challenge its truth. Instead, all I could manage was a slight deflection.

"Sir Clive does not discuss his business dealings with me. I don't think many gentlemen discuss such matters with their wives, much less their fiancées."

"And, in most cases, that's just as well, no doubt," Jack said. "But in this instance, I believe Sir Clive is missing an important asset. You are one of the most levelheaded creatures I have ever met, which I learned, much to my regret."

We looked steadily at each other in silence.

Regret? What do you regret, Captain Hatton? Do you regret proposing marriage to me? Do you regret proposing marriage in such an offhand, almost insulting manner? Or do you regret that I refused your proposal?

Jack shook his head and looked away.

"Be that as it may," his voice sounded strained and distant, "I do earnestly ask you to put your agile mind to helping me solve my problem. If opportunity presents itself, I am certain that you are more than able to pose a subtle question that might give us an important clue."

"I will do what I can, Captain, but please do not depend on my efforts alone for the success of your assignment."

He stood, smiled down at me, then took my hands, pulled me to my feet, and ceremoniously kissed each hand. Looking down at his bowed head, I could see a few pale strands among the golden curls.

"I knew I could depend upon you, Miss Fortesque. Don't bother to see me out, I remember the way."

I collapsed back onto the bench and retrieved the lilac sprig that had fallen.

Whatever your regrets are, Captain Hatton, they cannot be as deep or as painful as mine.

Chapter Eight

The sprig of lilac buds would probably wilt. But I couldn't bear to throw it away. So I put it in a small vase filled with water and was on my way to my room to freshen up when I passed Ada in a hallway. She paused in her labors, feather duster suspended over the small consul table she had been dusting.

"Hope I done the right thing, telling that gentleman caller where you was and letting him find his own way out to the back garden. Right sure of himself!"

I could not say if I was more amazed that Ada could speak so many words at a time or at the impertinence of the words she had spoken. But *gentleman caller* had an implied meaning that required immediate correction.

"*Captain Hatton* is an old family friend, and he had news from England that he was eager to tell me. Of course, it was perfectly permissible for you to let him find his way to the garden if that is what he requested. He has never been one to stand on formalities. And, no doubt, he did not wish to interrupt your work." I looked pointedly at the feather duster.

The Hattons are *an old family. And Jack Hatton* is *a friend. And he was eager to talk to me about a matter that* partly *concerned England.* I reassured myself that I had told the truth even though the message I had conveyed might not match actual facts.

I mounted the stairs with all the dignity I could muster, Medora trailing in my wake.

I placed the little vase containing the lilac sprig on the table beside my bed, returned *Sense and Sensibility* to the bookcase, and sat at the dressing table, meaning to tidy my hairdo, but was unable to muster the energy to lift my brush.

I stared at my reflection in the looking glass. Did regret show on my face? Had I aged noticeably since Jack Hatton had arrived in Boston? I detected no new lines or wrinkles, not a strand of gray in my mahogany hair. But I felt old and weary.

Cease your maudlin musings this instant, Drusilla! If you aren't careful, you will go into a decline, just like the overly romantic Marianne.

I picked up the brush, smoothed back some loose strands, and considered the assignment that Jack Hatton had maneuvered me into accepting.

How could I go about discovering the author of the note that had so disturbed Josiah Corring? Subtlety was required, but subtlety required time and patience, and time was of the essence.

What did I already know? Or what did I suspect?

Boston merchants all seemed to have suffered during the recent war with England. But what had Mrs. Prudence said?

My days in commerce are over, Miss Fortesque. Their end was hastened by the recent hostilities between our respective countries, which some of us supported in the spirit of true patriotism.

It took no leap of insight to know that, according to Mrs. Prudence, Josiah Corring and his ilk had *not* accepted their commercial losses in the spirit of true patriotism. But would she feel strongly enough about the matter to engage in what was essentially blackmail? And why wait three years after the end of the war to show her hand?

Whoever sent that note to Josiah Corring must have had some connection with people involved in breaking the British blockade of the American coast. Someone in shipping. Or in ship design. Successful privateers had to be swift and maneuverable. The image of *Flame Goddess* appeared in my mind's eye, along with her designer.

> *You really do not understand Boston, do you, Miss Fortesque? In England, you have all those titles that tell you who's who and where you belong. . . . Well, here in Boston, we have very much the same system, but without the titles. And, since you seem oblivious to it, the fact is that Mr. Benjamin Thornton is as good as a lord around here, and he has clearly shown an interest in Miss Jones. I'm not such a fool as to entertain the notion that a lady of Miss Jones's standing would care if I brought her the entire punch bowl, what with her prospects of Mr. Benjamin Thornton.*

Mr. Douglas Robertson had singled out Benjamin Thornton for particular dislike. But with his gesture toward Beacon Hill and his bitter remarks about Boston society, he seemed to have a general dislike for the class that Josiah Corring epitomized.

I would try to find a way to discretely inquire into Mr. Robertson's sympathies and activities during the recent hostilities.

Then there was Mr. Benjamin Thornton. And his father, Bradford Thornton—a cipher to me. A less likely son of daring revolutionaries like Gamaliel and Prudence Thornton would be hard to imagine. It was apparent that the partnership between the Corring and Thornton families was frayed, if not about to be severed. How was Benjamin Thornton's frustrated pursuit of Beryl Corring related to the business relationship between the two families? Had Bradford or Benjamin Thornton sent the anonymous note to warn Josiah Corring that the dissolution of the partnership would require greater compensation than he wished to give?

But in spite of all the talk about financial losses suffered during the war, I saw little evidence of any lack of funds. The Thorntons and Corrings were both comfortably ensconced in mansions on Beacon Hill, which required large staffs of servants to maintain.

And Josiah Corring had just celebrated the opening of an impressive new wharf: the Corring Wharf, not the Corring & Thornton Wharf. I recalled seeing the Bradford Thorntons and Mr. Benjamin Thornton at the opening reception, appearing to be quite content with their associate's new venture. But was that all a sham?

For the first time, I considered the cost of building such a wharf, one with sufficient warehouse and office space to attract enough tenants to pay off the investment and make a profit. I had assumed that Josiah Corring's opposition to war with England was because it was ruinous for him financially. But somehow, he had been able to produce sufficient funds to build and open an impressive new wharf—just three years after the war everyone knew was disastrous for Boston sea merchants.

Where did Josiah Corring get all that money? Did he have a secret partner?

I looked down at my ring. The facets of the ruby sparkled in reflected light.

Sir Clive, no doubt, had the wherewithal to back such a project. And his offices and warehouse were in the Corring Wharf, while Uncle Derrick's remained in the India Wharf.

If, indeed, Clive Brampton were a secret partner in the Corring Wharf, he would have no motive to blackmail Josiah Corring.

I felt a rush of relief, then a blanket of guilt.

What sort of lady are you, Drusilla, to suspect your fiancé of such nefarious behavior?

I resolved to give Sir Clive the loyalty he deserved as my fiancé. And I would do what I could to discover the writer of that simple but threatening note. It was the least I could do for Lord Chase, a gentleman whom I admired and respected.

The Thornton House was known to all Boston, even if it was not prominently situated for viewing. Set well back from Summer Street in more of an acreage than a city lot, bordered by tall yews, and visible only through a gate giving entrance to a wandering pathway leading to a sheltered front door, it was a relic of an earlier day, when Summer Street was a bucolic lane.

Hez, who was carrying my easel, discovered that the gate was unlocked and swung open easily, its hinges having been well oiled against salty gusts of easterly winds. Of gray clapboard with a deeper gray roof, the house nestled down among the trees and shrubbery within which it was embedded. Only dormers of upper-story windows offered its residents a view over the surrounding vegetation.

Although it might be expected for me to portray the front of the house with its off-center entrance, I asked Hez to set up my easel in the side garden. Hyacinths bordering the path where I worked filled the garden with fragrance. I sketched out east-facing French doors, which gave access to a small covered porch and seven shallow steps leading down to the garden. For descendants of stern-living Puritans, the Thorntons had built for comfort and beauty.

I painted in solitude until the sun, descending toward the roofline of the house, began to shine in my eyes, and I started to clean my brushes and prepare to depart.

"Miz Thornton would like for you join her for a cup of tea."

The speaker was dressed in calico covered by an apron rather than the usual servant's black or gray garb, and looked to be ten years older than her employer. She did not wait for my response, but disappeared through the French doors, apparently assuming that I would accede to "Miz" Thornton's wishes.

Having been entertained in some of the grandest houses in England, I had not anticipated being quite overwhelmed by the sitting room of an American revolutionary. But I was. The exotic luxury of Mrs. Prudence's surroundings contrasted with her unadorned, almost shabby attire. I entered a repository of objects, both decorative and functional, from legendary lands: the floor was covered in a carpet upon which a complex design in deep jewel tones must have been worked by Persian hands. Exquisite figurines from China graced the tops of fancifully carved tables and shelves. Intricate screens from Northern Africa were placed to fend off drafts. And everywhere, there was shining brass from India, polished to reflect the candlelight from two graceful chandeliers, which were likely to have hung in a Parisian *hôtel particulier* during the time of the *ancien régime*.

Mrs. Prudence was seated behind a tea service of austere elegance, set upon an ebony table sporting legs carved in the shape of sea serpents.

"Miss Fortesque. How kind of you to make good on your promise so promptly. I am eager to see your finished work, but I shall refrain from pestering you until you believe it to be complete."

"I do hope you will permit me to paint more than one view of your house, Mrs. Thornton. No doubt, I should have begun with the front, but I was so charmed by the prospect from the side garden, I could not resist beginning there."

"You are a young lady of good judgment, Miss Fortesque. And I believe your artistic gifts are of equal quality. Of course, you are quite welcome to paint as many views of this house as you wish."

"I shall do my best not to disappoint you, Mrs. Thornton. But I must admit that I am relieved my task is confined to painting a reasonable representation of the exterior of your house. How I could go about portraying this room in watercolors, I cannot imagine. It is a treasure box of delights for the eyes."

My hostess received my fulsome compliment with a nod, much as a declared beauty would receive a modest nosegay from a lesser swain.

"Of course, it takes more than one generation's curiosity, discrimination—and daring—to assemble a truly memorable collection of domestic accoutrements. That is why I fear I shall always find the furnishings of some of the grander and newer houses in Boston quite bland—elegant and costly as they are."

As she poured tea into a cup decorated with pagodas, a smoky aroma wafted in the air.

"I trust you drink Lapsang, Miss Fortesque?" she inquired as she handed me the cup.

But before I could assure her of my fondness for China tea, I heard a footstep from the doorway behind where I sat. A look of surprise—and perhaps irritation—flickered across Mrs. Prudence's face.

"Benjamin, my dear, to what do I owe the honor of your visit?"

"Nothing in particular, Grandmother, just thought I would stop by and say hello."

He kissed Mrs. Prudence on the forehead and then glanced at me.

"Miss Fortesque," he acknowledged me with a nod of the head, and returned his attention to his grandmother.

"Perhaps I have come at an inconvenient time."

"Don't be so punctilious, Benjamin," Mrs. Prudence instructed and waved in the direction of a table of decanters. "I doubt you are interested in tea. Help yourself and join us."

Mr. Thornton poured some brandy and raised his glass.

"Not as dramatic as the lion lying down with the lamb, but still quite reassuring to observe a true daughter of liberty serving tea to a loyal subject of the king."

"Benjamin enjoys teasing me about my past, Miss Fortesque. But I wonder if he has any notion of how much more *convenient* his life is because of the *inconveniences* so many endured before he was born."

"I believe this is where you, Miss Fortesque, should express undying loyalty to the Crown."

Mr. Thornton smiled at me with narrowed eyes.

"I was taught to be respectful of my hostess, Mr. Thornton. And, furthermore, I do believe that loyalty is best expressed in deeds, not words."

Mrs. Prudence raised an eyebrow and looked directly at her grandson, who once more saluted with his glass.

"It does seem as well that it is agreed that bygones be bygones, because the British are all of a sudden showing quite an interest in Boston. The most recent visitor from England, is, I understand, something of a family friend of yours, Miss Fortesque?"

"If you are speaking of Captain Hatton, his sister and I are close friends, Mr. Thornton."

"Seems a good sort of fellow, if perhaps somewhat at loose ends. But with peace breaking out everywhere, I suppose there's not much for a soldier—and a younger son—to do to occupy himself."

I took a sip of tea, futilely hoping that Mrs. Prudence would say something—*anything*—to steer the conversation in another direction. Then I chastised myself for cowardice. I needed to attempt to discover if there was any purpose beyond idle chitchat for Benjamin Thornton's introduction of Jack into the conversation.

"I had assumed that Captain Hatton was exploring commercial opportunities. Everyone knows that your country has the most agile trading fleet in the world," I offered.

"But I believe that men of Captain Hatton's background—he is the son of an earl, or so I've heard—consider commerce below them," Mr. Thornton parried.

It seemed likely that Benjamin Thornton had given considerable thought to Jack Hatton's reasons for being in Boston. Was it because he knew about the letter? Or was it simply because he was still hoping for Beryl Corring and saw Jack as his primary rival?

"Captain Hatton has never discussed his attitude toward commerce with me, Mr. Thornton. But as a fourth son, and a military gentleman facing what looks to be an extended time of peace, he might be of a mind to disregard older prejudices of titled families."

Once again, Benjamin Thornton regarded me with his narrow-eyed smile. "Or, he might be exploring the prospect of filling his coffers with the *proceeds* of commerce, without actually *indulging* in it."

"*Benjamin!* I will not have my parlor sullied with common gossip!" Mrs. Prudence chided.

"I apologize, Grandmother, but I wouldn't have thought you to be sympathetic with the idea of a hard-earned American fortune being married off to support the leisured nobility of England."

Mrs. Prudence's face flushed. "How the Corring family disposes of its assets is no concern of mine—nor of yours, I might add," Mrs. Prudence reproved.

Mr. Thornton shrugged off his grandmother's reprimand, and began to stroll about the room, picking up a vase or figurine, examining it briefly before moving on.

"You will kindly leave the valuation of my possessions to an auctioneer, after I have passed on, Benjamin," Mrs. Prudence said tartly.

"You misjudge me, Grandmother," the unchastened grandson replied as he picked up a carved model of a ship in full sail.

"I have always admired your collection, but especially this."

He drew a finger down the side of the miniature ship's hull.

I would not have believed Mrs. Prudence to be able to achieve the look of a misty schoolgirl, had I not seen the transformation before my eyes.

"Ah. *Fair Prudence.* Your grandfather had that built to his exacting specifications. It was the pride of his life, the sleekest, fastest ship of its time. How sad it is that he could not live to see all of the advances in ship design we have today."

Mrs. Prudence's opening was too opportune for me to ignore.

"I understand that Mr. Robertson is highly regarded for his innovations. I'm no great judge of the details of ship design, but I must confess that Sir Clive's *Flame Goddess* is the most elegant vessel I have ever seen," I offered.

"Ah, the estimable Mr. Robertson," Mr. Thornton commented as he replaced the ship model on its display shelf. "As they say, 'it is an ill wind that blows no good,' and we have the war to thank for the most recent refinements in shipbuilding. I am certain that Mr. Douglas Robertson, for one, is grateful that the war gave him the opportunity to make a reputation for himself as a ship designer—and accumulate sufficient fortune to leave the dreariness of Barnstable for the Colonnade. But why he bothered, one has to wonder. He is one of the least sociable fellows I have ever encountered."

"Sociability is all well and good, Benjamin. But Mr. Robertson's talent is rare indeed. All he lacks is a young lady who can see through his diffidence and balance it with a little social polish."

"Grandmother! I never suspected your having the soul of a matchmaker! Did you have a candidate in mind to offer as a bride for Robertson?"

Mrs. Prudence chuckled and patted her grandson's cheek as he bent to kiss her forehead.

"If I should decide to develop my skills as a matchmaker, I think I ought to apply them closer to home."

"No need for that, Grandmother. I believe I can take care of myself in that matter."

He bowed to me. "Miss Fortesque, a pleasure to become better acquainted." And departed.

Mrs. Prudence reached for the teapot, but her attention remained for a moment on the door through which her grandson had left.

"I believe another cup of tea is called for, Miss Fortesque. I never know whether to be concerned or amused by Benjamin."

When I returned to my room, the lilac sprig had not wilted. I refreshed the water in its vase from the washstand pitcher and strolled over to the window that looked down on the lilac in the back garden, and the bench under it.

I felt a sense of relief and pride as I reviewed my gleanings from the afternoon. I hadn't realized how much I wanted to show Jack that I could be of assistance in his collection of information—even if solving the mystery was beyond me. I now had stronger reason to believe that Mrs. Prudence, Benjamin Thornton, and Douglas Robertson were all potential sources for the note sent to Josiah Corring. *Fair Prudence* had not been a privateer, but it was evidence that both Mrs. Prudence and her grandson were aware of the finer points of ship design as they applied to privateers. And Mrs. Prudence's sympathies during the recent war would have been sufficient motivation for her to outfit such a ship. Furthermore, just as I had suspected, Douglas Robertson had designed privateers. He must have been deeply involved with the entire enterprise of capturing British vessels.

I felt a glow at the prospect of giving Jack my information. But I had no way of contacting him. I certainly could not trust Ada's discretion with a written message to him. I would have to wait for an opportune moment. If I knew anything about Jack Hatton, he would produce such a moment exactly when and where he chose to do so.

A knock on my bedroom door interrupted my musings. Ada handed me a note. For a moment I wondered if it was from Jack. But it was from Sir Clive. He had returned from New York City and was requesting the honor of my company for a short drive the following afternoon.

I dashed off a short acceptance while the maid waited. It was only after she left that I wondered if she had seen the lilac sprig and had any idea of how I came by it.

Chapter Nine

When Sir Clive started the curricle down Common Street, I thought he was taking me to see *Flame Goddess*, perhaps even tour her. But instead, he turned down the road leading to the new bridge to South Boston and tossed a coin to a lad to watch the horse and equipage before assisting my descent from the carriage.

Only a few mothers with young children and an older couple were strolling on the bridge that was a favorite destination of Bostonians on weekends and fine evenings. We walked some distance in silence before Sir Clive stopped and took both my hands in his.

"It is good to see you again, Drusilla. I forget how soothing a presence you are until I am actually with you."

Unsure of how I felt about being a "soothing presence," I turned the subject.

"I hope your journey was a complete success."

Sir Clive dropped my hands, grasped the railing and looked down into the waters of the outgoing tide.

"Yes. Yes. On the whole, I am quite pleased. *Flame Goddess* couldn't have been more of a joy." He laughed and shook his head. "Robertson might be the most taciturn and prickly of Scots, but the man is a genius designer of ships. And New York!"

He turned to me, his face a mix of intensity and uncertainty, or was it pleading?

"I hope it will not disappoint you too very much, Drusilla, if we do not settle here in Boston after we are married. I know you have family and friends and a place in society here. But I believe I have mentioned before that I cannot see myself settling in Boston. A major reason for my trip was not just to pursue some commercial prospects in New York, but more than that, to spend some time there, get a feel for the place. And I have decided it is much more to my liking than Boston."

He looked over the nearby wharfs to the city, with its hills whose green canopy of hundreds of trees were pierced by the steeples of a dozen churches, which in turn, were dominated by the dome of the statehouse.

"It's hard for me to put into words. But I feel freer in New York. And, although I could be mistaken, I think there will be a larger scope for commercial ventures there."

It wasn't until I started to reassure him and declare I would be happy to settle with him in New York that I realized how difficult it was to frame those words.

"I . . . I really have no permanent attachment to Boston," I could hear the uncertainty in my voice and realized as long as I was in a city that had grown familiar to me, a city that included my newly found, but sincerely loved family, I could picture being his wife. But go with him to settle in a totally unknown place? Just the two of us, with no friends or family for company?

How long have you regretted not agreeing to go with Jack Hatton to Russia? And you are hesitant about going to New York with Sir Clive?

"I am sure I will find New York as agreeable as you do," I declared with greater conviction than I felt.

He took my hands in his again. "You have my promise that I will do everything in my power to see that your life there is happy and pleasant."

He dropped my hands abruptly and crossed his arms.

"That is, if you still . . ."

He glanced back at the city and then cleared his throat.

"I'm afraid I have disappointing news. And although I did warn you it was a possibility, I now know it is a certainty. The Spanish orphan has been declared legal heir of the Brampton baronetcy. I am no longer entitled to be addressed as "Sir," and you, my dear Drusilla, will never be Lady Brampton, I fear."

The enormity of his loss hit me as if a rogue wave had suddenly crested the bridge railing. I grasped his arms, both to steady myself and reassure him.

"I am so very, very sorry. It seems quite unfair—and strange—that such a finding could be made. But, please understand: it in no way affects my promise to become your wife. Honestly, *Mr.* Brampton," I smiled, hoping to take the sting of the plain address, "I did not accept your proposal because you were a baronet. And I do not intend to reject you now that the English authorities have robbed you of your birthright."

He took my face in his hands and slowly lowered his lips to mine, kissing me firmly, even harshly, before embracing me as tightly as if I were a ship's timber and he were a drowning man in the middle of the ocean.

The laughter of a child at the end of the bridge prompted him to release me. Once more, he grasped the bridge's railing and stared down into the gray water.

"I do have a favor to ask of you, my dear. I doubt that news of my loss of title will spread very quickly, and I would prefer to wait until I—*we*—settle in New York, before acknowledging my changed status.

"We haven't discussed a date for our wedding," he looked into my eyes with a hint of a smile, "but I would very much like for us to be married in the summer. Perhaps July? That would allow time for a wedding trip and for us to settle in New York in the autumn."

I struggled to overcome the lightheadedness I felt at the necessity of committing to a definite wedding date. What had I been thinking? That our betrothal would go on for years?

"Yes, I see your reasoning," I was able to respond, hoping that my voice did not sound as hollow to him as it did to me. "Of course I must consult Aunt Camellia and Uncle Derrick about what dates might be convenient for them. I believe Uncle Derrick was thinking about traveling to Portland to discuss transporting timber, or was it potatoes? Some such, I cannot quite remember."

I stopped abruptly, realizing that I had begun to babble about irrelevancies. Not quite the expected response when one is setting a wedding date.

Sir Clive—I still called him that in my mind—smiled indulgently and ran a finger down my cheek.

"Don't fret, my dear. I have said quite enough to turn your world on its head. You need time to absorb it all before a specific date is set. And, I hope I am not disappointing you by asking that we have a small private wedding. Or did you have your heart set on something quite grand?"

The relief I felt might have been all out of proportion to Sir Clive's announced preference, but it was welcome to be able to express agreement with him without reservation.

"I couldn't be happier having a small, private wedding," I declared, smiling with relief. "The very idea of a grand occasion fills me with horror!"

Sir Clive smiled at me and tucked my hand under his arm as we walked back to the carriage.

"It is reassuring to be able to depend upon your good sense and loyalty," he said.

As I mounted the stairs upon my return from my outing with Sir Clive, I heard a masculine voice from the front parlor.

"No, Miss Ivy! Plato's Forms are not best thought of as ideal representations—even though his philosophy is called idealism. At least not in our common understanding of 'ideal,' that is to say—flawless or perfect. They are rather—how shall I put it, so that you might be able to grasp the concept . . ."

When I entered the room, I saw Ivy listening to Mr. Ellsworth Corring as if her very survival depended upon her understanding what he was saying. Annette Ware was regarding Ivy with a pitying smile. Evidently, Miss Ware had already mastered Plato's Forms to Mr. Corring's satisfaction.

Ivy was in need of rescuing.

"Miss Ware, Mr. Corring. What an honor it is to have you bring your discussion group to our home."

Ellsworth Corring glanced at me with a frown and turned back to Ivy, apparently to resume his lecture. Then, remembering his manners, stood and greeted me.

"Miss Fortesque. You will forgive my confusion," he inclined his head. "Mama does remind me that not everyone is as concerned with ultimate truth as some of us are."

"I fear that the only ultimate truth I know presently is a craving for a cup of tea. Ivy, darling, would you ring for Ada?" I concentrated upon following Lady Constance's example of dealing with social bores as dismissively as I could. Otherwise I very well might have slapped Mr. Ellsworth Corring across his smug face.

When Ada brought in the tea tray, Medora roused herself from her cushion by the fireplace and chose me as her most likely benefactor. I scooped her up, placed her on my lap, and rewarded her with crumbs of tea cake, an indulgence that I sensed did not meet with Mr. Corring's approval.

"I believe you are a student at Harvard College, Mr. Corring?" I inquired, offering a particularly large portion of cake to Medora.

Any reproval of my behavior died on his lips as he launched into what was clearly his favorite subject.

"Actually, I have completed my last year at Harvard College, Miss Fortesque. Even though I have studied there little more than two years, my professors believe I am more than prepared for greater challenges. I have hope of extending my education, both formally and informally, so to speak, in foreign parts, exploring the wellspring of the newer, advanced philosophical ideas. The University of Göttingen appeals—or, perhaps, Königsberg, Heidelberg, Berlin . . ."

"Any would be proud to have you as a student, I am certain," Miss Ware said.

But Ellsworth Corring was too absorbed in his subject to acknowledge her compliment with more than a nod.

"My plan is to brush up on my German this autumn and winter and tour about next spring and summer before commencing my formal studies in earnest."

"Will you be visiting England?" Ivy asked.

"I am not at all certain that I shall. Oxford and Cambridge are all well and good, but, to be honest—and you know, Miss Ivy, that at all costs I do try to be honest—English universities are much more the playgrounds for the sons of privilege than centers of serious philosophical inquiry."

Ivy looked crestfallen. "I didn't realize that."

"I can't imagine why you should, Miss Ivy," Ellsworth Corring reassured her. "The relative value of universities in the Old World is only discussed among those who are deeply involved in intellectual pursuits."

Miss Ware stood and shook out her skirts. Medora jumped down to gather up any crumbs that might have fallen. "This has been a most stimulating afternoon. Thank you, Ivy, Miss Fortesque. But I must be on my way."

Mr. Corring rose, too, and offered to escort Miss Ware home.

The sound of their footsteps could still be heard at the bottom of the stairs when Ivy sighed. "Have you *ever* encountered such a mind?"

I have never encountered such condescension and self-importance, I was tempted to say.

"I don't believe I have," I said instead, telling the truth, but not the whole truth. I wondered if I were becoming too skilled at speaking half-truths.

"Imagine, dedicating one's life to the most elevated of thinking and sharing it with others who are not as learned."

A certain way to be excluded from the guest list of any hostess who does not wish her friends to be bored to distraction, I thought.

"As long as those being instructed are willing students," was what I said.

"I suppose you have the right of it. Not everyone has the intellect and disposition for pursuing higher thought. I feel so honored that Mr. Corring believes I have potential for such a life. I have been thinking of how I can demonstrate to him that his faith in me is sound. I know he respects and admires original literary efforts. Did you know that Miss Ware is a poet? Sometimes she recites her poems for us. And I can tell that Mr. Corring is greatly impressed with her creations. Her example has made me decide to return to my own writing. Somehow, in all of the excitement of my party and the social whirl that followed, I've neglected my novel. I have now resolved to mend my ways and write some every day. In fact, I think now, before I must dress for dinner, is a good time to begin."

She twirled, kissed me on the cheek, and almost skipped from the room.

What was the child thinking? Not a child, I reminded myself. Closer to her eighteenth birthday than her seventeenth. What was Aunt Camellia thinking? Didn't she see the futility of Ivy's infatuation with Ellsworth Corring?

"I really do believe you are worried about nothing—or very little," Aunt Camellia said as she held up a pair of pearl drop earrings to her ears and studied the effect, then exchanged them for emerald earrings, shook her head, picked up the pearl drops, and fastened them in her ears.

Rummaging though the drawers of her dressing table, she pulled out boxes and velvet bags of pearl necklaces, rings, and bracelets, and began the critical task of selecting which would best set off the drop earrings.

"Ivy is still very young. I really never did imagine that she would make a splendid match in her first year out. Rather, I wanted her to begin to get her bearings in society. Boston is so very staid; I cannot imagine any serious harm coming to her. I've decided that Ellsworth Corring presents no real threat to her happiness. And as you say, his interests lie much more in gaining the approval of boring old philosophers among dreary, dusty libraries in out-of-the-way countries and cities no one has ever heard of than in settling down with a wife—much less chasing petticoats of a different type."

"But that is just my point, Aunt Camellia. Ellsworth Corring is quite likely to break Ivy's heart. I fear that she sees herself accompanying him on his European sojourn, perhaps taking notes during his profound discussions and being the helpmate she believes he needs."

Aunt Camellia finally abandoned her boxes and pouches, turned her attention to me, and took a breath.

"*Break Ivy's heart?* Drusilla, darling, you are making a piece of work out of nothing. I would never have expected such drama, from you, of all ladies. Ellsworth Corring is no heartbreaker. A true heartbreaker must possess a modicum of charm. Are you prepared to tell me that you have detected the smallest trace of *charm* in him?"

"Not an iota," I was forced to admit.

Aunt Camellia shrugged.

"The direst outcome of this little infatuation would be that Corring actually emerges sufficiently from the clouds and makes an offer for Ivy that Ivy insists upon accepting. Now *that* eventuality is something I would do all I could to forestall. Or rather, I would count upon your Uncle Derrick to forestall. It's amazing what a discreet word, mentioned in passing, about a will or a trust that ties up an heiress's funds until she is thirty, can do to cool the ardor of a suitor accustomed to a certain level of income. But on the whole, my confidence is with Ellsworth Corring's *amour propre*. I doubt I shall be worrying about a marriage proposal for Ivy coming from *that* quarter."

She laughed, but then looked almost stern.

"But I assure you, if Ivy fell prey to a *serious* infatuation that represented a *genuine* threat to her happiness, I would be the soul of vigilance. Take Captain Hatton for example. *There* is a gentleman whose charms would keep the most complacent of mothers awake at night, pacing the floor. I wonder if Ione Corring fully appreciates the dangerous shoals dear Beryl must navigate in her determination to bring him to the altar."

Aunt Camellia turned her attention back to the jewelry on her dressing table, so I was confident she missed the flush that I could feel suffusing my face.

She selected a triple strand of pearls and held them up to her neck, cocking her head to the side, studying their suitability before putting them down and choosing a longer, single strand of larger pearls, smiling, and fastening them.

"Much better, don't you agree?" she asked.

"Remarkable, Aunt Camellia. The difference between pretty and elegant. How I envy you your eye for perfection."

"We all have our gifts. Some would consider mine superficial. Your own gift of common sense—even allowing for a lapse to worry about Ellsworth Corring as a heartbreaker—is quite as enviable. And speaking of common sense. When are you and your admirable fiancé planning to set a wedding date?"

"We were just discussing that this afternoon. We have agreed to sometime in July. But I must caution you, dear Aunt. Neither of us wants a grand event. We both prefer a small, unpretentious wedding."

Aunt Camellia turned, beaming, and clapped her hands.

"Delightful, my darling. There is nothing to be recommended in pretentiousness. And small, in the proper hands, is the height of elegance!"

The first thing I saw when I entered my bedroom was the sprig of lilac that had inexplicably burst into full bloom. As I inhaled its fragrance, I remembered Aunt Camellia's words.

Take Captain Hatton for example. There is a gentleman whose charms would keep the most complacent of mothers awake at night, pacing the floor.

Or a foolish not-so-young lady treasuring a discarded sprig of lilac.

Was I being disloyal to the man I had promised to marry? What harm could it do to enjoy a sprig of lilac that had unaccountably opened after being torn from its bush and tossed on the ground?

My commitment to Sir Clive was irrevocable. I would never dream of deserting a man who was counting on my loyalty to face the loss of his fondest dreams.

But I couldn't bear to throw the sprig away or watch it slowly wilt. I selected two pages of writing paper and placed the lilac between them, put them into the middle of *Sense and Sensibility*, and told the little chiding voice in the back of my brain that I was doing so because lilacs are my favorite flower.

Chapter Ten

My fears that Aunt Camellia might perceive my lowered spirits and put me to an examination of their source were relieved by Ivy's excited announcement at dinner that Annette Ware's parents were hosting a house party at their country home in the hills of Roxbury.

Aunt Camellia's dedication to planning Ivy's wardrobe for this event was all consuming. Indeed, the intensity of her focus led to disaster, when, absentmindedly taking a step backward to assess the effect of new lace trim at the neckline of Ivy's green sprig muslin, Aunt Camellia caught her heel on a rug and fell, painfully twisting her ankle.

Of course the pain of her injury was nothing compared to the pain of being unable to accompany Ivy to the house party. But the doctor insisted that the ankle must be elevated and could tolerate no unnecessary movement. So, Aunt Camellia solemnly charged me with the care of Ivy's best interests.

"I know the party will be smotheringly chaperoned by eagle-eyed mamas, but not one of them would give a fig if Ivy were to place a foot wrong. You must be my eyes and ears, Drusilla. I am counting on you," Aunt Camellia whispered to me as Ivy and I wished her farewell.

As it happened, I did not find the task being Ivy's unofficial chaperone burdensome. Sir Clive was included among the guests, but he was frequently absent, finding business matters too compelling to spend all of his time in Roxbury. I suspected that he shared my lack of enthusiasm for much of the planned entertainment. And even when he was present, he most frequently could be found playing cards or billiards.

The last afternoon of the party, archery targets were set up on the front lawn. Never having had an opportunity to learn the sport and having no motivation to correct my lack, I took an observer's position at the foot of the stairs while the official chaperones remained seated on the verandah. Mr. Robertson, once more eschewing the gallantries expected of a gentleman, stood not far from me, arms folded across his chest, a bored look on his face.

There was the playing out of the ritual of gentlemen offering ladies instruction, with varying degrees of sincerity and necessity. Ivy, who had never before held a bow, was genuinely grateful for Ellsworth Corring's attentiveness and instruction. Susan Jones, as expert in the art as any of the gentlemen, bantered easily with Benjamin Thornton, who used witty remarks and asides to other participants to prevent accurate score keeping, which might have established Miss Jones's superiority in marksmanship.

Miss Beryl Corring, accompanied by Jack, pled ineptitude.

"Captain Hatton, how fortunate I am to have someone available to instruct me in the finer points of bowmanship, who, I am certain, is an accomplished archer."

"I do loath to disappoint you, Miss Corring, but I confess that I know nothing of bows and arrows, His Majesty's armies having abandoned their use so long ago. Perhaps you could help correct my ignorance?"

A laughing Miss Corring proceeded to instruct Jack in the basics of archery, to the amusement of the entire party.

About that time, Miss Ware, who in her role as hostess had been dispensing mostly disregarded directions and advice, realized that she was without a shooting partner.

"Mr. Robertson," I addressed the glacial presence near me. "I do believe duty is calling you to rescue a damsel in distress."

"I believe you have missed your calling as a governess," Mr. Robertson observed before ambling over to a distressed Annette and offering to assist her.

The single unused target was on the end, next to Miss Jones and Mr. Thornton.

Benjamin Thornton picked up his bow and locked an arrow in the string, but chatted with Susan rather than shooting.

There was a *thwam* sound from the next target. Mr. Robertson's first shot had hit the middle of the bull's-eye.

Benjamin Thornton flushed, raised his bow and shot. It landed on the line between the yellow bull's-eye and the red.

Douglas Robertson shot a second arrow. A second bull's-eye.

Benjamin Thornton's second shot was clearly in the red.

"I believe it is time that we gave the ladies an opportunity," Robertson said to his competitor, and turned his attention to Miss Ware, who looked awestruck at her partner's performance.

Thornton shrugged and motioned for Susan to shoot.

More impressive than a full bowl of punch, Mr. Robertson. I wonder if it will gain you anything with Miss Jones.

"Sorry to deprive you of the joys of bow and arrow, but I really did have some business to attend to," Sir Clive said as he descended the stairs.

Medora had wakened from her nap on the verandah and padded down the stairs in his wake. I scooped her up to prevent her from wandering onto the lawn amongst the shooters.

"I confess to having no interest whatsoever in archery," I replied. He took my hand and kissed it.

"That's good to know. I might have had to claim an arm injury or some such, had you been eager to join in. Shooting at a target with a bow and arrow has no charm for me. I much prefer live game and a musket—particularly if I have a trained hunting dog with me." He gave Medora a disparaging glance.

We stood in companionable silence, watching the archers. In the distance, the sun reflected on the water of the Charles River as it widened into the bay before flowing into the ocean. A gentle breeze rose from time to time to keep the heat from becoming oppressive.

"It is difficult to picture greater perfection," I said.

"Hmm," Sir Clive answered.

I glanced over at him, but his attention was focused on the archers—actually, on one archer in particular—Ivy. And for good reason. Even next to Beryl Corring, the declared beauty of the party, Ivy shone. Her green- and yellow-sprigged white muslin gown caressed her willowy frame as she aimed her bow. And when she hit the target instead of the lawn in front of the target, she glanced up at her instructor, Ellsworth Corring, with an enchanting smile framed by titian curls.

"Isn't Ivy stunning?" I said it more as a comment than a question. "And she is so fortunate that Aunt Camellia understands exactly how she should be gowned and coifed to set her unusual qualities to the best advantage."

"Yes, yes." Sir Clive slowly moved his attention away from his contemplation of Ivy. "I have long thought that the common complaints about ginger hair are rooted in envy. One can understand someone finding an abundance of freckles unattractive, but when paired with porcelain complexion, any shade of red, from golden to auburn, is, as you say, stunning."

"Aunt Camellia's fondest hope is that Ivy will make a great match, and I heartily agree that with her looks and sweet disposition, Ivy deserves to do so. Which is why it is so difficult for me to stand by and watch her exert all of her interests on Ellsworth Corring. He is so preoccupied with lofty thoughts, he seems to be incapable of appreciating Ivy for what she is."

"Insufferable pup! Your aunt cannot contemplate a match in that quarter with any cheer."

"She is depending upon Ellsworth Corring's self-absorption to head off any permanent attachment."

Sir Clive turned his attention back to Ivy, who was beginning to stroll back to the house, all the while chatting animatedly, while Ellsworth gazed down at her looking bored.

"She must have an uncommonly sweet disposition to tolerate such condescension in a gentleman," Sir Clive mused.

Before I could confirm my companion's surmise, Ivy and Ellsworth Corring had approached us.

"Miss Fortesque," Sir Clive bowed over Ivy's hand.

She responded with a breathless, "Sir Clive."

"You are in particularly fine looks today," Sir Clive said, causing Ivy to blush prettily. "Lucky man you are, to be in the company of such beauty, Corring," he added, taking the younger man's measure.

"Lucky? Oh . . . lucky, yes to be sure. However, I admire Ivy's fine mind more than any superficial beauty," Corring said.

Sir Clive raised an eyebrow. "But when a gentleman is in the company of either Miss Drusilla Fortesque *or* Miss Ivy, he does not have to make a choice between beauty and intellect."

"True, true," Corring said, placing his foot on the next step. "I would enjoy discussing the question further with you. Perhaps you could join our circle of philosophical inquiry in the blue salon," he offered without pausing for an answer to his invitation.

When Corring was out of hearing, Sir Clive gave a snort of a laugh and muttered, "It would be more agreeable to sit through a dozen Quaker Society meetings than to sit through five minutes of such drivel."

Ivy moved on in her escort's wake, but cast a smile over her shoulder as she reached the verandah.

"You were magnificent!" I exclaimed. "I have been quite concerned about the spell that Ellsworth Corring holds over Ivy, and had been meaning to ask you to pay her a little attention. To open up her horizons at least a bit."

Sir Clive and I followed the remaining archers back into the house.

"Your cousin is a creature of unique appeal. I can only think of …" Sir Clive's voice became soft, and trailed off. He paused for a moment, then continued in heartier tones. "It does not speak well for the discernment of the gentlemen of Boston that she is not deluged with suitors. Speaking of Boston gentlemen, I'm promised for a few hands of whist. I trust you will find some more engrossing way to pass the rest of the afternoon than joining Ellsworth Corring's circle."

Medora squirmed in my arms, so I headed for the gardens behind the house where I could put her down to romp in safety.

I strolled down paths covered in crushed seashells until I found a bench under a willow tree facing a small ornamental pond. Medora scampered about, occasionally pausing to follow the trail of some small creature or examine a hole leading to its abode.

I sat relishing the salty breeze on my face, enjoying a sense of contentment that had eluded me for some time. I realized just how concerned I had been about Ivy's infatuation with Ellsworth Corring and how grateful I was, not only to be able to share that concern with my fiancé, but to have him actually intervene with Ivy in precisely the manner I had hoped he would. Once more, I reminded myself that one did not have to be in love with a gentleman in order to share a rewarding life with him. Wasn't that what marriage was really for? To bring two people together who would act as a team to solve life's problems and concerns? And hadn't Clive Brampton and I just shown how well suited we were in doing that?

My reverie was interrupted by the sound of footsteps on crushed shells announcing the appearance of Beryl Corring and Susan Jones.

"Trust you to find the perfect spot, Drusilla." Susan bent to pat Medora, who had run to greet her with sharp, happy barks.

Beryl Corring took a seat beside me on the bench, removed her hat, and raised her face to catch a refreshing breeze.

"What a curious little dog you have, Miss Fortesque," she observed. "Did you bring her with you from England? Wasn't there anyone who could have cared for her in your absence?"

"I suppose I could have left her with my aunts. But, actually, she's not my dog, at least not entirely my dog. So I didn't feel comfortable leaving her in anyone else's care."

Beryl Corring looked confused.

"Her other owner couldn't take her?"

"It's really an amusing story," I said, resigning myself to recounting the history of Medora. "Two years ago, as I was walking near Hyde Park in London, I spied a street urchin throwing stones at a filthy little dog. Of course, I intervened as best I could, but I was not making much headway until a quartet of elegant horseback riders approached from the park. Two of the riders were Lady Constance Hatton and her brother, Captain Hatton. Captain Hatton took charge of the situation in true military fashion, dispatched the urchin with an expedient toss of a few coins, scooped up the dog, and handed her to me. My acquaintance with

Lady Constance and Captain Hatton would have ended then and there, had not a threatening storm unleashed a torrent of rain at that precise moment. Lady Constance insisted I accompany them back to their home, and that was the beginning of our friendship. I assumed Medora was my responsibility, but I wasn't sure of her safety with my great-aunt's cat. So Medora stayed with Lady Constance."

"But how, then, did you happen to bring the dog with you to Boston?"

Miss Corring was clearly engrossed in my story, but I didn't believe Medora—or even Lady Constance—was the focus of her curiosity. Reluctant as I was to relive any part of the fateful weekend of Lady Constance's wedding, I sketched out the mishap that left me holding Medora as the Marquis and Marquise de Rochmont departed for their wedding trip.

"I knew you were acquainted with Captain Hatton and his sister, but I had no idea how close your friendship is."

A new respect sounded in Miss Corring's voice. She wasn't the first lady whose interest in me was directly related to my friendship with Lady Constance—and Lady Constance's charming brother. "It is my understanding that Lady Constance—or however she is styled now that she is married—is one of the brightest lights of London society. Haven't you missed being there for this past season? Of course, maintaining family relationships is not unimportant. And it is generous of you to support your Aunt Fortesque and your Cousin Ivy as Ivy enters society. But quite frankly, I cannot imagine anyone faulting you for choosing a London season over a Boston season."

Just as I had suspected, it was clear where Beryl Corring's ambitions lay.

"I have experienced but one London season, Miss Corring, and I admit it was all one could wish for. However, I suspect that year after year, London seasons would become almost dull in their repetition of balls and gossip."

"I find that difficult to believe, Miss Fortesque. Everyone knows that London is the center of all that the rest of the world emulates. Surely after you are married to Sir Clive, you will wish to take your place in London society. Your friendship with Lady Constance and Captain Hatton alone would guarantee your entrée to the most select circles."

"I do hope to spend some time with Lady Constance before too long," I admitted, "but that certainly does not require me to plunge into the full social whirl of a season. As for Captain Hatton, I cannot think of a hostess who does not welcome him—when he chooses to appear. His acceptance of invitations is erratic, but as an eligible bachelor, his sins of omission are forgiven."

"But once he is married and settled down, I am quite certain he will take his place in society, Miss Fortesque." Beryl Corring smiled knowingly. "His charm and easy manners would be wasted in some backwater."

So Beryl Corring had ambition to enter London society—on the arm of Jack Hatton. In spite of the warm sunshine, I felt a chill and a dampening of my spirits.

Oh Jack! Please don't let Beryl Corring turn you into a dull fixture of London clubs, whiling away your life gambling and striving to keep up with the latest fashionable folly.

"I see that you take my point, Miss Fortesque," Beryl Corring said, misinterpreting my glum expression.

She patted my hand.

"No need to worry about your friend's brother, Miss Fortesque. As my mother has often said—and has demonstrated over the years: even the best of men are in need of gentle guidance from the distaff side. A man of Captain Hatton's attributes will find just such a wife before too long, I am certain."

My weak smile must have satisfied Miss Corring. She glanced at Susan, who was throwing a stick for Medora to retrieve.

"I envy you such energy, Miss Jones," Miss Corring said as she put on her hat and tied its ribbons. "But I believe I shall rest a bit before dinner."

Susan watched Beryl Corring's retreating figure.

"I suppose Captain Hatton's fate is sealed," she mused as she scooped up Medora and took the seat next to me. "Miss Corring is *so* beautiful and *so* confident."

"You seem to have attracted more than one admirer yourself," I replied.

Susan flushed. "You noticed Mr. Robertson, too? Miss Corring insists that he was challenging Benjamin Thornton for my attention. She believes that if I 'play my cards right'—those were *her* words—I can induce Mr. Thornton to propose marriage by encouraging him to believe that I am interested in Mr. Robertson." She shook her head. "Am I too simple? Too naïve? Miss Corring's advice sounds so cold and calculating. And, furthermore, I am not at all certain that I would relish a marriage proposal from Mr. Thornton, at least if what I suspect is true actually *is* true."

"Just what do you suspect is true?" I asked.

"What I suspect is that Benjamin Thornton is still determined to attach Miss Corring and is using me in very much the same way Miss Corring suggests that I use Mr. Robertson to secure Mr. Thornton." Susan laughed. "Does that sound impossibly complicated? Do I sound as if I have a slight fever of the brain?"

The conversation between Mrs. Prudence and Benjamin Thornton played over in my mind. What was it that Mr. Thornton had said?

I wouldn't have thought you to be sympathetic with the idea of a hard-earned American fortune being married off to support the leisured nobility of England.

It did seem that Benjamin Thornton had an opinion about where a hard-earned American fortune might be better put to use. And when Mrs. Prudence suggested that he might need her services as a matchmaker, Mr. Thornton had declared himself quite capable of taking care of himself.

"Am I being impossibly far-fetched?" Susan asked in response to my silence.

"No, not at all," I reassured her. "I'm sorry for woolgathering when you needed a reaction. I was just considering your impression and I think there is a possibility that you are on to something."

Susan nodded. "I am quite certain that most people think that I am the luckiest lady in Boston to attract Benjamin Thornton's attention, but it has never felt that way to me."

Neither of us spoke for a while, the silence broken only by Medora's occasional snores as she slept on Susan's lap.

"What did you think of the other impression Miss Corring spoke of?" Susan's voice was soft and a little hesitant.

"The other impression?"

"That Mr. Robertson was trying ... attempting ..." Susan flushed.

"Of course he was! I've never seen anything so obvious."

"You really think so? You're not just trying to make me feel better?"

I laughed. "But I thought *you* thought Mr. Robertson was quite disagreeable and standoffish!"

Susan's flush deepened.

"Well, when a gentleman is abrupt and apparently not interested in making polite conversation, one, of course, makes certain judgments. But, have you ever seen any of the ships he has designed? They are pure poetry. There must be more to his character, his soul, than his lack of social address reflects."

Dear Susan. Of all ladies, perhaps you will actually make a love match. No one is more deserving, I thought.

"If anyone can discover and encourage hidden resources in a gentleman's character, it would be you, my dear friend," I said.

Chapter Eleven

When we returned to the house, Susan went directly to her room. I was restless, but the droning of Ellsworth Corring's voice coming from the blue salon discouraged me from joining the discussion circle formed around him.

Eventually, I made my way to an empty library, where the quality of the books compensated for the small selection.

I selected a slender but elegantly bound volume of Shakespearean sonnets and settled into a small sofa facing an empty fireplace. Medora curled up beside me. But no sooner had I begun to read than Medora jumped down and ran to greet Captain Hatton, who had opened and then shut the door so quietly I wouldn't have heard him, had Medora not alerted me.

He picked her up and addressed her face-to-face.

"You miserable cur. Whatever possessed me to rescue you from certain death on the mean streets of London?"

"*You* rescued Medora? That is not at all the way I remember things," I protested.

Jack tucked Medora under his arm, took the place next to me on the sofa, and set Medora by his feet.

"I see your point. Actually, *I* rescued *you* while *you* were rescuing *her*. Not that I have ever been properly thanked for my efforts—by either of you."

He glanced down at my lips, which I closed in a firm line. I also had to remind myself to take my next breath. The idea of running for the door flashed through my brain, but I was brought back to my senses by the sound of my book slipping from my lap to the floor.

Medora scurried to hide under the sofa while Jack retrieved my book and read the title.

"Shall I compare thee to a summer's day . . ." he began to recite.

Perhaps you should. I certainly am uncomfortably warm.

Matters were getting out of hand. I had to regain control of the situation—or at least of myself.

"I cannot believe you are here to recite poetry," I said, trying to imitate the voice of a disapproving governess.

Jack looked at me with narrowed eyes, but said nothing for a moment.

"You have it right, of course. I needed to speak to you privately about the matter we discussed at our last meeting. The matter of the note. Have you been able to discover anything?"

"I'm afraid I haven't been able to discover the identity of the writer of the note, but I have given the matter a great deal of thought. And perhaps what I have observed will give you no new information . . ."

"Just tell me what you have observed, what you think, and *I* will assess its value. After all, it's *my* responsibility to come up with an answer."

I could hear the tones of Captain Hatton addressing a junior officer.

I stood and began to pace. Jack, of course, stood also, ignoring my gesture that he remain seated. He pulled a cheroot from his pocket, shrugged, replaced it, and leaned against the mantel of the fireplace, crossing his arms over his chest.

"I have thought seriously about motivation," I began. "At first, it seemed quite obvious that the writer of the note was on the opposite side of the recent war from Josiah Corring and wanted him to suffer exposure. The contents of the note led to that assumption. But enough time has passed, it is possible that the potentially treasonous letter to which it refers has changed hands and is being used for some purpose not at all connected with the war."

"Hmm. For example?"

I wanted some encouragement, some signal of understanding. But Jack's face was blank.

I sat down before continuing. "Pressure to join some business venture? Make some sort of risky investment? Or, remain in a partnership that is no longer as lucrative as it once was?"

"Thornton," Jack nodded.

"But which Thornton is the question," I replied.

A flicker of amusement on Jack's face encouraged me.

"You have a candidate?"

"Not really," I admitted. "I would like to say Benjamin, just because . . . but I really know little about his father, Bradford, and *he* would be the one with the longer history of partnership with the Corrings—Josiah in particular."

Now Jack began to pace.

"One of the Thorntons is the obvious suspect, I agree. But how would a Thornton come by Corring's letter to my father? I've picked up no hint of Bradford's involvement with privateers. And his son—Benjamin—does not strike me as one to undertake an adventurous cause."

"But there *is* Mrs. Prudence!" I felt a glow of one who had played the winning card in a game of whist.

"Ah. I do want to hear all you know about Mrs. Prudence." Jack sat almost facing me, leaning on the side of the sofa, stretching an arm along the back.

I concentrated on recounting my visit to Mrs. Prudence's house and tried to ignore Jack Hatton's proximity.

"I had occasion to take tea with Mrs. Prudence in her parlor not long ago. Are you acquainted with her?"

"I know who she is. Doesn't everyone in Boston know who she is? And I have been formally presented to her. But I don't think that someone who has drawn a sword in the service of the king is much to her liking. Indeed, it is extraordinary that she would invite *any* loyal subject of the English monarch to take tea with her. It really is regrettable that our Foreign Office does not employ female diplomats. Had I not observed firsthand your ability to radiate a quality of trustworthiness and integrity that disarms even the most obdurate, *your* invitation would have astounded me."

For once, I could detect no hint of teasing in his steady, blue-eyed gaze. His sincere compliment was more unnerving than all his flirtatious gambits, and I had to marshal my wits to maintain a matter-of-fact tone.

"You know, then, the plain, almost shabby appearance Mrs. Prudence presents. It would be difficult to imagine a greater contrast between her appearance and the setting in which she holds forth. Everywhere I cast my glance in her sitting room, I saw extraordinary treasures from all over the globe, a testament to generations of seagoing merchants from whom both she and her husband were descended. Delicately carved tables and chairs, draperies of exquisite silk brocade, carpets of subtle colors and intricate design, and vases, figurines, all sorts of fanciful *objects d'art*. According to Mrs. Prudence, the finest way to furnish a house is not to follow the latest fashion, but to *inherit* one's possessions. I found it amusing that her point of view is more like an English aristocrat than a revolutionary.

Jack gave a snort of a laugh. "Exactly who is the aristocrat and who is the revolutionary can be a bit confusing from time to time. Do go on."

"While I was considering how to direct the conversation in a way that would help your investigation, who should appear, but Mr. Benjamin Thornton."

Jack raised an eyebrow, encouraging me to continue without interrupting my stream of thought.

"Mrs. Prudence did not seem surprised to have him drop in unexpectedly. Her manner with him was an odd mix of indulgence with mild irritation. I had the impression that they were something of old sparring partners."

"They sparred that afternoon?"

Jack folded his arms across his chest and cocked his head. Again I had the picture of what he must have been like as an officer, but this time, an officer listening intently to a report from a scout who had been behind enemy lines.

I quite liked being in that role and continued my story.

"Benjamin roamed about the room, picking up various vases and figurines—looking for all the world like an auctioneer assessing what they might bring. Mrs. Prudence gave him a stunning rebuke, to the effect that he should wait until her departure from earthly climes before disposing of her possessions."

"How I would have liked to have witnessed *that* exchange!"

"You would have been amused. But more than that, you would have been intrigued by Benjamin Thornton's maneuver to reinstate himself in his grandmother's good graces. He picked up a miniature model of a sailing ship—*Fair Prudence*—named, of course, for none other than our hostess. And what was even more interesting about this turn in the conversation was that it led to an exchange about ship design, privateers, and the ship designer, Douglas Robertson."

Captain Hatton's response to this bit of information was the raising of *both* eyebrows. I knew I had impressed him with my report, so I didn't wait for his encouragement to continue.

"So now we know for certain that Douglas Robertson designed privateers. I also suspect Mrs. Prudence was involved in financing American privateering during the recent war. And if that is the case, it is highly likely that her grandson knows of her involvement."

Jack's eyes narrowed. "It seems you have discovered three very different individuals with close connections to privateers. Do you have a favorite suspect for our note writer?"

I laughed. "It's impossible for me to be objective, considering my fondness for Mrs. Prudence and my antipathy for Benjamin Thornton."

"I happen to believe that objectivity is overrated, Miss Fortesque. Tell me what you think."

"Well," I temporized, trying to organize my thoughts. "First we have Mr. Robertson, who appears to be the least likely to have a motive to do Josiah Corring harm. But shortly before my visit to Mrs. Prudence, I had an exchange with him in which he expressed resentment of the established families of Boston—the denizens of Beacon Hill. And who typifies that privileged group more than Josiah Corring?"

Jack smiled and shook his head.

"I shouldn't be surprised at your ability to gain people's confidences, but I confess I am amazed someone as guarded as Robertson let that slip to anyone. Do you suspect he has a particular fondness for you?"

"Not at all. His attachment is for Susan Jones! And he resents that Benjamin Thornton's position in society makes him the clear favorite for Miss Jones's hand."

Jack laughed. "I won't bother to ask you how you discovered *that*. And I am not at all sure *how* or *if* Robertson's unrequited fondness for Miss Jones fits into our puzzle. But his antipathy for the established families of Boston might be important."

"Then, there is Mrs. Prudence," I continued. "I hope my liking for her doesn't make me underestimate her motivation to do Josiah

Corring ill. If she financed privateers, she would have been privy to the auctioning of their cargoes. She seems to be the most logical person to have come into possession of the letter. But somehow, it is difficult for me to see her as the author of the blackmailing note to Corring. I know she despised his opposition to the war and probably considered him to be a traitor to the cause she and her late husband had fought for, but . . ."

"And Benjamin Thornton?"

"I admit that he is my favorite for the blackmailer. But I understand I could very well be influenced by what might be an unfair appraisal of his manners."

"And just what has put Benjamin Thornton into your black book?"

Jack sounded as amused as curious.

"There is a presumptuousness I cannot like. His way of assuming that Susan Jones is flattered by his attention. And his proprietary air about his grandmother's house and possessions. He doesn't strike me as someone who would stand idly by and let the Thorntons be eclipsed by the Corrings. Furthermore, there is the matter of Beryl Corring."

"How on earth does she figure into this situation?"

My spirits dropped, hearing the sharpness in Jack's reaction to the mention of Beryl Corring. So it was true that he was seriously interested in her. Why else would he have spoken so abruptly upon hearing her name in connection to her father's being blackmailed? I felt like weeping at the thought of Jack Hatton being in her thrall. But I reminded myself that, as an engaged lady, I had no right to judge his romantic attachment. I concentrated on giving an accurate account of the parting conversation I had heard between Mrs. Prudence and Benjamin Thornton.

"Somehow, I cannot quite recall how, the exchange between Mrs. Prudence and Benjamin Thornton ended with Thornton suggesting . . ." I knew I was entering sensitive territory, but I was committed and couldn't retreat. "Suggesting that Mrs. Prudence would not want to see a hard-earned Yankee fortune used to pay for the indulgences of the progeny of the British aristocracy."

This time, it was Jack's turn to flush. And I saw a flash of steel in his usually lipid blue eyes. But he made no comment, and I was eager to move on with my account.

"Mrs. Thornton suggested that, perhaps, her grandson might need some matchmaking assistance. But Thornton assured her he had his marriage prospects *well in hand* and needed no help from her or anyone else to assist him. It may sound far-fetched, but it occurred to me that he might have sent the note to Josiah Corring in an effort to pressure him into aligning his family even more closely with one that had impeccable loyalty during both wars with England, namely, the Thorntons."

"Hmm," Jack said, as he resumed his seat next to me, drumming his fingers on the back of the settee as he responded to my theorizing. "For Benjamin Thornton to be the culprit, as satisfying as that would be, he would have to have at least read, or better yet, come into possession of Josiah Corring's incriminating letter. And we both agree it is unlikely for him to have had any role in the privateering enterprise."

"But look at the situation from the perspective of motivation," I countered. "While Mrs. Prudence appears to have had the most opportunity to come into possession of the letter, that doesn't necessarily mean that she wrote the note. Mr. Robertson has some motivation, but how he could have come into possession of the letter stretches the imagination. And as far as opportunity is concerned . . . I believe that Benjamin Thornton's access to and interest in his grandmother's furnishings might be suggestive. Is it too far-fetched to conceive of him, finding himself alone in her parlor or sitting room, doing pretty much what I witnessed him doing—but going a little further? Not being content to examine vases and figurines, but opening a drawer or a letter box?

"Oh you darling girl! I do love the way your devious mind works!"

Jack's eyes held me as if I were mesmerized.

Careful, Drusilla, or you will drown in their blue depths, a voice murmured in the recesses of my brain.

But I could not summon the strength to turn away. Indeed, I might have leaned a tiny bit toward him. Regardless, he was ever so slowly lowering his lips to mine.

At last, I was enveloped in his embrace and was being thoroughly kissed. I wrapped my arms around his neck. I *was* drowning, after all, and needed to hold on to *something*.

"There is no lady in the world like you," Jack whispered. "Believe me, I have tried to find one. We belong together. You know that as well as I do."

I closed my eyes and laid my cheek against his shoulder, feeling free of the cloud of regret the first time since that fateful scene in the breakfast room at Hatton Court.

"All you need do now—you must do now—is to let Clive Brampton know that you have made a dreadful mistake in agreeing to marry him."

Jack might just as well have tossed cold water in my face.

Clive Brampton! Sir Clive Brampton, who was soon to lose his title. Mr. Clive Brampton, who was depending upon my loyalty to see him through the social embarrassment that loss would bring. The gentleman to whom I had given my word.

I disentangled myself from Jack's arms. His eyes narrowed as he watched while I took deep breaths, trying to regain my composure.

"How . . . how can you say, 'All you need do'? You are asking me to go back on a solemn promise."

"Da . . . dash it, Drusilla!" Jack raked his hair in frustration. "Ladies break engagements every day of the week. Right up to the moment of the wedding! Just look me in the eye and tell me that you do not love me and that you *do* love Brampton!"

"Don't!" My voice sounded like a whimper. "Don't make this even more painful than it already is."

I had to get away from Jack before I dissolved into tears. But as I stood, Jack did, too, gripping my arms and turning me to face him. It took all the courage I could muster to look him in the eye. "You have no idea of what you are asking me to do, to just casually break my engagement to Sir Clive."

Jack let go and looked down at me, disgust etched on his face.

"I consider myself to be a bright lad. But with you, I never learn, do I? How could a fourth son with no hope of a title, much less a fortune, compete with a titled Midas?"

"That's not at all . . ."

I reached toward him, asking him to understand, but he turned away and left the room.

I collapsed onto the sofa, too numb to shed the tears I could feel behind my eyelids.

Chapter Twelve

Here you are! Cousin, I've been looking high and low for you! Cuz . . .? Whatever is the matter? Are you ill?"

Ivy's voice summoned me back to my surroundings.

"I . . . I must have gotten too much sun."

I was relieved to discover I had sufficient wit to invent any excuse for what I suspected was my less than immaculate appearance.

"It looks to me as if you fell into a shrubbery! Look at your hair! *I* am the one whose Psyche knot is always threating to tumble. Let me help you pin it back up. You really do need to lie down before dinner, but you can't risk leaving this room without some serious repairs."

While Ivy busied herself making me look presentable, I searched for a distraction from any further questions about my state of dishabille.

"Was there some particular reason you were looking for me?"

Ivy took a last hairpin from her mouth and placed it as the final anchor for my reassembled hairdo. "I had just wanted to talk to you about . . . I had wanted to . . ."

She sat beside me and studied my face. "You do look a *little* bit more the thing, but, perhaps you should lie down for a bit. I could get a lavender compress for your forehead. I would wager that you have a headache."

Nothing to match my heartache.

"I'm feeling much better," I reassured her, hoping that I had produced a convincing note of brightness. I needed to distract both Ivy and myself from my distress.

She looked around the room, apparently gathering her thoughts. "Oh, what is this?"

My heart plummeted. Surely, Jack had not left some small personal item behind—an initialed handkerchief, or that cheroot he had been playing with?

But, mercifully, Ivy was looking at the volume of Shakespearean sonnets I had been reading before Jack arrived and shattered my world.

She began to turn the pages of the slender book, pausing now and then to read a few lines. I picked up Medora from the floor and began to pat her to disguise the trembling of my hands.

Don't be melodramatic, Drusilla. Ivy is the most innocent, least suspicious creature on the face of the earth.

"Do you think our hosts would object if I took this to my room?"

"I cannot think why they would. It scarcely seems that the books here are in much demand."

"Except by you." Ivy chewed her lower lip before continuing. "When you were seeking a place to recover from sun sickness, you automatically retreated to a library and looked to great literature to make you feel better. *That* is the sign of a truly educated, elegant mind!"

"Dear Ivy! Don't flatter me!"

"It's true! I mean it! Ever since I met Mr. Corring—Ellsworth Corring—and Annette Ware, I have been trying my best to cultivate my higher faculties. They are very kind and patient when they try to explain things to me. But I never quite feel that I am on their level of advanced thought."

"Ivy, dear Ivy." I took her hands and Medora jumped back to the floor, not willing to share my attention. "You really do not give yourself sufficient credit. You have a very lively mind. Just think of that fascinating novel you are writing—about the times of knights and fair maidens. I am certain that there is no one else in Boston, much less at this house party, who has attempted anything so imaginative."

"But Ellsworth Corring and Annette don't *make things up*. They read very enlightened books and essays and *understand* and *discuss* them."

"Ivy darling! You are tempting me to tear out the hair that you have so kindly arranged! Please understand. There are many different kinds of intellect. The type that Ellsworth Corring and Annette Ware display is quite worthy, but it's not the only kind there is. Just think! Your own mother would fall asleep in less than a minute should she take it into her head to try to follow Ellsworth Corring's philosophical discussions. But is there *anyone* you know who can arrange a more inviting room or a more pleasing bouquet than she? And then there is your father. Do you think anyone lacking in brain capacity could have made the fortune in commerce that he has?"

"Hmm. I hadn't thought of it like that." Ivy laughed and gave me a quick kiss on the cheek. "If what you say is true, Sir Clive must be a *genius*! Aren't you lucky!"

But before I could struggle to affirm my good luck, Ivy became sober once more.

"That's all well and good for Mama and Papa and you and Sir Clive. Mama and Papa clearly appreciate each other's particular talents. As do you and Sir Clive. But Ellsworth Corring seems to be absorbed in philosophical pursuits to the exclusion of almost everything else."

Was this the opening I had been hoping for? Could this be an opportunity to help Ivy discover Ellsworth Corring's shortcomings as a potential husband?

Choose your words carefully, Drusilla. A word of implied criticism of that tedious young man will have Ivy rushing to his defense.

"I am certain that we all are most inclined to follow the interests that come naturally to us, Ivy. And Ellsworth Corring is clearly brilliant in his grasp of higher philosophy."

Ivy nodded.

"And in the academic world, his gifts shine. But there are other worlds. Just look at how many different interests you have."

Ivy cocked her head.

"He *does* seem to appreciate the poems that Annette Ware recites. Including a poem she wrote herself."

Ivy smiled and tapped her lower lip, just as Aunt Camellia did when she was deep in thought.

"Perhaps I could help him expand his horizons."

She hugged me and glided from the room.

At least your misery hasn't prevented you from furthering someone else's happiness, I told myself.

There was a chance that Ellsworth Corring would respond positively to Ivy's efforts to "expand his horizons." In which case, he might have potential to be a more interesting human being than he had heretofore shown himself to be. If, on the other hand, he reacted negatively, her preoccupation with him might diminish.

I tried to console myself with having furthered Ivy's happiness. My only other consolation was that the house party would disband the next morning. All I had to do was muster the fortitude to face the evening with Jack no more than the length of a room away, but lost to me forever.

I dressed for dinner with particular care, resorting to the rouge pot to compensate for my pallor and placing my best topaz broach at the V of my décolletage to distract from my generous rouge application.

Jack Hatton's back was to the door as I entered the drawing room. Over his shoulder, I could see Beryl Corring looking up into his face adoringly. I stifled an urge to turn and run back to my room and searched for my fiancé. He was conversing with Benjamin Thornton. Ordinarily, I wouldn't have dreamed of interrupting, but my pride wouldn't let me risk the possibility of Jack's turning around and seeing me look as lost and forlorn as I felt.

"How unfeeling for the two most distinguished gentlemen present to withdraw their company from the ladies," I said, smiling my brightest smile.

"Drusilla, my dear," Sir Clive tucked my arm under his and patted my hand, "You are in looks this evening."

"I do believe that the fresh air does all of us good."

"I must say you have the right of it, Miss Fortesque," Benjamin Thornton replied, looking toward the door.

Sir Clive and I turned in the direction of Benjamin Thornton's gaze. Ivy stood framed in the doorway. Her apricot gown gave a glow to her creamy complexion and set off her soft, red-golden curls.

Thornton murmured a quick, "You'll excuse me," before leaving us to secure Ivy as his dinner partner. I stifled a frisson of concern. Never had I imagined the possibility of Benjamin Thornton pursuing Ivy. What would Aunt Camellia think about such a match?

Don't let your imagination run wild, Drusilla. No harm could come of Benjamin Thornton escorting Ivy to dinner, and it might pull Ellsworth Corring's head out of the clouds.

My fiancé turned his attention from Ivy and raised an eyebrow.

"I do hope *that* was not lost on Ellsworth Corring," I said.

"He's hopeless," Sir Clive replied, nodding toward the sofa where Mr. Corring was talking with Annette Ware. Apparently, Ellsworth Corring was the only gentleman in the drawing room who was oblivious to Ivy's entrance.

Mercifully, Sir Clive and I were seated at the far end from Jack and Beryl Corring at dinner, so I was able to avoid the painful sight of them engrossed in each other's company. Ivy and Benjamin Thornton were opposite us, and I silently blessed my fiancé for keeping up a general flow of conversation that included Ivy without condescension, while also putting Benjamin Thornton on notice that my cousin was not to be trifled with. Sir Clive was letting Thornton know that Ivy's absent father wasn't the only gentleman concerned about her best interests. Once more, I reminded myself that Clive Brampton—with or without a title—was a true gentleman and he deserved my loyalty.

Only the occasional sound of Miss Corring's high laughter and Jack's low drawl drifting from the other end of the table were reminders of the pain I felt just below my topaz broach.

When the gentlemen rejoined the ladies after dinner, Beryl went to the pianoforte. Jack followed her and volunteered to turn pages—a task I had never before seen him agree to do. I was just thinking of how best to make my excuses and escape when Sir Clive asked me to join in a game of whist with him, Susan Jones, and Douglas Robertson. I couldn't find the heart to refuse him, in light of his chivalrous behavior toward Ivy at dinner.

Of course, I knew that Sir Clive was a serious card player. I soon learned that Douglas Robertson matched him in intensity—and rivaled him in ability. Susan seemed to have caught their spirit and was playing above her usual game. Only years of dreary evenings playing with my whist-mad aunts kept me from disgracing myself during the first trick. But I marshalled my forces, concentrated on the game, and endeavored to ignore Beryl's soprano—I vow she was a tiny bit sharp—floating across the drawing room.

I was congratulating myself on the quality of my play when I glanced up while Susan was shuffling, and spied Ivy chatting animatedly with Benjamin Thornton.

Was Benjamin Thornton truly pursuing Ivy? Should I be concerned? Why did this situation have to present itself when Aunt Camellia was absent? Why did this have to happen when I was so immersed in my own misery I could scarcely think straight?

"Drusilla, my dear?" Sir Clive prompted.

I glanced down at the unsorted cards in my hand, and at the two cards that had been played. Diamonds. Sir Clive had led with an ace. Didn't I have the jack? I ruffled through my cards, selected the jack, and was about to play it when I realized I was holding the jack of hearts. Shaking, I replaced it, and laid down the ten of diamonds.

Sir Clive frowned and scooped up the cards from the trick.

"I hate to walk away from a game when it's at a draw, but I find that I need a breath of air. Drusilla, my dear, would you care for a turn on the terrace?"

It sounded like a summons to an inquisition, but there was no escape. I mustered a smile in return for Susan's sympathetic glance and concentrated on walking toward the doors opened to the terrace with as much dignity as I could muster.

"I have never pried into your private thoughts, Drusilla. But something is clearly troubling you enough to intrude on your usual ability to perform basic social functions. So I do believe that you owe me some explanation for your marked preoccupation this evening."

Sir Clive was leaning against the balustrade, arms folded across his chest. Light from the drawing room showed his stern face as he studied mine, which, turned toward the garden, was mercifully obscured in shadow. Of course I had understood that a gentleman of my fiancé's business acumen had a harsh, unrelenting aspect to his personality. But why, oh why, did I have to encounter it for the first time tonight, when my dreams had just been shattered—in order to protect this grim interrogator, of all ironies.

The truth is, Sir Clive, or should I say Mr. Brampton, had I not given my word to you and had you not told me of the imminent loss of your title, I would be the happiest lady in the world right now instead of the most miserable.

What could I say? I felt as if I were drowning.

"*Something* clearly distracted you at the card table," Sir Clive prompted. What was it?"

A lifeline. I wouldn't even have to exaggerate all that much to speak of my concern about Ivy. And I *had* meant to talk to him about it anyway.

I took a deep breath and placed my hand on his arm.

"It's about Ivy."

Not really a lie at all!

"*Ivy?* I'm afraid I don't understand."

To my relief, the frown on my companion's face had turned into a look of puzzlement.

"Yes, Ivy. You know that since Aunt Camellia twisted her ankle and was unable to come with us, she counted upon me to look after Ivy and be certain that Ivy made no missteps. My main concern for Ivy has been her infatuation with Ellsworth Corring."

Sir Clive grimaced. "What a self-important, wet-behind-the-ears bore! Surely, your aunt and uncle would not countenance their only daughter being wasted on such a specimen!"

He turned and looked out over the garden. "She is a rare beauty."

His voice was so soft, I had to strain to hear him.

"Aunt Camellia is well aware of Ivy's unique beauty and she seems confident, almost to the point of complacency, that Ivy will make a splendid match. *I*, on the other hand, have worried that Ivy would more or less stumble into a marriage with Corring—one that would prove to be stultifying for her when she inevitably wakes up to her full potential."

Sir Clive regarded me with narrowed eyes.

"Have you no faith in your Uncle Derrick's ability to lay conditions upon Ivy's inheritance that would discourage such an eventuality?"

I laughed. "Aunt Camellia suggested just such a maneuver."

"Your aunt is a lady with a brain to match her charm. And the wit to conceal it. So, you'll pardon me if I am unable to understand your near-disastrous preoccupation this evening—particularly while we were playing whist."

"I suppose I focused my concerns upon Ellsworth Corring to such an extent, I failed to consider who might take his place in Ivy's affections."

Sir Clive looked startled. "You have a candidate?"

"Benjamin Thornton."

I was answered with a shrug.

"Escorting the lady who makes the most dramatic entrance into dinner is something Thornton would do without much thought. I wouldn't put a great deal of store by it."

"But what distracted me from whist was the sight of Mr. Thornton and Ivy chatting cozily. I have an impression that Benjamin Thornton does little without forethought. I'm sorry for almost ruining our card game, but wondering how my sweet, naïve cousin would manage with the likes of Benjamin Thornton gave me pause."

"Thornton." Sir Clive tapped the balustrade. "Well, well, well. You think your aunt would approve?"

It was my turn to shrug. "It's difficult for me to come up with an objective reason for her not to. But I cannot shake a sense of uneasiness."

"It's not like you to make a piece of work out of nothing—or at least not very much."

I couldn't permit Sir Clive to delve any further into the state of my mind.

"I suppose I'm making too much of my responsibilities as an alternate chaperone for Ivy." I laughed to assure him that I was well on my way to a restored perspective. "Anyway, we will all be returning to Boston tomorrow and I can gladly restore total responsibility for Ivy to Aunt Camellia. By the way, I must say how much I appreciated your engaging her in conversation during dinner. I think it is helpful for her to have such a model of gentlemanly behavior."

Sir Clive bowed his head and raised my hand to his lips.

"Always happy to help a fair lady."

As I slipped into my nightgown, I congratulated myself for having negotiated the most terrible evening of my life. For a reward, I decided to forgo my usual one hundred strokes of hair brushing and seek the oblivion of sleep as soon as possible. But a knock on the door and the appearance of Ivy let me know that I would have to postpone oblivion yet a little longer. I wearily took up my hairbrush and began my nightly ritual as Ivy settled herself on a slipper chair and carefully arranged the skirts of her apricot gown about her.

"You were a triumph tonight, Ivy. I only regret that Aunt Camellia was not here to witness it."

"I don't know if I feel triumphant." Ivy cocked her head to the side and thought a moment. Then she stood, slowly walked to the cheval mirror, and turned, looking at her reflection over her shoulder. "What I feel is older, more self-assured."

"I can well understand that. Not many young ladies in their first season would attract the attention of a gentleman of the sophistication of Benjamin Thornton."

Ivy laughed. "Mr. Thornton! I cannot be certain that he was actually interested in *me*. Oh, he was very flattering in asking to take 'the most stunning creature in this assemblage' into dinner. But when he sought me out after dinner, all he really wanted to talk about was *you*."

I put my brush down. Suddenly the conversation required my entire focus.

"Why in heaven's name did Benjamin Thornton want to talk about *me*?"

"Oh, I suppose, not *you* precisely, but your life in England. Especially your time in London. Your friendship with Lady Constance—and Captain Hatton." Ivy frowned in thought, which would have prompted a caution from Aunt Camellia, but I was too tired and confused to issue the caution in my aunt's stead.

Why was Benjamin Thornton interested in Lady Constance? Or was it more likely that Captain Hatton was the true focus of his interest? But before I could formulate an innocent-sounding question, Ivy continued.

"Perhaps the established families of Boston are intrigued by the English? Or perhaps Mr. Thornton is still holding out hope for Beryl Corring and he wants as much information about Captain Hatton and his family as he can find."

No wonder Ivy felt older and more self-assured. She was thinking—and speaking—like a true daughter of Camellia Fortesque.

"But I really didn't stop by to talk about Benjamin Thornton," Ivy continued. "I wanted to tell you how much I admire your fiancé. I don't think I have ever enjoyed dinner conversation as much as I did tonight. Sir Clive is the perfect gentleman, isn't he?

I am beginning to see that, even though I don't seem to be able to grasp all of the higher philosophy Ellsworth Corring discusses, I am perfectly able to carry on polite conversation—even with a gentleman of Sir Clive's polish and sophistication."

Ivy kissed me on both cheeks and wished me good night.

The next morning, I was the last lady to descend the front stairs to present myself for departure. Sir Clive and Benjamin Thornton each stood next to their curricles. The Joneses' family landau waited its passengers as did the Corring town coach.

Ivy, wearing the freshly trimmed sprig muslin that had occasioned Aunt Camellia's accident, was chatting with Sir Clive as they both admired his handsome pair of matched chestnuts waiting patiently for the return trip to Boston.

"Whatever has become of Captain Hatton?" Beryl Corring inquired.

"He left early this morning with Mr. Robertson for a tour of Mr. Robertson's shipyard," Susan Jones told her.

Hmm. I wonder how Miss Jones came by that bit of information. I caught her eye and she blushed.

"There you are at last, Cousin!" Ivy hailed me. "Have you ever in your life seen such an elegant pair of horses, so perfectly matched?"

"Sir Clive has exacting standards. They move as well as they look," I said before brushing her cheek with a kiss and greeting my fiancé. "I am certain that Sir Clive would be happy to take you for a drive so that you can judge for yourself."

"Good morning, Miss Fortesque, Miss Ivy." Benjamin Thornton strolled over from his equipage and doffed his hat.

He had addressed me first, but all of his attention was directed toward Ivy. "Lovely morning for the journey back to Boston," Thornton observed.

He is going to ask Ivy to be his passenger on the drive home.

Both Ivy and I looked to Sir Clive, who had no difficulty receiving our unspoken message.

"Indeed," Sir Clive replied. "I was just about to grant Miss Ivy's request for a spin behind my team. I know you will appreciate the well-sprung ride of the Joneses' landau, my dear," he said to me in parting.

"You don't strike me as a lady who opts for sedate comfort over a perch on a curricle, Miss Fortesque," Benjamin Thornton said, turning to me. "I would be pleased to have your company, and promise to deliver you to the Colonnade in perfect safety."

There was no way I could refuse his offer, but I did wonder why Mr. Thornton had extended it. Perhaps his invitation was related to the sullen look on Beryl Corring's face when she saw him hand me up to the seat on his carriage.

Chapter Thirteen

It was only after I had succeeded in rescuing Ivy from being Benjamin Thornton's companion for the trip back to Boston that I realized how little *I* wished to be his companion for the journey. The events of the past twenty-four hours had left me physically and emotionally drained, and I needed to be at my best for any encounter with this gentleman, whom I regarded as devious as any I had ever met. Medora curled up in my lap and went to sleep. I patted her absentmindedly as I tried to gather my thoughts.

Mercifully, no conversation was required as Mr. Thornton maneuvered his team out of the driveway and onto the narrow road leading to the Neck connecting Boston to the mainland. To my amazement, he managed to accomplish this task ahead of Sir Clive, whose curricle had been at the head of the line of carriages in the driveway. There was a self-satisfied smile on Benjamin Thornton's face.

"Perhaps you are now assured that my driving skills would have been sufficient for Miss Ivy's safety, Miss Fortesque. I assume that is why you were so eager to prevent her from driving back to Boston with me."

I was certain that he assumed nothing of the sort, but if a battle of wits was coming, I didn't want to use all my ammunition on a small skirmish.

"Perhaps I have been a little overprotective of Ivy these past few days. But Aunt Camellia charged me with looking after her, and as you well know, Aunt Camellia sets a very high standard when it comes to seeing to the well-being of her daughter."

"But I have never noted your aunt to be overly cautious regarding Miss Ivy's association with unmarried gentlemen of adequate fortune and good family. And I would have thought, in all modesty, that I am such." Mr. Thornton cast me an aggrieved look while maintaining the pace of his horses.

"On the other hand, I do understand your caution, Miss Fortesque," he continued, studying a turn in the road with narrowed eyes. "Your cousin is a *rara avis*. Not at all what is commonly thought of as 'pretty,' much less, 'beautiful.' More like 'stunning.' And that, combined with an apparent lack of artifice, makes a compelling combination for certain gentlemen, particularly those who are somewhat bored with more traditionally attractive females. But, clearly, your Aunt Camellia is well aware of all that. And so, I would think she would be quite favorably disposed to someone like me, a steady sort from a known family, who has already settled down to a respectable routine in the city where Ivy feels at home. I should think her concern might be much more easily aroused if a less—shall we say—*dependable*—gentleman were to show interest in Miss Ivy." He turned his gaze from the road and looked directly at me. "Captain Hatton, for example."

Ivy and Jack? Such a pairing was beyond contemplation.

"I have never noticed Captain Hatton singling out Ivy for any particular attention." The words tumbled out before I could stop them.

"And you *would* notice if Captain Hatton were to pay particular attention to your cousin, wouldn't you, Miss Fortesque?"

"Of course I would." I struggled to sound as matter-of-fact as possible. "I told you that I have been charged by Aunt Camellia to look after Ivy's best interests."

"But there is more to your vigilance than just your concern about Ivy, isn't there, Miss Fortesque. I'm guessing, and, actually, I would be willing to wager a considerable amount of money, on your being better acquainted with Captain Hatton than you have let on."

"I don't believe I like the tone or implications of what you are saying, Mr. Thornton. And I would prefer to cease all conversation for the balance of our journey back to Boston."

"Oh, for pity's sake, I do apologize if my tone or implications—as you put it—offended your fine sensibilities, Miss Fortesque." Benjamin Thornton managed to sound just a tad bored, which placed me in the uncomfortable position of seeming to be an overreacting prude. "I wasn't implying anything in the least unsavory. But it occurs to me that, given your relationship with Captain Hatton's sister, you have had an excellent position from which to observe him. And one thing has had me wondering for some time, Miss Fortesque, just niggling at the back of my mind."

Once more, he looked directly at me. But this time there would be no shock. I steeled myself for any revelation, question, or assertion.

"What I have been wondering is why Captain Hatton just happened to come to Boston this spring? Why would a son of the crème of the English aristocracy decide to visit the center of successful rebellion against the king, when there are so many quiescent colonies where he might have chosen to seek his fortune?"

"Perhaps you are underestimating Boston's place in the world of commerce, Mr. Thornton. You of all people know that the very life's blood of your city flows with the spirit of competition in markets all over the globe," I responded, expecting my verbal dueling partner to acknowledge a hit.

I was quickly disabused that any such acknowledgment was forthcoming.

"But that is exactly the point of my puzzlement, Miss Fortesque. And I suspect that you are 'too close to the forest to see the trees,' as the saying goes. There is no question that adventurous competition—some would say cutthroat competition—to travel the world establishing trading empires is what built the fortunes of Boston. And, I must say, it is clear that your fiancé, Sir Clive Brampton, personifies that competitiveness. But that quality is missing in Captain Hatton."

"How can you say that, Mr. Thornton? Perhaps he has never mentioned it to you, but Captain Hatton fought for years against Napoleon's armies in the Peninsula. I can't think of anything more adventurous than *that*. And as far as 'cutthroat competition' is concerned, I imagine that phrase becomes quite literal on the battlefield."

"Of course, he has never breathed a word to me about his battlefield exploits, Miss Fortesque. An English gentleman wouldn't dream of doing so. But I suspect it is only in those life-and-death situations that someone like Captain Hatton becomes completely engaged with the outcome of a competition or confrontation. You must understand, I do not say this as a criticism, just an observation. While he does not exude the disdain of commerce usually found in his class, I am sure that he sees its pursuit as an avocation, not a main focus, a life's driving purpose that burned in my grandfather—or does now in Sir Clive, I believe."

"And you, Mr. Thornton? Are *you* consumed with extending the Thornton name and fortunes in commerce?"

"Perhaps not in the same manner as my forbearers, Miss Fortesque, but never doubt that I have every intention of expanding my family's scope and influence. No doubt that is why I can see the lack of commercial ambition in Captain Hatton. Which brings us back to my initial question. Why did your dearest friend's brother come to Boston? I understand there is a friendship between his father and Josiah Corring going back to the early days of our republic. And Corring, supposedly, offered to take Hatton under his wing, so to speak. Show him the ropes of outfitting seagoing ships, selling shares in cargos, all that sort of thing. But I'll let you in on the most poorly kept secret along the wharves of Boston: it's been quite some time since Josiah Corring risked any of his capital directly in seagoing commerce. His most recent venture was a disaster. Sailed directly into a hornets' nest of Barbary pirates. Even the magnificent new wharf that bears his name is rumored to have been partially financed by a much more active, risk-taking sea merchant."

Benjamin Thornton half-smiled at me and raised an eyebrow. *And we both know the name of that gentleman, don't we, Miss Fortesque.* He didn't have to say the words for me to hear them.

"Speaking of your esteemed fiancé," Mr. Thornton continued, "he represents another little piece of the puzzle. Why, I wonder, when Hatton arrived in Boston and found that you, his sister's very best friend, were engaged to be married to the most successful shipping merchant, not just in Massachusetts, but probably in all of the United States, was there apparently no effort on your part, Brampton's part, or Hatton's part, to enlist Sir Clive's sponsorship of Hatton's fledgling interest in commerce?"

"I would not presume to interject myself into Sir Clive's business pursuits."

I thought that my prim tone would serve to repress Benjamin Thornton's speculations, but, instead, he guffawed.

"You'll pardon me for doubting your protestations of propriety, Miss Fortesque. I must remind you that all my life, I have known a female who is capable of daring anything she decides is in her best interests. Or in the interests of matters and people who concern her. None other than my estimable grandmother. And I believe it is her recognition of, and admiration for, that faculty in you which explains her otherwise inexplicable fondness for you."

Every time I thought I understood where Benjamin Thornton's assertions were heading, his questions went off in another direction. Clearly, he was suspicious about Jack's motivation for being in Boston. Did he suspect Jack was on the lookout for an heiress to marry, specifically, Beryl Corring? In light of what Thornton had said in Mrs. Prudence's parlor that might be the case. Or did he know about the letter and suspect Jack's real purpose? If so, how could I warn Jack, since I was unlikely to have anything beyond perfunctory, civil conversation with him? Or was Thornton hinting at something more than friendship between Jack and me? That thought turned me cold. Perhaps he was just jealous of his grandmother's kindness to me, I tried to reassure myself. Whatever he suspected, I had been a fool to try to deflect his suspicion without finding out what it was.

"I am flattered to be compared with your grandmother, Mr. Thornton, however unworthy I am of such a comparison. Certainly, by this point in the conversation, *she* would have discerned what you are trying to tell me that I have been too dull to understand."

"I am truly not trying to *tell* you anything, Miss Fortesque. I promise you. If I had any message to deliver to you, I am perfectly capable of doing so." To my surprise, I could detect no hint of duplicity in his voice. "The thing is, Miss Fortesque, I prefer to live a calm, predictable life. I suppose I am like my father in that regard. My family has lived in Boston for generations. Despite revolution and war, families here who have known each other forever rub along quite easily, conducting business among themselves. But for some time now, things have been less sure, less predictable. And the beginning of those uncertain times seems to have started with the arrival of Sir Clive Brampton, then continued with your arrival, and in ways I can only sense, but cannot articulate, culminated with the appearance of Captain Hatton."

"Certainly you are not—"

"No, no, Miss Fortesque! Perhaps I phrased my observation badly. I do apologize. I am certainly not making any allegation of skullduggery of any sort—by you or either of your compatriots. What I have been trying to express is my frustration in attempting to understand the relationships among the three of you and the effect those opaque relationships has had on both business and social interactions in what has always been my predictable corner of the world bounded by Beacon Hill and the wharves."

To my amazement, I found myself feeling a deep bond of sympathy for Benjamin Thornton. Was he feeling as much pain over the loss of Beryl Corring as I was over the loss of Jack Hatton? What could I say to put him off the trail of discovering Jack's true mission, my ambivalence about my engagement, or, most importantly, my tangled and ill-fated romance with Jack? How much truth could I actually speak?

"I wish I could provide answers to your questions, both specific and implied, Mr. Thornton. It is difficult to explain the apparent lack of rapport between Sir Clive and Captain Hatton. Although they are very different gentleman, they share the attribute of keeping their own counsel. Sir Clive by reserve and Captain Hatton by sociability. And, of course, in addition to their very different personalities, there are always the arcane habits of English social classes—but I am certain that subtle social distinctions are familiar to a son of Boston."

"Touché, Miss Fortesque." my companion treated me to a genial smile, which I had never before seen.

"It is not clear to me just how grave your concerns are regarding Captain Hatton, Mr. Thornton, but I can assure you that I have never detected the taint of malice in him."

Anger, yes. Presumption, yes. But never malice.

"Do I detect a whiff of 'damning with faint praise,' Miss Fortesque?"

"Only if you hold to your Puritan forbearers' strict standards of conduct, Mr. Thornton."

"My forbearers were no doubt austere and unbending, but those were apparently the qualities needed to carve out a living here in this anything-but-gentle land, Miss Fortesque. However, I imagine that in spite of their preoccupation with avoiding eternal damnation, they were as capable of acting in malice as any of us. And leaving malice aside, I assure you that the congenial captain has a temper."

Once more, my companion looked at me directly. "I have no idea of what set him off, but I assure you that I have seen Captain Hatton as angry as I have ever seen any man—just yesterday afternoon—as a matter of fact."

"Did . . . did you ask him . . .?"

"No more than I would have asked him about his battlefield exploits, Miss Fortesque."

I had been so engrossed in our exchange that I was surprised to see that we had turned onto Common Street. As we passed Douglas Robertson's house, Mr. Thornton glanced at it with narrowed eyes. Perhaps not all of the individuals responsible for the disruption of his orderly world were from England.

He brought the curricle to a halt in front of Uncle Derrick and Aunt Camellia's town house. I saw a slight flutter of curtains in Aunt Camellia's bedroom window.

Mr. Thornton helped me down from my perch, holding Medora until I had managed the descent.

"Thank you," I said, offering my hand, "for a safe and instructive drive home."

Benjamin Thornton bowed over my hand and returned Medora to me.

"You are more than welcome, Miss Fortesque. I do hope I have convinced you that I am not at all your adversary. Quite to the contrary, I suspect."

Ada opened the door. Mr. Thornton tipped his hat, leaped onto the seat of his curricle, and drove his team up Common Street at a smart clip.

If I had any message to deliver to you, I am perfectly capable of doing so.

I watched as Mr. Thornton turned his rig onto Summer Street. Was he paying another surprise call on his grandmother? Were his parting comments the message he had wanted to deliver from the beginning of our trip? How did he see himself as my ally?

"Miss Fortesque," Ada prompted. What she might be thinking of me, staring up the street at Benjamin Thornton's receding carriage, I didn't wish to contemplate.

"Good morning, Ada," I said, heading up the stairs with as much dispatch as I could while preserving what shreds of dignity I could muster.

"Mrs. Fortesque would like to chat with you in her *boodrwar* as soon as you have refreshed yourself, Miss Fortesque." Was that malice that I detected in Ada's voice?

Aunt Camellia greeted me while reclining on her chaise lounge.

"So happy to see you back, Drusilla, my dear, but what have you done with Ivy?"

Medora, who had followed me, jumped up on the chaise hoping for a treat, but went unnoticed.

"I entrusted her to the safekeeping of Sir Clive, Aunt Camellia, so I am certain that she will arrive safely any moment now."

"Why . . .?" Aunt Camellia was so puzzled she forgot to keep from a momentary wrinkling of her brow.

I settled in a fauteuil covered in pale pink satin and gathered my thoughts on how best to explain my decision to keep Ivy from driving home with Benjamin Thornton.

"Last evening, Ivy made a stunning appearance for dinner," I began.

Aunt Camellia beamed. "The apricot gown? I *knew* it would set off Ivy's attributes to perfection!"

"She attracted the attention of every gentleman present, particularly, Benjamin Thornton, who asked to escort her into dinner."

"So he has cooled toward Susan Jones, or was he using Ivy as a foil?"

"I couldn't be certain, Aunt Camellia. Believe it or not, Douglas Robertson managed to insinuate himself between Benjamin Thornton and Susan during the party. But this morning Robertson left early with Captain Hatton—presumably to show off some new ship design. And when Thornton, ignoring both Susan and Beryl Corring, seemed intent on inviting Ivy to drive with him back to Boston, I looked to Sir Clive to intervene. Luckily, he read my unspoken signal and invited Ivy to drive with him before Thornton could. Then Thornton invited me to drive with him. I am still not sure whether he wanted to reassure me that he would be an acceptable suitor for Ivy or if he was just making a point to disoblige Susan—or even Beryl Corring, for that matter. Sir Clive and Ivy should be arriving at any moment."

"I do appreciate your diligence in looking after Ivy's best interests, Drusilla. I am certain you acted wisely in this case. But I cannot tell you how frustrated I am not to have been able to witness all the goings-on at that house party."

"It is really too bad that you couldn't have seen Ivy's blossoming, Aunt Camellia. She might still retain some interest in Ellsworth Corring, but, clearly, she is gaining in confidence, and I would be surprised if he can continue to monopolize her interests."

"And what is your impression of Benjamin Thornton, after traveling from Roxbury to Boston in his company?" She sat up, reached for a box of bonbons and finally rewarded the persevering Medora.

"I like him better than I did, Aunt Camellia, but I'm not sure I can explain just why. Certainly, if he has a genuine interest in Ivy, I can see no reason why he wouldn't make an excellent suitor for her. But, happily, my responsibilities as her chaperone are now at an end."

"It was quite selfless of you to sacrifice what would have been a pleasant idyll for you and Sir Clive in favor of looking after Ivy, Drusilla. And I do want to hear everything else that happened at the party when you've had a chance to settle in."

While I unpacked, I listened for Ivy's arrival, but I was able to empty my traveling case and change frocks and still she had not returned.

As I descended to the parlor, bracing myself to hear Aunt Camellia's fears of a possible carriage accident, I heard Ivy's and Sir Clive's voices as they ascended the staircase from the entryway. They sounded carefree, totally oblivious to the anxiety their delayed arrival had provoked. I paused for a moment and repressed the rebuke I felt for their thoughtlessness.

Aunt Camellia was ensconced on her chaise while Ivy recounted her adventures.

"Oh Mama!" Ivy exclaimed. "I am so sorry that you were not able to be at the party. It was delightful. And then, Sir Clive was kind enough to listen to my pleas and take a detour on the way home so I could see his yacht—*Flame Goddess*."

Meanwhile, Sir Clive had the good grace to quietly greet me and murmur, "Sorry if we caused any concern, my dear. I found that I could not withstand Ivy's importunities."

"How delightful!" Aunt Camellia exclaimed, any recrimination banished from her mind. "Won't you join us for luncheon, Sir Clive?"

"I would like that of all things, Mrs. Fortesque," he declared, bowing over her hand, "but I fear I have been away from the wharf too long."

"And Miss Ivy." He took her hand and patted it. "Thank you for your very pleasant company this morning."

"My pleasure, Sir Clive. Your skills as a driver are only excelled by your tastes in sailing vessels."

Was this composed lady my naïve cousin?

As the sound of Sir Clive's footsteps faded down the stairs, Ivy settled herself into a wing chair with all the grace one could hope for of a daughter of Camellia Fortesque.

"Drusilla, I cannot thank you enough for permitting me to drive back with Sir Clive. He is the most considerate of gentlemen. Only Captain Hatton rivals him for polish. And, quite frankly, although I know he is the brother of your dearest friend, I confess I wonder about his *sincerity*. He is so handsome and dashing, he must have become accustomed to female attention from the moment he was breached. I fear he might take feminine approval for granted."

Color drained from Aunt Camellia's face. "Captain Hatton sought you out for particular attention at the party?"

"Oh no!" Ivy laughed. "When Sir Clive and I stopped by Mr. Robertson's shipbuilding wharf to see *Flame Goddess*, Captain Hatton was there in deep conversation with Mr. Robertson, and they chatted with us for a bit. Captain Hatton might be envied for his easy charm for ladies, but I do believe he envies Sir Clive's *Flame Goddess*."

Ivy stood, shook out her skirts, and kissed her mother. "It is wonderful to be home and I am eager to tell you all about the party, but I do need to freshen up before luncheon."

"Good heavens!" Aunt Camellia exclaimed after Ivy had departed. "I sent off a girl to that party and have welcomed home a young lady. How cruel of fate that I was not there to witness the transformation."

Chapter Fourteen

During luncheon, Ivy made a fulsome report of the party to a delighted Aunt Camellia. They were so absorbed in their discussion, any comment from me was unnecessary, which was fortunate, because my brain was full of my conversation with Benjamin Thornton. Neither Aunt Camellia nor Ivy paused for more than a moment when I excused myself for a much-needed nap. But I couldn't rest. I kept reviewing the questions that Benjamin Thornton had raised.

There is nothing your worrying can do about any of your questions, Drusilla. Whatever partnership you had with Jack in the solving of the mystery of the note has been permanently dissolved. If there is a connection between the note and Sir Clive's business arrangements with Josiah Corring, you had better leave that for Jack to discover on his own. Sir Clive has never given you the least indication that he wishes to share that part of his life with you. And now that Ivy is back home, even Benjamin Thornton's intentions toward her are a question for Aunt Camellia to worry about, not you. Obviously, Benjamin Thornton saw Jack right after Jack left the library. But surely, if Thornton had any suspicion of the cause of Jack's anger, he would have at least hinted at it. And Susan Jones is more than capable of sorting out Benjamin Thornton and Douglas Robertson. Unlike you, she is the most sensible of females.

Dinner was spent bringing Uncle Derrick up to date with as much party news as he could tolerate until he withdrew to his study for brandy and cigars.

Sheer fatigue finally permitted me to sleep that night. I awoke early feeling refreshed and I was happy to find the breakfast room empty, giving me a chance to collect my thoughts. As I was sipping my second cup of tea, Uncle Derrick arrived.

"Good morning, Drusilla, my dear," he said as he bent to kiss my cheek before taking his seat. "I must say, you are much more in looks this morning than you were at dinner last evening. I suppose chaperoning duties were a little wearing for you, although Ivy couldn't have been all that difficult to keep track of. But pleasing Camellia can be a demanding proposition."

"Ivy is the best behaved of young ladies, to be sure. However, I am relieved to hand back all responsibility for her well-being to Aunt Camellia. She can cope with deciding if Benjamin Thornton's interest in Ivy is sincere or not."

Uncle Derrick piled his plate with ham slices. "I'd rather negotiate with a heathen for a cargo of gimcracks and gewgaws than try to keep up with the loves and losses of the young. But Camellia is engrossed by such matters. You will not be surprised to learn that last night she was all atwitter about Benjamin Thornton's true motivations. Is he really interested in Ivy for her own sake? Is he using Ivy to tell Susan Jones that he will not tolerate her encouraging Douglas Robertson? Or, for heaven's sake does his true interest remain with Beryl Corring? I am not at all certain she appreciated my advice on the matter."

I stifled a laugh. "And just what was your advice, Uncle Derrick?"

"Why, to wait and see what the young man does. Benjamin Thornton strikes me as someone who knows the workings of his own mind, even if he isn't always eager to share those workings with the rest of the world."

"Following your advice might deprive Aunt Camellia of one of her favorite occupations—speculating on marital prospects for Ivy—but I think you are right. Having spent most of yesterday morning in Mr. Thornton's company, I find that I am no better able to read his thoughts, but I am in better charity with him. I *had* taken him for being something of an indolent, entitled recipient of fortune and family, coasting on the earnings of his forbearers. He disabused me of *that* judgment."

Uncle Derrick nodded. "Not too long ago, common wisdom was that the Thornton branch of Corring & Thornton was fading away to commercial irrelevance. Bradford Thornton, Benjamin's father, always seemed to move in the shadow of Josiah Corring. But Benjamin is a bird of a different feather. Going into private banking, and doing quite well for himself from what I hear. More involved with the mills that are springing up on just about every river and stream than with the seagoing concerns of his forbearers."

"So he genuinely had no ill will, no envy of Josiah Corring's showy new wharf?"

"Now don't go leaping to conclusions about *that*, Drusilla. I know of no one with any ambition at all who does not keep a running balance sheet in his mind of where he stands *vis-à-vis* his peers. I would be more than a little surprised if young Thornton didn't find it galling to witness all the to-do about the opening of Corring Wharf—particularly since it was the first Corring endeavor in three generations that did not include a Thornton. And I am certain that Camellia would remind me that the opening of Corring Wharf came just about the time that Beryl Corring began to ignore Benjamin in favor of Sir Clive Brampton." Uncle Derrick paused in layering butter on a piece of brown bread and looked up at me. "I wouldn't wonder if Sir Clive's favoring you over Beryl Corring didn't go some way to soothe Benjamin Thornton's wounded pride."

Was that why Benjamin Thornton had suggested that we might be allies? No, that was too long ago to be of any importance now. Best to follow Uncle Derrick's advice and watch what Mr. Thornton would do to discover the solution to puzzle he presented.

That afternoon, Ivy went to call on Annette Ware, no doubt more with the intention of discussing the house party than higher philosophy. Aunt Camellia announced that her ankle was sufficiently recovered to permit her to accompany me to Mademoiselle's to select material for my wedding gown. The expedition took on the atmosphere of a royal progress with Ada and Hez holding Aunt Camellia's arms as she made her way to the landau and then boosted her into the carriage and arranged pillows under the afflicted limb. The same procedure was followed at Mademoiselle's, where Aunt Camellia was settled in a wing chair, pillows at her back, and a hassock to elevate her foot.

I had never considered how I would feel about choosing a pattern and material for the dress I would wear on my wedding day. But I suspected that I was lacking in the romantic mistiness of many perspective brides. As I examined various plates illustrating the newest fashions that Mademoiselle had selected as possible choices, she and Aunt Camellia addressed the serious problem of color. Greens and golds were best suited for my hair, eyes, and complexion, they agreed. But the interplay of color and fabric was essential to consider.

I left it to them to solve the problems that they raised and tried to decide on the design. Rounded or V-shaped neck? Puff or somewhat longer sleeves? A slightly fuller skirt than I had previously worn? A train? Many drawings featured elaborate drapery on the bottom third of the skirt. Mademoiselle would have to modify any such embellishments, or I would look like a squat teapot. I sighed inwardly. It seemed that the relatively simple, slim gowns of past years that had served me to advantage were being replaced by fuller skirted, decorated offerings that required the wearer to be tall and rail thin. It would take the height of Lady Constance or Ivy to show them to any advantage.

Eventually, Aunt Camellia and Mademoiselle announced that rich crème silk shot through with gold would suit me best. Having been unable to find a plate that I thought suited my requirements, I left the final design of my gown in Mademoiselle's capable hands.

"I understand *completement!*" the dressmaker declared. "I will make you a gown that will be as memorable as the occasion demands! Something understated, that shows your figure to advantage."

"You were wise to leave the design of your gown to Mademoiselle, Drusilla, my dear," Aunt Camellia said when we were settled back in the landau. "These new fashions are not going to be kind to any but the tallest ladies. For once, my Ivy will be at a distinct advantage—if, indeed, she does not waste herself on a husband who has no appreciation of feminine apparel. You certainly have avoided that pitfall. I believe that Sir Clive has as subtle and discriminating appreciation for fine distinctions in craftsmanship of all sorts as any gentleman of my acquaintance, including your Uncle Derrick."

Upon our return, Aunt Camellia retired to rest and I set up my easel on the balcony overlooking Common Street. It had been weeks since I had addressed the subject of the elm trees marching along the Mall that bordered the Common. They were now in full leaf and my cardinal friends had been joined by other birds with nests, whose tiny inhabitants could be heard chirping encouragement to parents busily offering meals of worms and bugs.

But I didn't want to concentrate on nesting. I concentrated on painting as many of the shades of green of the leaves as I could detect. As I was putting the finishing touches on the bark of the tree trunks, two figures emerged, crossing the Common from Beacon Hill. Their exceptional height immediately disclosed their identities: Ivy and Ellsworth Corring. They were engaged in conversation, with Corring doing most of the talking. Neither glanced up as they approached Common Street, so I pulled my easel back into the shadow of the doorway, my curiosity overruling my conscience that reminded me that eavesdropping is evidence of poor character.

They crossed Common Street, but instead of Mr. Corring accompanying Ivy to the door, they paused just in front of the house.

"I well appreciate your hesitance, Miss Fortesque." Ellsworth Corring was evidently so accustomed to giving public lectures, he had forgotten that a lower register is preferable for more personal communication. "Indeed, your reticence speaks well for your character. No young lady of wisdom rushes into such matters, willy-nilly. Take the time you need to consider the clear advantages of our nuptials. There is no need for me to discuss the matter with your father until I have your acceptance."

If Ivy made a reply, it was too soft for me to hear. Corring patted her cheek, turned, crossed the street, and headed back in the direction of his home on Beacon Hill. I heard the door open and Ivy's footsteps in the stairwell. She did not stop to see if I was in the parlor as was her habit when returning from an outing, but continued on up to her bedroom on the next floor.

I stood transfixed by what I had heard.

A splash of brown paint on the floor of the balcony beside my foot interrupted my reverie. I took a rag and wiped the end of the dripping brush and dried the small puddle on the floor. Fortunately, the paint matched the dull brown color of the weathered floorboards.

This is what happens to eavesdroppers. Well, not precisely. Eavesdroppers are supposed to hear unwelcome news about themselves. But it is difficult for me to think of anything anyone might say about me that would trouble me more than what I have just heard. What is Aunt Camellia going to say? She has been confident that such an eventuality was remote. What will Uncle Derrick say?

Uncle Derrick! The picture of the self-important Ellsworth Corring informing Uncle Derrick of Ivy's acceptance of his proposal was sufficiently bracing to restore me to some degree of normalcy. I reminded myself that Ivy was Aunt Camellia's and Uncle Derrick's daughter and that they would handle this situation as they saw fit. Did I have an obligation to tell them what I had heard? My official duties as chaperone were over.

What had Aunt Camellia said about Ivy just a few hours ago?

If . . . she does not waste herself on a husband who has no appreciation for feminine apparel.

The real problem, as I saw it, was that Ellsworth Corring had little capacity for appreciation for *Ivy*—apart from her willingness to applaud his own intellectual brilliance. At least she had not immediately accepted, and it was possible, given her hesitation, that she might not. I decided that if she was old enough to receive a marriage proposal, she was old enough for me to permit her a little privacy while she contemplated it. I hoped that she might seek out one of her parents, or even me, for advice.

Ivy's pallor and lack of conversation piqued Aunt Camellia's concern at dinner. "Whatever is the matter, Ivy, darling?" she asked.

"I think I must be feeling belated fatigue from the excitement of the party, Mama."

Ivy was so convincing, I would have believed her, had I not been witness to her exchange with Ellsworth Corring.

"Be sure to retire early, darling. This is no time to miss social engagements because of illness," Aunt Camellia advised and let Ivy's silence pass without comment for the remainder of the meal.

I went to my room early, too, and tried to occupy myself with a letter to Lady Constance, describing my wedding dress, a subject that I knew she would consider to be of first importance. But all the while I was listening for Ivy's knock on the door.

Perhaps she will have the good sense to confide in her mother. That would be the best possible thing for her to do. Or her father. Uncle Derrick's common sense would cut through any misty-eyed idealism she might still be harboring.

I was about to extinguish the lamp and try to sleep when I finally heard the soft knock, almost a scratch, on the door.

"Drusilla! I was so relieved to discover your light still on. I just must talk to someone and I've decided you will be the most objective."

If Ivy's intention was to talk, she did not do so immediately. Instead, she paced the width and then the length of my room, her ruffled white lawn dressing gown swirling around her, green ribbon moving gently in the breeze her agitation created, her titian hair floating around her face.

She came to a halt abruptly and sat on my dressing table bench facing me. "I know I can trust you, Cousin, but please don't be offended if I ask you to swear you will not breathe a word of what I am about to tell you to a living soul."

I nodded. "Of course." Thank heavens I had resisted any temptation of telling either Aunt Camellia or Uncle Derrick what I had overheard from the balcony.

She took in a deep breath. "Ellsworth Corring proposed marriage to me today!"

I widened my eyes and lifted my eyebrows in what I hoped would be a convincing display of surprise.

"I know, I know. After his blatant neglect of me the last night of the party, it came as a complete shock to *me* when he asked to walk me home from Annette's. From the look on her face, Annette was surprised, too. But, evidently, she had encouraged him to do so by pointing out that I might be 'falling into the clutches'—that is how Ellsworth expressed it—of a 'mercenary soul' like Benjamin Thornton."

Ivy stood and began to pace again, coming to rest against the windowsill on the far side of the room.

"Oh, Drusilla! I feel as if I have aged years in such a short time! It seems only yesterday when receiving a marriage proposal from Ellsworth was my fondest wish—one I scarcely dared contemplate! Now..."

She shrugged and held up her hands before clasping them under her chin, apparently contemplating the ironies of life.

"If you no longer wish to marry him, then you must refuse him—as gently as possible, of course," I said.

"Of course you are right, Drusilla. You are so dependably sensible about everything." Ivy moved to the side of the bed and sat facing me. "But that's the problem. I am having a most difficult time untangling just how I feel about Ellsworth, and, therefore, whether or not I should accept his proposal."

"Do you love him?"

She cocked her head and pursed her lips. "I *thought* I did. But now I wonder if it was just infatuation. He *is* quite the most brilliant thinker imaginable. I *still* know *that*. And he wants me to go to Europe with him where he will pursue philosophical studies with the great scholars who are leading the advance of human thought." She hugged herself. "*That* could be quite thrilling, perhaps."

"Perhaps?" *Please, Dear Lord, help me to help this child see what life with Ellsworth Corring would really be like.*

"Well . . ." Ivy chewed on her lower lip. "Europe is very far away and I only speak a little French. Ellsworth says that I must learn German. That's the language of the important scholars. And I wonder: what if he gets so absorbed with talking to all those great thinkers and forgets about me? And I will be so far away from home and . . . but it might be a glorious adventure, and if I don't . . ."

"I believe the key to a successful marriage lies in the quality of devotion that the husband has for his wife. Ellsworth Corring's lack of attention to you at the party is very telling." I felt as if I had played an ace that would take the trick and therefore the game.

Ivy nodded. "That really disappointed me. All the other gentleman were very kind and attentive. Ellsworth apologized most sincerely for that lapse and promised he would not neglect me like that ever again. But . . ."

"But he *does* become distracted with his *philosophical* pursuits," I completed her thought for her. "And you *don't* want to be tied to a husband for whom you are an afterthought."

"Noooo. But how thrilling to be the wife of a *great thinker* and to be his *inspiration*—that is what Ellsworth says I would be."

I resisted the urge to take her by the arms and give her a good shake. What would my vaunted common sense recommend?

"I understand you want to keep Mr. Corring's marriage proposal a secret, Ivy. But, ordinarily, a gentleman contemplating marriage first asks permission of his lady's father. I assume Ellsworth Corring has not done that. So, perhaps your father's guidance in this instance might be of great value to you."

"Ellsworth says that tradition is very old-fashioned. He says, of course, after I give my consent, he will speak with Father. But Ellsworth believes that following old traditions—just for the sake of traditions—stands in the way of social progress. And really, Drusilla, it is very important to me to come to this decision on my own."

My spirits dropped. I had felt so close to leading Ivy to a decision to reject Ellsworth Corring. Now, it seemed as if she had circled back to where our conversation had begun.

"Well," I said, trying to set a demanding standard for Ivy's suitor, one that I was confident he could not meet, "in order to be happy with Ellsworth Corring, you must believe, beyond any shadow of a doubt, that he not only enjoys your company and your wholehearted admiration, but he also returns your admiration in kind. That he respects and admires you for who you are."

"Hmmm." Ivy narrowed her eyes. "Sort of a test. . . . I think I have one in mind. Thank you, dear Cuz." She hugged me and left the room with a bounce in her step.

Chapter Fifteen

I had not been successful in my attempt to convince Ivy to turn down Ellsworth Corring's marriage proposal. But, at least, she was going to do something to test his feelings for her. It was reasonably certain that young Mr. Corring would fail any fair test of devotion to anything other than his own brilliance. I turned over my pillow, gave it a good thump, and decided to let time work out Ivy's romantic dilemma.

At breakfast the next morning, Ada handed me a note from Susan Jones inviting me for tea and a chat in the afternoon. It was likely that Susan would want to discuss *her* romantic entanglements. I suppressed a moment of envy. Why was *I* everyone's confidant, but no one was *my* confidant? *Just be grateful that no one knows the truth of your romantic entanglements*, I scolded myself as I wrote a brief note of acceptance of Susan's invitation.

"Strange, isn't it?" Susan said, stirring milk and sugar into her tea. "The Wares rarely rouse themselves to be part of the social scene, but their house party will be the talk of Boston for the rest of the season. It must be just the few miles away from our usual haunts and activities that make people act differently. Take Ivy, for example. The last evening of the party, she was almost unrecognizable from the shy miss who attended Beryl Corring's ball. I trust Ivy now has sufficient insight and confidence to send Ellsworth Corring on his way."

"I hope she has," I said, wishing I could share Ivy's confidences and feeling quite righteous for resisting.

Susan continued to stir her tea. Then she selected a cake and proceeded to turn it into a pile of crumbs with her fork. At last, she placed the fork on the edge of the plate of ruined cake and looked up with a most uncharacteristically pensive expression.

"I had quite a strange encounter with Benjamin Thornton yesterday afternoon, and I fear it might have inadvertently led to entirely false conclusions on the part of someone else. How does life get so complicated?"

"I suppose the only preventative against life's complications is to retire to Bath, as my dear aunts have. And I am quite certain that such a life would drive you to distraction."

Susan brightened and took a sip of tea.

"You are the most sensible, levelheaded lady I have ever met, Drusilla. How I envy you!"

I preferred to hear about Susan's strange encounter with Benjamin Thornton than to dwell on my common sense, so I tried to steer her thoughts back in his direction.

"I have come to think that Benjamin Thornton is a more complicated person than I had previously understood him to be."

Susan nodded. "When he asked to take me for a drive yesterday afternoon. I must confess that I was surprised. After the scene at archery during the party, he had given me a curt nod, walked off, and hadn't exchanged a word with me for the rest of our stay in Roxbury."

She returned to stirring her tea for a moment.

"Did he apologize for his abrupt behavior?" I had never before had to nudge Susan to continue telling any story.

She rested her spoon in the saucer and cocked her head. "Yes, yes he did. Most unlike him, I thought. And not only for that particular instance of discourtesy, but for 'monopolizing my time' this spring and, possibly 'raising my expectations' that a marriage proposal was in the offing."

She pushed her cake plate aside, folded her arms on the table, and leaned toward me. "For heaven's sake! I felt as if I were being placed in the position of a spinster whose last hope had been crushed!" she laughed. "I guess I conveyed my feelings and he fell all over himself apologizing if he had sounded 'presumptuous' about my 'expectations.' I assured him that he was worrying needlessly, that I had made no assumptions whatsoever as far as his long-term intentions were concerned. I assumed he would then thank me, escort me back to his carriage—we were walking down the South Boston Bridge at the time—and bring me back home."

"He didn't?" I was so engrossed in Susan's recitation, I had abandoned any interest in tea and cake.

She took a deep breath and shook her head. "It is fortunate that I am of an iron constitution, with the blood of generations of canny Yankees flowing in my veins, or I might have fainted dead away right there on the South Boston Bridge. Because at that point, Benjamin Thornton took my hand and said, after careful consideration, he thought, perhaps, it might be a 'sensible decision'—those were his exact words—for us to 'contemplate marriage.'"

Susan sat up straight and slapped the table so hard the silver and china rattled. "Can you *believe* that? Not even anything to the effect of, 'My dear Miss Jones, I have come to respect and admire you and hope, with time, you will learn to return my sentiments.'"

"Wha . . . what did you say?" I managed in a whisper.

"Well. I resisted the urge to storm off and walk back to Boston on my own, and managed what I understand is the polite formula of 'I am mindful of the honor of your kind offer etc., etc.' Thank heavens I have read a sufficient number of novels, or I wouldn't have known *what* to say. Then to add insult to my wounded pride, I saw a look of what could only have been profound relief on his face when he realized that he had been rejected."

"You poor thing," I sympathized. "The drive back to your home must have been excruciatingly painful."

"Strange, but the drive back was actually the most pleasant part of my time with him. I suppose, because, for the first time, we actually knew where we stood with each other. Although the ending of our afternoon was . . ." Susan took another deep breath and squared her shoulders. "He asked me if I minded explaining to him why I was so certain that we would not suit. And, of course, I pointed out the fact that he did not love me, nor I him."

Dear, dear, Susan. How fortunate you are to have understood the importance of love in a marriage. How I wish, when I made my decision, I had understood it.

"What did he say to that? Did he condescend to you for being a romantic?"

"As soon as the words were out of my mouth, I expected just such a reaction," Susan said. "But he actually thanked me for knowing my own mind."

"It almost sounds as if he doesn't know *his* own mind, which is passing strange. Especially because I witnessed an exchange between him and Mrs. Prudence not long ago in which he declared that he could take care of his own marital prospects. In fact, if I recall, she was recommending you as a potential wife for him," I said, stilling a little voice that cautioned me not to gossip about a conversation that was really quite personal between grandmother and grandson.

"That is precisely what he told me. He said that he had come to rely on his grandmother's judgment and she was delighted that he had singled me out for attention. I'm terribly flattered, but much as I admire Mrs. Prudence, marrying her grandson to make her happy doesn't sound like a sound foundation for life."

"Something puzzles me," I said, thinking out loud. "I would have wagered a great deal when I heard Benjamin Thornton tell Mrs. Prudence he could take care of his personal life on his own, that he knew his mind quite well. And Uncle Derrick, an astute judge of character if I have ever met one, has said just how well Benjamin Thornton knows what he is about. But you are telling me that he offered for you and was relieved to be rejected? That is not the picture of a gentleman who knows his own mind at all. What could have happened?"

Susan folded her arms on the table and leaned forward. "You know what I think?" she said in whispered tones. "I think Benjamin Thornton is and always has been in love with Beryl Corring, and watching Beryl Corring with your friend, Captain Hatton, acting the happy couple all during the house party has upset him much more than he can even admit to himself. I *always* suspected that when he was paying attention to me, Miss Corring was his audience."

My friend, Captain Hatton. I raised both eyebrows in feigned surprise to keep dismay from my face. *Jack and Beryl Corring. You had better get used to the idea, Drusilla.*

"And you believe . . ." I began.

"That Benjamin Thornton thought he could better endure losing Beryl to Captain Hatton if he had already announced his engagement to another lady." Susan finished the sentence.

To my relief, she began to busy herself stirring her now-cold cup of tea, which gave me time to fix as bland an expression on my face as I could manage. The last thing I wanted my perceptive friend to notice was my dismay over Captain Hatton and Beryl Corring making a match.

"It sounds as if you managed a potentially awkward situation quite smoothly," I said, to turn the subject.

She looked up from her teacup, crestfallen.

"That is precisely what I was thinking as we made our way up Common Street. But then, who just happened to be walking down from Summer Street as Benjamin Thornton was lifting me down from his curricle, but Mr. Douglas Robertson. He tipped his hat, greeted us, gave me the frostiest glare imaginable, and walked on. Clearly, he assumed that I had encouraged Benjamin Thornton's attentions, when nothing could be further from the truth. And, after the way the house party ended, I had such hopes. . . . But Mr. Robertson left the party early with Captain Hatton and hasn't made any effort to speak with me since. And then our first encounter had to be spoiled by Benjamin Thornton!"

"Mr. Robertson has a thriving business to run, and I am sure he has been preoccupied with it since he took those days off for the party. As for his coming to the wrong conclusion about you and Benjamin Thornton, time should reveal the true state of affairs to him before too long. It will do Douglas Robertson no harm to worry about where your affections lie."

As if on cue, Josie, the family maid, entered with a note for Susan. I watched her blush as she read it. She looked up, her face glowing.

"Mr. Robertson has asked to take me for a drive tomorrow afternoon," Susan announced. "You are so wise, Drusilla. I was worried for nothing."

As I stepped out of the front door of Susan's house, I noticed a stylish gig with a sleek chestnut pair standing in front of Uncle Derrick's house, a young lad tending the horses. It seemed that I had an afternoon caller. I wished I could go to my room to consult my looking glass, smooth my coiffure, and apply a bit of color to my cheeks, but the stairs leading to my room passed the landing just outside the parlor, so I pinched my cheeks, patted my hair, hoped for the best, and began to mount the stairs.

Halfway to the landing, I became aware of a murmured conversation taking place in the parlor. I could not distinguish what was being said, and I paused for a moment to be sure of the identity of the two speakers. One was Ivy, the other—whose soft, soothing tones were so unlike any I had heard from him before—was the owner of the smart gig and chestnut pair, my fiancé, Sir Clive Brampton. I hesitated for a moment, feeling strangely awkward to interrupt a private exchange, when Medora emerged from the parlor yipping a happy greeting. I picked her up and entered the parlor.

Ivy and Sir Clive were standing side by side in the middle of the room.

"Cousin Drusilla!" Ivy said in a breathless voice.

"Drusilla, my dear," my fiancé greeted me and planted a kiss on my cheek. I was close enough to see what I first took to be a red-gold thread on his usually immaculate lapel. Medora slipped from my hands, but landed on her feet and ran toward Ivy.

"I . . . I was just showing Sir Clive my manuscript," Ivy said, picking up a thick stack of writing paper from a nearby table. "I . . . I'll just run along now. Thank you, thank you, Sir Clive, for encouraging me to continue writing." She cast him a glowing smile, realized that she was about to tread on Medora, and dropped the papers she was holding, which scattered across the floor.

All three of us bent to collect Ivy's manuscript.

"Please don't bother . . . thank you . . . I can . . . thank you," Ivy whispered as Sir Clive and I handed her what we retrieved.

Finally, the entire manuscript was restored to Ivy. "Thank you, thank you, I'm so sorry to have been such a bother," she said blushing, curls fallen loose from her Psyche knot framing her face. "I . . . I think I need to get these pages in order right away."

How long Sir Clive and I stood watching the door through which Ivy disappeared, I am not sure. But, eventually, I did remember my manners and suggested that he might like a glass of sherry.

Declining a glass myself on the grounds that I had just come from tea and cakes, I settled into one of the wing chairs that flanked the fireplace and waited while Sir Clive examined the decanters on the sideboard, selected the brandy instead of sherry, poured himself a generous tote, and took the wing chair opposite mine.

He sipped his drink before placing it on the table next to his chair and cleared his throat.

"I would not be at all surprised if you found the scene you just happened upon to be a little . . . strange." He glanced down at his lapel, grimaced, and brushed away the red-gold strand I had noticed. "But there really is a very simple explanation of how it came to be." He paused for a moment, collecting his thoughts. "I was driving up Common Street, when Miss Ivy, coming from the Common, stepped into the road, clutching what I learned was a book manuscript, completely oblivious to her surroundings." He paused, shook his head, and took another sip of brandy. "That I was able to bring my chestnuts to a halt in time to prevent catastrophe is beyond miraculous. Miss Ivy, was, by that time, totally incoherent. I intended to simply escort her across the street and place her in the care of your aunt. But, apparently, Mrs. Fortesque had gone on an errand taking the maid with her. Ivy . . . Miss Ivy was in no state to be left alone. Eventually, she calmed down and I was able to learn that she had read a portion of a romantic novel she had written to some sort of literary or philosophical discussion circle at Miss Ware's house," Sir Clive gazed at the ceiling and shook his head. "Miss Ivy must have the kindest of hearts to put up with such nonsense. And how was she repaid for her naïve enthusiasm, but to have her efforts ridiculed."

I was relieved that Sir Clive's explanation was quite believable.

"I cannot tell you how grateful I am that you were driving up Common Street at the precise moment Ivy was in need of rescue. It is nothing short of the greatest of good fortune—and quick action on your part—that kept her from being seriously injured as the result of her preoccupation. And . . . and I *do* know that she can be quite . . . impulsive . . . in her expressions of gratitude."

Sir Clive raised his glass saluting me. "You have an understanding heart to go with your sensible mind, Drusilla, my dear. I suppose you have guessed the major offender in this story is none other than that arrogant pup—"

"Ellsworth Corring." I nodded.

"He had the temerity to propose marriage to her." Sir Clive's eyes narrowed as if he were taking aim at the hapless suitor. "I cannot imagine what your Uncle Derrick would have to say about such a scheme. But apparently, he wasn't apprised of young Corring's intentions."

"That is true. Uncle Derrick was not consulted. According to Ivy, Mr. Corring believes such customs are vestiges of old traditions, which the new, enlightened generation would do well to abandon. But what Ellsworth Corring has no way of knowing, and I am not at all certain Ivy knows, is that Uncle Derrick, himself, never favored *his* prospective father-in-law with a formal request for Aunt Camellia's hand. They eloped, much to the distress of her family. Of course, I have no doubt that little fact wouldn't have kept Uncle Derrick from asking Ellsworth Corring some penetrating questions and generally letting him know what he expected his daughter's husband to do to ensure her happiness." I stopped suddenly. *What on earth had made me babble on about family secrets?* "Oh dear! Please forget that. But I know I can count upon you to keep a confidence."

"It seems to have been an unsettling afternoon all round," Sir Clive mused. "Of course you can rely on my discretion. At the very least, Miss Ivy has been spared a disastrous marriage."

"And you seem to have found a way to encourage her writing, too." I said. "Did she read any of her novel to you? I believe it takes place in medieval times and concerns castles and knights in shining armor."

"No, no. I told her that the masculine mind cannot fully appreciate the subtleties of ladies' writing and it is futile for a gentleman to try. And Ellsworth Corring should know that."

"Perhaps you should share those thoughts with Benjamin Thornton," I said, laughing. "I think it's likely that he will be Ivy's new suitor. He seems to meet Aunt Camellia's standards, and, I must say, I am more positively disposed to him after chatting with him on our trip home from Roxbury than I had been."

Sir Clive cleared his throat and stood to leave.

"I must be on my way, my dear. I am once more struck by your remarkable reasonableness. When I think of what might have ensued if almost any other lady discovered her intended husband in the scene you encountered here this afternoon ..."

He took both my hands, kissed me, patted my cheek, and left.

I sighed a deep sigh of relief as I listened to his footsteps descending to the front door. Even though Sir Clive and I might not be in love with each other, we could navigate life's eddies and even whirlpools with rare equanimity. And the absence of emotional intensity in our attachment to each other actually helped us maintain a cordial relationship. He had just acknowledged that I had been exemplary in my composure. *What might have ensued if almost any other lady discovered her intended husband in the scene you encountered here this afternoon.* I knew he meant it as a compliment, even though his voice had sounded fatigued. It *was* fatigue. Certainly not wistfulness. It wasn't possible that Sir Clive would have tolerated, much less excused, an emotional display on my part. That was what drew Sir Clive to me in the first place—my reliable emotional composure.

Your reliable emotional composure, Drusilla? What if it had been Jack? What if Jack and I were engaged to be married and I discovered him alone in a room with a breathless Ivy, a strand of titian hair on his lapel?

I was surprised by the tears that threatened to fall. What I needed was a nap before dinner. It had been an exhausting day.

Chapter Sixteen

Ivy betrayed nothing of the afternoon's dramatic events in her demeanor at dinner that evening. I could not help but contrast her composure with the anxiety and uncertainty she had displayed mere weeks earlier over much less stressful challenges.

But the contrast became even greater when, after dinner plates were cleared, and before Uncle Derrick excused himself for a cigar and brandy in his study, Ivy said, "I think I need to let you know that Mr. Ellsworth Corring proposed marriage to me. But after due consideration, I have rejected his proposal. I do not think we would suit."

Both Uncle Derrick and Aunt Camellia, neither, to my knowledge, ever before being at a loss for words, stared at their daughter in shocked silence.

"I believe you have made a very wise decision, Ivy, my dear," I said, as much to disguise my own lack of surprise as to fill the awkward silence.

"Yes . . . yes . . . of course," Aunt Camellia's voice sounded unnaturally strained. "Drusilla has the right of it. You made the only decision you could have made to ensure your future happiness. But why did you not consult me—or your father, in the matter?"

"And what possessed that young jackanapes to presume to address you without letting me know of his intentions, much less asking for my approval!" Uncle Derrick sounded as if he was beginning a long recitation of his thoughts about the lack of basic manners in certain young men, but a quick reproving glance from Aunt Camellia cut short what more he was going to say. He coughed into his napkin and cleared his throat. Did Ivy know that her parents had eloped? That her own parents had failed to consult *her* mother's parents about their intention to marry? Regardless, it was clear that Aunt Camellia did not want to risk the mention of the subject at such a delicate moment.

"Please do not think that my failing to discuss Mr. Corring's marriage proposal with you is any indication of a lack of confidence in your judgment. I just felt . . ." Ivy's voice faltered into uncertainty for a moment, but she took a breath and continued. "It seemed to me that if I am old enough to receive a marriage proposal, I should be developing sufficient maturity to rely on my own counsel."

I wondered if Aunt Camellia and Uncle Derrick saw the quick look Ivy sent my way. I assumed it was a request that I not betray the fact that she had confided in me. She needn't have worried. I meant to do my best to bring the painful scene to an end by saying as little as possible. But my intentions were futile. Ivy had more to say to her astonished parents.

"And, additionally," Ivy continued, "Ellsworth—that is, Mr. Corring—believes that the practice of a suitor asking his prospective father-in-law's permission for his daughter's hand in marriage is a tradition too old to be followed by the new, enlightened generation."

Uncle Derrick studied Ivy with one raised eyebrow. "What a cold, dispassionate reason for dispensing with a time-honored tradition. Romantic impetuosity, I can understand as a reason for a suitor forgoing such an interview, but—"

"Let's not dwell on the matter," Aunt Camellia said, apparently still concerned about raising the specter of hers and Uncle Derrick's example. "Your father and I are relieved that you made the decision you made, Ivy, darling. It speaks to your maturity and good judgment."

"Thank you, Mama." Ivy crossed to where Aunt Camellia sat and embraced her, then embraced and kissed her father, who patted her on the shoulder.

Without any formal request from any of us to be excused, we all wandered from the dining room and went our separate ways. Uncle Derrick to his study for a much-needed cigar and brandy. Aunt Camellia to her boudoir to adjust to the idea of a daughter who had suddenly found her counsel unnecessary. Ivy to her room to revel in her newly acquired independence—or perhaps to pen another chapter in her novel. And I to my room, to thank heavens that a thoroughly trying day had finally come to an end. I did not expect a visit from Ivy, and I received none.

The next day, Aunt Camellia declared that Ivy's wardrobe required freshening and Ivy went off with her mother in search of new bonnets and gloves and, perhaps, even a new gown or two—decisions about which Aunt Camellia's counsel was still essential. I hoped that the mother-daughter expedition would serve to restore a sense of normalcy in the household after the previous evening's awkwardness.

But a sense of normalcy in the household and a sense of normalcy in my own state of mind were not the same. In fact, I tried unsuccessfully to remember when I had been truly relaxed and at peace.

Not since Jack Hatton walked into the drawing room and set your world at sixes and sevens.

I told myself not to be dramatic. I walked out onto the balcony and gazed at the familiar but ever-changing landscape: the Common, the roofs of the houses on Beacon Hill, and the statehouse dome standing sentinel above it all. Boston would never rival London, but Mr. Bulfinch had created buildings worthy of any English city. The terrace of Park Row marching down from Beacon Hill and the Colonnade facing the Common were a perfect framing of the park that had once been a pasture. Whether it was the similarity to my own country or some indefinable difference from it, I couldn't say, but I was suddenly taken by overwhelming homesickness.

When would I see England again? *Would* I see England again? In a few short weeks, I would be married to Clive Brampton and we would live in New York City. Having lost his baronetcy, *Mr.* Brampton would be in no hurry to return to our home country. The embarrassment of having lost his title was too excruciating. How long would it take before his sense of loss eased sufficiently for him to face his reduced status among those whose esteem he most coveted?

But as homesick as I felt, I was reluctant to leave Boston. At least I *knew* Boston. I had family and friends in Boston. What would it be like living in New York City with not so much as one acquaintance, much less a friend, other than Clive Brampton?

I started to blink back tears, but was distracted by the sight of a gig pulling up in front of the house next door. Mr. Douglas Robertson descended from the driver's seat and assisted Susan Jones down from the passenger's seat. When her feet were safely planted on the ground, they remained facing each other, gazing into one another's eyes, oblivious to their surroundings.

That is love, Drusilla. That is what true love looks like. Susan Jones would go happily to New York City—or to the far reaches of India, for that matter—with Douglas Robertson. Because she loves him, and he loves her. And . . . you would willingly go to the far reaches of India with Jack. . . . Stop it! Stop these maudlin, disloyal thoughts this instant!

Tears were again prickling my eyelids. I walked as briskly as I could up the stairs to my room, Medora trotting behind me. At least my fervent prayer that I would not encounter the inexplicably hostile Ada before I reached my destination was granted.

I lay down, a dampened washcloth pressed on my eyes to remove any trace of tears. Medora snuggled up next to me and licked my fingers. The little dog was capable of loyalty after all. I stroked her silky coat and reviewed my options. I could marry Clive Brampton as I had promised and go with him to New York City. Or, I could go back on my promise to Clive Brampton and leave for England and my aunts' home in Bath. Break the promise I had made in order to return to my aunts' home, when I had refused to break it to marry Jack? That would be foolish beyond measure. Of course I would marry Clive and we would have a very pleasant life together.

Medora fell asleep, snuffling softly from time to time. I drifted off and dreamed that Medora and I were lying in a ship's berth, but where we were sailing, I had no idea.

It was bitter cold in the tower room. Even at high noon, little sunshine and warmth penetrated the thick stone walls and slits that served for windows. Marceline shivered, and tried to ignore the gnawing hunger that made her thin frame tremble. Now, coming on for midnight, only the faintest light from a crescent moon relieved the blackness of her prison. It was just sufficient light for her to see the bell resting on the table across the room, if she had looked in its direction. However, she steadfastly refused to turn her head so that she could see it, for fear of losing courage. All she had to do was ring the bell. And she would be warm and fed and . . . she shivered more violently, at the very thought of the price she would pay for those creature comforts. Neville de Boufe would have his way with her.

She would rather die! Surely, though, Lucien de Lux would rescue her. Surely, he was, even now, assembling an army to march on Castle de Boufe and restore her to her uncle's custody.

Ivy looked up from the manuscript she was reading aloud to me. "I'm undecided, Drusilla. Should I have Lucien attack the castle with a band of his loyal followers, or should I have him rescue Marceline all by himself? Swim the moat—I could put vicious fish in the moat. Do you know of any vicious fish? I'm sure there are some. Then he could scale the tower and . . ."

Deciding to ignore the challenges Marceline's knight would encounter scaling the sheer face of a stone tower, I was considering whether or not to point out the problem of the small window slits and the difficulty of a grown man getting through one to enter Marceline's place of confinement when the strident voice of Annette Ware rose from the downstairs vestibule, "Do ask if Miss Ivy is at home, Ada. Although I am certain she is, in both meanings of the expression."

Ivy blanched. She hurriedly gathered up the pages of her manuscript. "I don't want Annette to see these. It's not that I am at all ashamed of my writing, I just don't want to endure her . . . her supercilious attitude toward what I write."

She looked about frantically for a place to hide her manuscript, and, as footsteps approached the door to the parlor, she dived for the bottom drawer of the large chest close to her chair, opened it, threw in the stack of pages, and was just closing it as Ada announced, "Miss Ware to see you."

I was bereft of words. Ivy's opening of the bottom drawer of the large chest had evoked a paralyzing memory. The memory of the day I was alone in this room, painting the portrait that had risen, unbidden, in my mind. The portrait of the only man I had ever loved, Jack Hatton. Fearful of being discovered, I had hurriedly hidden the painting in that very drawer, meaning to remove it at the first possible moment. But distractions had intervened, and I had forgotten to retrieve the incriminating evidence. Somehow, I would have to extract Ivy's manuscript before she could discover Jack's portrait, which lay beneath it. Explaining its presence there would, without a doubt, create a challenge beyond my skills in deception.

A less self-absorbed lady might have found it odd to enter a room where one hostess was crouched by a large chest and the other was sitting frozen, pale, and mute. But fortunately, Miss Ware was too full of her mission to notice such trivial details.

Ivy and I recovered simultaneously, both stood slowly, found our voices, and said in unison, "Please do be . . ."

But Annette Ware was already seated and arranging her heliotrope skirts around her before we completed our sentence. I turned to Ada and requested cakes and tea. Sustenance was needed to maintain one's equanimity during a visit with Miss Ware.

"I have come on a most urgent matter, Ivy, my dear." Miss Ware cast me a glance that I read as a discreet request that I excuse myself for what she intended to be an intimate *tête-à-tête* with Ivy. But Ivy sent a pleading look, which I interpreted as "Please do not leave me to the mercies of this harpy." I smiled at Ivy and remained seated. She could interpret my refusal to leave as cousinly loyalty. But in truth, only a pistol pointed at my head or a saber pointed at my heart would have moved me from the parlor. I couldn't leave without somehow restoring Ivy's manuscript to her while preventing her from discovering Jack's portrait. And I admitted to myself that I was anticipating Annette Ware's conversation, which could be counted upon to be diverting in a way she never intended it to be.

"Whatever can be the matter?" Ivy prompted Miss Ware.

"It is Ells . . . Mr. Corring. He has not ventured into public for at least two days, and when I wrote him a note inquiring about when I would see him again, his answer was disturbing. He said that he had received a 'severe blow to the heart from a friend in whom he had placed all of his confidence.' Other than myself, I could think of no other person than you, Ivy, who could be thus described." Annette sighed and clutched her hands to her bosom. "The last time I saw or spoke to him was the day that you brought that bit of trumpery writing to our meeting. I knew he was deeply grieved by your ungrateful reaction to his reservations about its suitability as appropriate reading for ladies who wish to cultivate higher thinking. Frankly, Ivy, my dear, I was greatly disappointed in you. After all the hours that dear Ells . . . Mr. Corring had so generously invested in improving your understanding of new philosophy, for you to have thought for one second that he would place his imprimatur on such shallow entertainment!"

Oh no! Precisely the topic of conversation Ivy had feared. I hoped she would not dissolve into tears—a reaction that would only serve to make Annette Ware feel more justified in her sense of moral superiority. While I was mentally trying to formulate a rebuke to our obnoxious guest that did not violate every standard of propriety, I witnessed the most remarkable transformation in my cousin.

Ivy flushed, straightened her spine, and lifted her chin. "Just because *some* people hold ladies' fiction in low esteem, does not mean that there is no *worth*, no *value*, in such writing. *Some* readers find what is written *by* and *for* ladies to be of considerable subtlety."

Ivy had taken Clive Brampton's words so much to heart that she pronounced them as her own, with conviction.

Annette Ware could not have looked more shocked if Ivy had uttered a sailor's oath. "You didn't say anything like that to Ells . . . Mr. Corring, I trust! He has such confidence in your ability to appreciate the nobility of higher thinking. He takes great pride in the progress you have made in that regard."

"How generous of him." I wondered for a moment if Miss Ware detected the irony in Ivy's voice, but I should have known better.

"Generous to a fault, I fear," she responded. "Too generous, it seems to me. It appears that you have dismissed his gentle admonitions about the frivolity and superficiality of your jottings."

"To be honest with you," Ivy said, "I did not say to Mr. Corring anything like what I just said to you, Miss Ware. Indeed, his criticism of my work cut me to the quick and had I not received wise counsel from someone quite knowledgeable in the ways of the world, I would still be weeping over Ellsworth Corring's words."

Annette Ware's eyes narrowed. "Then what could have caused . . . Benjamin Thornton! It must be Benjamin Thornton! Everyone at the house party saw him singling you out the last evening, Ivy. Everyone, that is, except poor Ellsworth. His thoughts were so elevated from ordinary concerns, he alone did not take note, either of Mr. Thornton's marked attentions to you, or, what I must admit, was every indication that you were encouraging them."

"I most certainly was not 'encouraging' Mr. Thornton's 'attentions,' as you put it!" Ivy's aquamarine eyes flashed steel. "Furthermore, if, as you claim, Ellsworth Corring was oblivious to them, how can Mr. Thornton's 'attentions,' much less my alleged encouragement of those intentions, be responsible for whatever is ailing Mr. Corring?"

Miss Ware studied her skirt and brushed at something that I could not detect. It couldn't have been dog hair, because Medora was curled up in *my* lap.

"Well, if you must know," she began in such a low voice that I strained to hear her. "As a true friend of Ellsworth Corring, I felt it was incumbent upon me to apprise him of what had transpired between you and Mr. Thornton at the house party. As soon as I had informed him, he announced that he must speak to you immediately. So naturally . . ." Miss Ware punctuated her disclosure by brushing a few more invisible blemishes from her skirt.

Ivy and I exchanged glances. Now we knew what had prompted Mr. Corring's impetuous marriage proposal.

"I am sorry if you believe that I gave Mr. Thornton excessive encouragement at your house party," Ivy said, apparently moved to sympathy by Annette Ware's obvious discomfort. "But let me assure you, that I was only trying to be polite. And, evidently, Mr. Thornton was actually not pursuing a particular interest in me, because I have not so much as laid eyes upon him since we have returned to Boston."

"Oh . . . oh," Annette Ware said. I had never heard or seen her so subdued. "I . . . I am truly sorry if I spoke precipitously, Ivy. I do hope you will take no offense. I must be off."

While Ivy walked her to the parlor door, I retrieved her manuscript, congratulating myself on my quick action.

"Thank you, Drusilla!" Ivy took the manuscript, sat, and began to arrange the pages in order. "In spite of her . . . abruptness, I feel sorry for poor Annette. I do believe that her feelings for Ellsworth Corring are more than just admiration for his intellect. Now where was I? Oh, yes, getting Marceline rescued from the tower of the awful Neville de Boufe."

She closed her eyes. "Now let me think. . . ." Then she smiled and opened her eyes. "I know what she will do! Why have I never thought of this before? Marceline will not sit idly by waiting for her rescue. Here's what will happen. When Lucien's forces lay siege to de Boufe's castle, de Boufe's henchmen are called upon to defend it, and a kindly maid is the only one left to bring Marceline her pitiful portions of bread and water. Filled with sympathy for Marceline's plight, she lends Marceline some humble maid's clothing, and in such disguise, Marceline is able to escape the castle and rush into the waiting arms of Lucien de Lux!"

Ivy returned her attention to her manuscript, and frowned. "I seem to be missing that last page I was writing on."

And before I could register what she had said, she was opening the bottom drawer of the tall chest.

"Here . . . what? What is *this*?" Ivy rose, the missing page of manuscript in one hand, the portrait of Jack Hatton in the other.

"When? When did you paint this, Drusilla? When did he sit for it? Why . . . why was it in . . .?"

"It was supposed to be a . . . a surprise." My voice was a whisper. "A . . . a surprise for . . ." *Oh dear, who was the surprise for?* "Lady Constance," I continued.

Bad choice, Drusilla. Why would you need to hide a surprise for someone in England?

But Ivy didn't ask that obvious question. She was studying the portrait.

"You must know him well—much better than you ever led us to believe." The tone of accusation was clear in her voice. She looked up and fixed me with a steady gaze. "Why did Captain Hatton come to Boston, Drusilla?"

"Whatever his reason for coming to Boston had nothing to do with me!"

"But you wish it did, don't you, Drusilla? I know you think I'm a hopeless romantic, but I don't think someone would have to be a romantic at all to see that the person who painted this portrait loves Captain Hatton. He's a handsome man, but there is more than handsomeness in this portrayal of him. There is a depth of character that *I* certainly have never seen in him. A wistfulness that is totally lacking to those of us who know him in society."

Ivy handed me Jack's portrait, but I could not bear to look at it while she was watching my face. I placed it on the tea table. Ivy sat down and picked up her manuscript again, then set it aside.

"Does Sir Clive know?" she sounded sad, as if she were asking about the death of a close friend.

"Sir Clive and I have agreed that we will not burden each other with tales of past attachments. And, really, Ivy, you are investing much more into my relationship with Captain Hatton than it deserves." I tried my best to put just the right degree of conviction into my declaration.

Ada chose that precise moment to arrive with the tea tray. Before I could remove Jack's portrait from the table, she saw it and recognized the subject.

"Handsome man, that," she said, studying the painting. "The friend of your family who didn't want me to announce him when he visited you in the garden—when was it? Some time ago, I'm thinking."

"Try not to spill any tea on it," I said, snatching the portrait from the table. "It is a special gift for his sister," I added, looking at Ivy, who did not even try to hide the recrimination on her face.

Ada shrugged and trundled off.

I stood, making an effort to keep both my voice and my knees from shaking.

"I don't believe I care for tea and cakes at the moment, Ivy, dear. But I do think your novel is moving along nicely."

It took an effort for me to walk at a normal pace to the safety of my bedroom. When I arrived, I realized that I had made the journey from the parlor to my room with Jack's portrait in my hand for anyone to see. I blessed fate for sparing me an untimely encounter with Aunt Camellia and set about finding another hiding place for the picture. What could I do with such incriminating evidence of my lost love? Sending it to Constance was out of the question. If Ivy read my feelings so easily, Constance would see them in an instant. I pulled out a stack of paintings of the trees lining the Common and placed Jack's portrait in the middle of them. Certainly no one would have sufficiently sustained interest in dull paintings of trees to discover my secret.

Chapter Seventeen

Clive Brampton and I had set our wedding for July 15 at 10:30 a.m. I happily turned over every detail of planning for the ceremony to Aunt Camellia, who promised its exquisite perfection would be the talk of Boston for years to come. Not that I would have the satisfaction of hearing such talk, because I would be removing to New York City. But Aunt Camellia would be living in Boston for the rest of her days, and it gave me some degree of satisfaction that the occasion of my wedding would provide ongoing social cachet for her.

My gown provided another source of satisfaction. Mademoiselle proved herself equal in discernment and skill to any London or Paris modiste. In my secret heart, I knew that I looked forward to wearing her elegant creation more than I looked forward to my actual wedding. I might not be a glowingly happy bride, but I would be the epitome of fashion—which I knew to be a requirement for the wife of Clive Brampton.

To my great relief, Ivy refrained from further mention of Jack's portrait. She spent her days writing her novel, going for walks to clear her mind and work out problematic points of plot. She took a notebook and pencil with her for moments of inspiration. Sometimes Medora accompanied Ivy on these excursions, with Ada plodding along behind them.

Shedding her dependence upon the approval of Ellsworth Corring and Annette Ware gave Ivy new self-confidence. She no longer sought advice from either Aunt Camellia or me about questions of fashion, but made choices of gowns and accessories that were uniquely her own, and unfailingly flattering.

While I was relieved that Ivy had lost any illusions about finding happiness as the wife of Ellsworth Corring, I was becoming a little bit concerned that no other suitor appeared to take his place. Certainly, I had made it clear to Benjamin Thornton that he would face no opposition from me if he chose to pursue Ivy. More than that, I really didn't believe any disapproval on my part would prevent him from doing precisely as he wished. However, he had made no effort to contact her. But Ivy seemed to be blissfully unconcerned about her suitorless state, apparently too absorbed in writing to care.

The first day of July brought oppressive, damp heat. It was also Ivy's actual eighteenth birthday, which, having been so lavishly celebrated two months earlier, had to be acknowledged quietly, within the family. Uncle Derrick and Aunt Camellia gave Ivy a single strand of flawless aquamarines that were the perfect complement to her eyes. I gave her a small portable writing desk equipped with two silver pens and pale green writing paper. Sir Clive, the only one outside our immediate family who knew Ivy's true birthday, had been invited to a small family dinner in her honor, but sent regrets because of pressing business, arranging for departure for New York.

I had intended to begin packing for my own move to New York, but decided I didn't want to sort through my possessions on such a miserably hot day any more than I thought Hez would want to manhandle my large trunk up from the cellar.

As it turned out, Aunt Camellia was eager to discuss details for the wedding ceremony, which was to be held in the front parlor.

"The obvious place for you and Sir Clive to stand is here," Aunt Camellia stood in front of the French doors leading out to the balcony. "The clergyman—Mr. What's-His-Name from Trinity—will be facing you, Drusilla, she nodded in my direction, and, of course, Sir Clive," she waved her hand in the direction she thought he should stand. It was clear that Aunt Camellia did not consider grooms to be of the most vital consideration when planning a wedding.

She turned and looked up at the curtains covering the French doors. "Those will have to be drawn so guests can see the canopy of green trees behind you." She paused for a moment in thought. "We must have something more than those simple curtains. Nothing ostentatious . . . but not too modest, either. Hmmm. Ribbons. Satin or taffeta? Taffeta, I believe, drawn up in a large bow above the center of the doorway leading out to the balcony. But what color? A pale crème, perhaps—a subtle contrast with the gold in your gown. That way *you*, my darling Drusilla, will stand out as the centerpiece of the entire arrangement!"

She sat down, then, as if having just been relieved of an enormous burden, sipped some tea to restore her strength.

"For you, Miss Ivy," Ada's voice was muffled behind an enormous bouquet of white lilies and white roses. Their fragrance filled the entire parlor.

"Magnificent!" Aunt Camellia exclaimed.

"For me?" Ivy whispered. The flowers overwhelmed the tea table where Ada set them. Ivy's hands shook as she opened the envelope. "Happy Birthday . . . from Sir Clive!" she read.

"You are so fortunate to have such a thoughtful fiancé, Drusilla," Aunt Camellia said.

"I am going to write him a thank you note right now," Ivy announced, picking up the flower arrangement. "I'll use that beautiful writing paper you gave me, Cuz."

"It would have been lovely to have had that bouquet here in the parlor to enjoy," Aunt Camellia murmured as Ivy departed. "Although, I suppose it might have been awkward explaining its presence if any guests dropped by, since everyone believes Ivy turned eighteen in the spring. But I cannot regret having had Ivy's birthday celebration in May. She has become remarkably polished in these short months. I had almost despaired when she became infatuated with Ellsworth Corring. But having seen through him, I do believe her judgment in gentlemen is much improved. And I must thank your Sir Clive for providing such an excellent pattern for her to use to evaluate future suitors."

She languidly wielded a fan decorated with elaborately robed Chinese figures, which Uncle Derrick had brought her from one of his voyages. "Mercy, but it's sultry. Reminds me of my childhood summers, almost. But it should break well before your wedding. It would be a shame for your big day to be spoiled by thunder and lightning storms. At least everything will be held indoors. Garden weddings can be charming, but why take the chance? However, it looks as if this time, the weather is much more likely to inconvenience Fourth of July celebrations than your wedding. I daresay Clarissa Jones is fretting over her big party."

"It will seem strange to witness the celebration of the defeat of my country," I said. "Although, I suppose, in time, I will become accustomed to it. How does Uncle Derrick feel about the Fourth of July?"

Aunt Camellia shrugged. "Your uncle is a walking, breathing paradox. He is the most English of men, but he seems to be able to blend into any setting. I believe your Sir Clive might very well be like him in that respect. In any case, don't fret yourself about Independence Day festivities. There are parades, fife and drum corps, patriotic speeches, and much eating and drinking, all finished off with fireworks. But you should know by now that Americans—particularly those with whom you are most likely to associate—still look to England as the arbiter of all things civilized."

As it turned out, the spell of oppressive weather broke the afternoon of July 3, with an alarming clap of thunder that sent Medora scurrying for shelter under my bed. Nature continued a display of wind, rain, thunder, and lightning well beyond nightfall. But by morning, the city appeared washed and sparkling, with a freshening wind off the bay, creating a perfect setting for the day's festivities.

Immediately after breakfast, Cook, Ada, and Hez departed to spend the holiday with family. Aunt Camellia, Ivy, and I went out on the balcony to watch the parade make its way down Park Row and turn down Common Street passing directly below us. A color guard dressed in uniforms of the Continental army, which had inexplicably beaten His Majesty's army, led with the Stars and Stripes and the flag of the Commonwealth of Massachusetts. The crowd below cheered and waved handkerchiefs and miniature Stars and Stripes, as did Aunt Camellia and Ivy. I held Medora, hoping that my lack of participation would be assigned to concern for my dog. Uncle Derrick appeared as a fife and drum corps marched by. He put an arm around my shoulders and softly sang to the tune they were playing:

> *Yankee Doodle went to town*
> *A-riding on a pony,*
> *Stuck a feather in his cap*
> *And called it macaroni.*
> *Yankee Doodle keep it up,*
> *Yankee Doodle dandy,*
> *Mind the music and the step*
> *And with the girls be handy!*

"Don't worry, Drusilla, my dear. Such foolishness is reserved for once a year. You'll become accustomed to it. And the fireworks can be quite enjoyable."

Sir Clive seemed to be even less enthusiastic about the Fourth of July than I was. And he had our departure for New York as an excuse to limit his participation in the celebration. So we agreed that I would accompany Aunt Camellia, Uncle Derrick, and Ivy to the Joneses' party next door. And he would put in a late appearance. When we arrived, it was already what Constance would have called "a sad crush"—the ultimate compliment for a successful social gathering. We were ushered into the back garden where tables were set up for feasting and drinking.

Mrs. Prudence sat at a table of honor, along with a small group of aging revolutionaries who were old enough to have participated in the events that led to the Declaration being celebrated. I went to pay my respects to her. She received me graciously, but seemed subdued, lacking the fire and confidence I had observed in her only weeks before.

"Miss Fortesque. How little I dreamed forty-two years ago that loyal subjects of the king would be attending a celebration of our independence, and there would be no ill will."

Was it just the inevitable change that time brings that had sapped Mrs. Prudence of her verve? The stocktaking that comes with birthdays and anniversaries? I followed her gaze and saw Susan Jones, her preferred candidate for granddaughter-in-law, chatting with Mr. Douglas Robertson. Benjamin Thornton strolled over, greeted me, bent to kiss his grandmother on the cheek, and murmured something in her ear. She patted his hand, which rested on her shoulder.

Our host, Hollis Jones, mounted to the top stair leading from the house to the garden and asked for his guests' attention.

"Thank you for helping us celebrate the birthday of our glorious country," he began. "I trust that no one will let this day pass without saying a prayer of gratitude to our Maker for the freedom that is in the very air we breathe. Furthermore, I know that we all want to express our particular gratitude to the stalwart citizens that we honor today, who played a vital role in securing our independence."

He motioned to Mrs. Prudence and her companions, who nodded and beamed as guests applauded.

Mr. Jones cleared his throat and continued. "In addition to the happiness of our national day of celebration, Mrs. Jones and I have a more personal reason for happiness. It is our very great pleasure to announce that our daughter, Susan, is engaged to be married to Mr. Douglas Robertson!"

"Does it strike you as odd to be announcing an engagement to be married on a day called Independence Day?" I flinched, turned cold, but steeled myself and turned to face the questioner, Captain Jack Hatton.

"Didn't your mother tell you that it is impolite to startle a lady?"

"You, of all ladies, know that my mother despairs of having the slightest influence over my behavior," he said, taking my arm and steering me toward the back of the garden and a solitary table empty of guests.

"I don't see your intended amongst the crowd. Are his patriotic sensibilities more easily bruised than yours or mine?"

"Of all men, Sir Clive is able to accommodate local customs. He plans to make an appearance later, but he is quite preoccupied transferring his commercial interests from Boston to New York. You must have heard that we plan to settle there after our wedding."

"Ah yes. Your wedding is quite soon, isn't it? I received a charming invitation from your Aunt Camellia, but I had to send regrets. I'm planning a visit to Cape Cod, which Douglas Robertson assures me should not be missed. I might stop by New Bedford and see how those Quakers have managed to dominate whaling."

Jack squinted and looked off into the distance. The bright sunlight revealed creases at the corners of his eyes and a weariness on his face that made me want to reach out and smooth away the cares etched there.

"I plan to leave in the morning," he said. "And since you'll be gone before I return, I thought I owed you an apology for my words and behavior the last time we spoke. I had no right to presume . . . to cast aspersions on your motives . . ."

"No, no," I whispered, but Jack didn't seem to be listening and continued as if he were delivering a prepared speech.

"And I felt that you deserved a progress report on my mission here, what with my enlisting your assistance. I have to thank you for putting me on the right trail. It turned out that Robertson *was* the designer and builder of the *Bon Esprit*. And he was able to give me all the information I needed about its financing and the bidders for its prize cargo. What he told me makes it quite clear who must have been involved with the note to Josiah Corring. I haven't approached that person yet. I find the situation delicate. But I don't think there is any urgency, and I want to handle it with a reasonable degree of discretion. I'll have time while I'm away to figure out what to do to give Corring the assurance he needs that nothing will come of the implied threat in the note."

"No doubt, he will be quite grateful to you," I said.

"Captain Hatton! There you are! And Miss Fortesque! We've found a fiddler for country dancing. Please join us," Beryl Corring said, extending her hand to Jack.

"A pleasure, Miss Corring." Jack smiled and took her hand. "But you'll have to show me the steps. Won't you come along, Miss Fortesque?"

"Thank you, but I believe I shall wait here. I'm expecting Sir Clive at any moment." I was in no mood to witness Jack, the most proficient of dancers, pretending ignorance of any dance steps.

Neither Beryl Corring nor Jack urged me to change my mind.

Watching them as they made their way to where the fiddler was tuning up, I thought what a striking couple they made. With the contrast of Jack's fair hair and Beryl's raven locks, they each set off the other's best features. There was no doubt Josiah Corring would welcome Jack as a son-in-law, and Jack would not need to exert himself to earn Miss Corring's dowry. Her mother would never tire of introducing her handsome son-in-law: "Even though his father is an earl, we find him to be totally unaffected by the privilege to which he was born."

I felt someone's eyes on me and was dismayed to find Benjamin Thornton looking at me and then to the couple I was studying and back again to me. How could I have let down my guard so completely? I marshalled my wits as best I could, because he was making his way to where I sat and other than bolting out the back gate of the garden into the mews, I could not avoid speaking with him. At least he had brought some refreshment.

"I hope you like ginger beer, Miss Fortesque. You look as if you need a brandy, but there was no way I could provide it without causing talk." He took a seat opposite me and placed the drink on the table. I cautiously took a sip. It was a little raw, but I needed it every bit as much as Mr. Thornton suspected. I set it aside, though. I required all my wits about me for this encounter.

He slowly quaffed from a large tankard while I tried to think of something to say that would divert his attention from the subject of Jack, Beryl, and me. But all I could think of was Susan and Mr. Robertson's newly announced engagement, another topic that I did not wish to broach with him.

"I am the least fanciful of men, Miss Fortesque." Mr. Thornton spoke before I could formulate a comment on the lovely weather. "But even *I* could see the unhappiness—almost pain—on the faces of both you and Captain Hatton as you were chatting with each other just now. I could have sworn that I was witnessing—not a lovers' quarrel—nothing that dramatic. More like the *aftermath* of a lovers' quarrel, I would wager."

If he had reached across the table and hit me on the side of my head, I could not have been struck dumb more effectively. But he continued in soft, silky tones that belied the pain that he must have been aware he was inflicting. "You know what I think, Miss Fortesque? I think that the actual quarrel took place the last afternoon of the house party. *That* would explain the uncharacteristic anger I saw in Captain Hatton in the hallway outside the library and his obliviousness to my presence. And if that guess is right, then what I witnessed today was some sort of rapprochement. The necessary papering over of the breach, so that if you encounter each other in the future—and since Captain Hatton is the brother of your best friend, such an encounter is likely to happen—you can maintain a façade of civility."

"I believe you have missed your calling, Mr. Thornton," I said with as much conviction as I could, without shouting. "You should have been a barrister—or whatever the person who prosecutes criminals here is called—the gentleman who assembles and presents accusations in court, and declaims to impress a jury."

I should have known that Benjamin Thornton would be unmoved by my protest. He settled his elbows on the table, folded his hands under his chin, and narrowed his eyes.

"But if I were presenting this case in court, Miss Fortesque, if I were putting the pieces of this puzzle together for a jury, there is one that wouldn't fit—*you.* You must have rejected Captain Hatton that afternoon. Otherwise, why would he have been so angry? But if you rejected him, why did you look so longingly after him just now when he walked away from you with Beryl Corring? Someone else might believe that you turned down Captain Hatton for Sir Clive's wealth. The fourth son of an earl, a soldier in peacetime, can't offer anything approaching Brampton's fortune. Perhaps underneath everything, you *do* have the heart of a mercenary, but even in my most cynical moments, I find that hard to believe. Then again, perhaps my insights are off the mark."

He fell silent and looked over to where Beryl Corring and Jack Hatton stood waiting to begin the first dance.

"One thing I am certain of, though, is that Miss Corring has no idea of the complexity of the gentleman she has set her sights on. And I am the last person who could warn her, more's the pity."

Benjamin Thornton studied the contents of his tankard as if looking at scene of utter despair. He shrugged, drained it, and stood to leave.

"I hope it doesn't offend you if I wish you a happy Independence Day, Miss Fortesque," he said, and strolled off.

Sir Clive appeared just before dusk, and we watched the fireworks before he escorted me home.

"I am sorry that I arrived at the party so late, my dear."

"I do understand, really," I assured him.

He drew a finger down my cheek and brushed my lips with a kiss. "You are the best of ladies, Drusilla. Much better than I deserve. But never doubt that your happiness is of great importance to me."

Chapter Eighteen

When I entered the breakfast room the next morning, I encountered Cook, red faced, cup and saucer in one hand, plate in another.

"I don't know what to think, sir," she was saying to Uncle Derrick. "Not a sign of her! Not the most pleasant lass by a long shot, but dependable as rain—dreary as rain, too—but never late, much less absent."

"I am certain she will appear sooner rather than later," Uncle Derrick said, casting a wary eye on the cup, which was sliding around on the saucer, as Cook gesticulated in her agitation. "And I do appreciate your filling in for her," he added, reminding her that the proper place for the cup, saucer, and plate was on the table in front of him. "Also some silverware, if you please, and the same for Miss Drusilla."

"Seems our Ada has taken an unauthorized holiday," Uncle Derrick raised an eyebrow. "Actually, I never would have thought the girl had it in her. What do you think? Spirits or romance?"

"I cannot say which is more unlikely," I had to admit.

Cook came trundling back with a full place setting for me. "Sent Hez over to her family's place. She'll probably be there, but what could have kept her, I can't think. Oh sir! You don't s'pose something could be amiss? Perhaps her mother taken ill? Oh sir, I feel awful for having judged her so cruelly."

The smell of burning ham wafted from the kitchen.

"Mercy!" Cook exclaimed and ran to rescue our breakfast, Uncle Derrick's silverware in hand.

He pressed his fingers to his forehead. "I suppose I didn't need that cutlery anyway, in that it might be some time before we have anything to cut."

"Don't fret yourself, Uncle. I trust I am capable of finishing the table settings and even fetching something to drink from the kitchen." I took myself off to calm Cook.

As I returned to the breakfast room with crockery and cutlery, the church bells of Boston began to chime.

"At least it's the Sabbath," Uncle Derrick mused, "so no one will be wondering why I'm not at the wharf."

"And I'll be absent from Morning Prayer, but I imagine I won't be the only absentee, what with the celebrations yesterday," I said.

"What in heaven's name is the matter?" Aunt Camellia inquired from the breakfast room door. "Why hasn't Ada brought me my toast and tea?"

"You might as well sit down and wait with Drusilla and me, my dear," Uncle Derrick stood and pulled out a chair for his agitated wife. "It seems that Ada has extended her holiday."

I went to get a place setting for Aunt Camellia. When I returned, she was mulling over the maid's ingratitude.

"I vow I was the only lady in Boston who would hire that girl, what with her sour disposition. But I never knew anyone more skilled with mending and ironing. I should turn her off without a reference the moment I see her glum face, but how could I find another maid who would never scorch even my finest voiles?" she wondered, fingering the sheer, deep ruffles on her pale green dressing gown.

Cook finally arrived with breakfast and I helped her serve.

"Would you like for me to fetch Ivy?" I asked before sitting down to my own meal. "Isn't it late for her to be sleeping?"

"Oh don't disturb her," said Aunt Camellia. "The fireworks gave her a headache and she planned to take a sleeping powder before she went to bed. Might as well let her rest until we get the household back to rights."

The three of us ate our meals in silence. Uncle Derrick resolutely sawed and chewed dried out, burned ham. He surreptitiously offered a bite to Medora, who sniffed at it and turned away. Aunt Camellia nibbled and crumbled blackened toast. And I ate the occasional spoonful of cold porridge. As if our spirits weren't sufficiently depressed, Hez appeared just as Uncle Derrick was swallowing his last bite of ham and informed us that Ada's family had not seen "hide nor hair" of her the previous day.

Aunt Camellia blanched. "Derrick! You don't think there's been foul play!"

"I am certain there is nothing of the sort, my dear! After all, this is Boston! There must be a perfectly benign explanation, but I do believe I will search out the night watch and see if he can offer any helpful information."

Aunt Camellia and I slowly mounted the stairs together.

"I'll just look in on Ivy before I go on up to my room," Aunt Camellia said.

I had scarcely closed my door when I heard a scream from the other end of the hallway. I rushed to Ivy's room and discovered Aunt Camellia standing over the bed, looking at what I initially took to be Ivy's inert body, but upon closer examination discovered it was bedsheets, rolled and fashioned in the general form of a body. A lacy nightcap lay on the pillow, crowning this creation. Aunt Camellia swayed, as if to faint. It took all my strength to get her up the stairs and into her bed. Then I went next door to Uncle

Derrick's room, found a brandy decanter, and encouraged Aunt Camellia to take a sip. Finally, I was able to settle her among her pillows and I sat, holding her hand, wondering what more I could do.

"I should have known." Aunt Camellia's voice was a hoarse whisper. "She's run off with that dreadful Ellsworth Corring. All that acting as if she no longer cared about him. It was all a ruse. Oh, my darling, darling little girl! Throwing herself away on such an unworthy, head-in-the-clouds dreamer."

She covered her face with trembling hands, sighed, and took a deep breath. "At least they won't starve—no thanks to *his* ambition! But she could have done so much better! She is such a rare beauty!"

There was a soft knock at the door.

"Derrick?" Aunt Camellia asked.

But it was Cook who appeared. "Miss Ware is in the parlor and insists that you will want to hear her news," Cook announced.

"Was Job as plagued as I?" Aunt Camellia wailed. "Say whatever needs to be said to get her gone, Drusilla."

I plumped the pillows and arranged the covers around my weeping aunt and ordered Cook to sit with her while I went to face our inopportune guest.

"Where are Ivy and Mrs. Fortesque?" Annette asked as soon as I entered the parlor. She was wearing a mustard ensemble, the sight of which exacerbated the slight queasiness I had felt since eating my breakfast of cold, lumpy porridge.

I scooped up Medora, who had followed me, having rightly assessed the unlikelihood of any bonbons from Aunt Camellia for the time being. I clung to the little dog as much for comfort as to disguise my trembling hands and concentrated on finding something to say to encourage Miss Ware's earliest possible departure.

"I fear they are both indisposed," I said, reassuring myself that, at most, it was only a half lie. "The fireworks . . . gave them both terrible, blinding headaches. I believe it is an inherited malady." I stopped myself short before continuing on with a recitation about the condition running for generations in Aunt Camellia's family. Was I just giddy from all the stress, or was I really in danger of becoming a candidate for bedlam? I should have told Miss Ware that Aunt Camellia and Ivy were suffering from something contagious.

"It is really too unfortunate that they are ill, because I know they would have wished to hear my news directly from me. And I wanted the Fortesque ladies to be the first to know. Except for my parents—and the Corrings, of course." Annette took a deep breath and straightened her back. "Mr. Ellsworth Corring and I became engaged last night! I suspect there was a time when Ivy entertained hopes of an offer from Mr. Corring, but I am certain that she will understand that dear Ellsworth and I are perfectly matched. And his parents are *so* pleased! Mrs. Corring just beamed with pleasure. Ellsworth tells me that his family is anticipating another similar announcement before long, as soon as Captain Hatton returns from his trip to the Cape. Ellsworth thinks the captain is exploring some investment opportunities in whaling, so that it won't look as if he would be totally dependent on Beryl's fortune."

Medora whimpered. I realized that I was almost squeezing the air out of her small body. "Sorry, my dear," I patted her on the head and put her on the floor. She curled up next to my feet, for once seeming to sense my need for comfort and companionship.

"I know Aunt Camellia and Ivy will both be eager to wish you great happiness. You must have ever so many friends who will want to hear your news as soon as possible," I said.

"Of course, that is so true, and I wouldn't want to keep you from your task of tending to the invalids. Do tell them I hope they both have speedy recoveries. I'm sure that my happy news will lift their spirits. Don't bother to get up. I will see myself out."

The best aspect of Annette Ware's visits were their brevity.

So Aunt Camellia is wrong. Wherever Ivy went, it was not with Ellsworth Corring. He is not the most admirable of gentlemen, but he is not capable of proposing marriage to Annette Ware on the same night that he plans to elope with Ivy Fortesque. Should I go upstairs and inform Aunt Camellia?

"Drusilla?"

It was Uncle Derrick.

"No sightings of the elusive Ada, I fear. Whatever was that creature in mustard doing here? I almost collided with her at the front door." He tossed his hat on the sofa and strode over to the brandy decanter.

"She was announcing her engagement to Ellsworth Corring," I said.

"I'll drink to that," Uncle Derrick raised a generous tot of brandy. "At least I won't have to introduce that twit as my son-in-law."

"I'm afraid there's no reason for celebration, Uncle," I choked out. "Ivy has gone—disappeared! Aunt Camellia assumed she had eloped with Corring, but now . . ."

Uncle Derrick paused for a moment, poured himself more brandy, then lifted the decanter, asking me if I would join him. I nodded. He placed the drink in my hand, sat down next to his discarded hat, drank down half the contents of his glass, and put it on the table next to him.

"Tell me," he said.

I told him about the rolled-up sheets and the lace cap resting on the pillow.

"At least we know she was not abducted. The silly girl, wherever she went—and with whom—she went of her own accord. And, of course, this solves the problem of the disappearance of Ada. Clearly, she accompanied Ivy on her adventure."

"I suspect that Ada provided Ivy with some servant's attire as a disguise. She wrote a scene in her book where that happened. She was particularly pleased with that scene." I took a sip of brandy and set the glass aside. Unless I planned to retire to my room and hide myself under my bedclothes, I needed to keep my wits about me.

"Poor Camellia! And she doesn't even know this latest news about Corring's betrothal."

"I settled her in bed and left Cook watching over her. I suppose there's no point in disturbing her just to deepen her distress."

Uncle Derrick stood and began to pace.

"What is the saying? 'Cast your bread upon the waters?' I am receiving from my daughter precisely what I gave to Camellia's father. We eloped, you know. And he never spoke to me again—disowned Camellia. But, come what may, I could never inflict that punishment upon Ivy. All I want to know is that she is alive and safe."

"Oh Derrick! Thank heavens you are returned!" Aunt Camellia rushed into Uncle Derrick's embrace.

"Aunt Camellia! I thought Cook was looking after you and you were resting."

"Cook fell asleep in her chair and began to snore. And who could sleep with *that* racket! Anyway, my mind was racing. I am sure Drusilla has told you, Derrick, that Ivy is missing, too, and it's clear that she has eloped with Ellsworth Corring. So you must organize a search immediately. I cannot imagine that between them they could formulate, much less execute, much of a plan . . ." Aunt Camellia paused, looking from Uncle Derrick's face, to mine, and back to Uncle Derrick's before collapsing on the sofa. "There's news, isn't there?" she whispered. "Dreadful news . . ."

Uncle Derrick tossed his hat on the floor and sat next to Aunt Camellia, taking her hands in his.

"It seems, my dear, that Annette Ware and Ellsworth Corring are engaged to be married. She just left, having imparted the news to Drusilla."

"Then who . . .? Surely . . ."

There was a loud knock on the front door that prevented us from hearing Aunt Camellia's certainty.

Uncle Derrick rushed downstairs. Aunt Camellia and I listened attentively as a male voice said, "I was instructed to give you these." We sat in silence as Uncle Derrick climbed the stairs back up to the parlor.

When he appeared in the doorway, he was holding three envelopes and a flat box. His face was inscrutable.

"I believe that we have good reason to assume that Ivy is alive and well," he announced. "That was Starnes, Sir Clive's man."

Uncle Derrick handed me the box and an envelope with my name on it written in Ivy's hand. He then sat next to Aunt Camellia and gave her the second envelope, keeping the third for himself.

"If you need to be alone, Drusilla, your aunt and I will understand."

Precisely the words said to the bereaved after delivering the news of the death of a loved one.

But this loss has nothing to do with love, and everything to do with pride.

I kissed my aunt and uncle. Her cheek was damp with tears. His was bristling with whiskers he had not had time to shave that morning. As I made my way to my room, I heard Medora padding by my side. When had she acquired any softer feelings for me? I was amazed but beyond grateful for her newly discovered loyalty. I picked her up before sitting in the chair by the window, and gave her a swift kiss on her topknot, receiving a lick on my cheek in return. Which to open first, the box or the envelope? I set the box on the little table next to the chair. I would deal with its contents when I had read what Ivy had to say.

July 4, 1818

Dearest Drusilla,

By the time you read this letter, I shall be aboard Flame Goddess *sailing to New York with Sir Clive Brampton. As you will have guessed, Ada is with me and will serve as chaperone until Sir Clive and I are wed shortly after our arrival in New York.*

Many people will judge me harshly for this decision. But I believe in my heart of hearts that you not only will withhold judgment, but will forgive and understand.

I know that you and Sir Clive entered into your engagement with the best of intentions to build a marriage based upon mutual respect, both of you having given up hope of finding true love. And had you been married by the time Sir Clive and I discovered our feelings for each other, I would not have dreamed of coming between you, but would have simply entered a convent to spend the rest of my days in prayer and meditation.

However, fate saw otherwise, and from our first opportunity to actually spend time together—on our journey back to Boston from Roxbury—we found that there was nothing either of us enjoyed more than being in each other's company. I couldn't have dreamed of a more gallant, thoughtful knight. How wrong I was ever to have judged him on physical appearance alone. How superficial I was in my judgments! At least all those dreary hours I spent listening to Ellsworth Corring drone on about "higher knowledge" were not totally wasted and I came to look beyond the surface. Now I see my dear Sir Clive as the very image of the complete gentleman.

In spite of the strong feelings for each other Sir Clive and I discovered, I still might have hesitated to have permitted us to follow them to their natural conclusion had I not become convinced that not only were you not in love with Sir Clive, but, in all likelihood, you continue to hold fond feelings—dare I say love—for another gentleman. Furthermore, I must tell you that Ada informs me that you have participated in at least one assignation with that gentleman since you became engaged to Sir Clive Brampton! I am not judging you for this act of disloyalty, knowing as I do the enormous pull of love. But how could I stand idly by, knowing that agreeing to elope with Sir Clive was not, in the long term, creating unhappiness, but actually preventing great unhappiness, not only for him and me, but you, also? So now, not only will Sir Clive and I be entering into a marriage where both partners truly love each other, you will be free to eventually find happiness with a new love—perhaps someone you have yet to meet!

Although I loath to keep any secrets from him, I have chosen not to tell Sir Clive about your clandestine meetings during your engagement. His esteem for you is as high as can be. It would be needlessly cruel of me to disabuse him of your loyalty.

I am so looking forward to this thrilling new chapter in my life. Sir Clive believes that New York City will provide a perfect setting for me to have a salon where writers and artists will feel welcome. He has decided to settle permanently in America and even plans to become a citizen of the United States. This means, of course, that he will forswear his title, so we will be just plain Mr. and

Mrs. Clive Brampton. I do admire him for this decision. But even without his title, he will always be my true knight in shining armor.

I hope you wish me well, dear Cousin, as I do you.

Fondly,
Ivy

I folded the letter, placed it on the table, and took up the box. Inside was an envelope with my name on it in Clive Brampton's writing. Underneath the envelope was a strand of rubies set in gold, and a pair of ruby eardrops, clearly a set to match the ring that still sparkled on my finger.

The note was brief:

My Dear Drusilla,

Because I know you as a lady of generosity of spirit and uncommonly good sense, I am confident that you will come to understand that Ivy and I have made the best of a most difficult situation. Believe me when I say that I know I was more fortunate than I deserved when you agreed to marry me. But I find that a love match such as I had long since ceased to hope for was something I could not resist.

What I told you at our last meeting will always be true. Your happiness is of great importance to me. Please accept this gift, which was intended for you on our wedding day. I trust it will ensure your independence, if not serve as a dowry, if you too have the good fortune to marry for love.

Your servant,

Clive Brampton

I took the ruby ring off my finger, placed it in the box, and, too numb to cry, sat patting Medora.

Chapter Nineteen

edora whimpered. I walked downstairs through a silent house and opened the door into the back garden to let her out. The lilac had shed all but one of its shriveled blossoms.

What would I do? What would Aunt Camellia, Uncle Derrick do? Most unwelcome events had a protocol. Priests are called to the patient's bedside. Death notices are written. Crepe is hung. Condolence visits are made.

The betrothal of Miss Drusilla Fortesque to Sir Clive Brampton has been terminated by mutual consent. Therefore, the wedding scheduled for July 15, 1818, will not take place.

Aunt Camellia had written the invitations. I hoped she would write the retractions for the invitations.

Of course, I would return to England, to Bath, to the home of my aunts. But not immediately. It would be unseemly for me to abandon Aunt Camellia and Uncle Derrick before they received confirmation that Ivy had arrived safely in New York City—and was duly wed to Clive Brampton. But as soon as feasible, I wanted to leave Boston. I could endure the public humiliation of being abandoned by my fiancé after wedding invitations had been sent. It was my pride—not my heart—that had been wounded. But witnessing betrothal celebrations for Jack and Beryl Corring was another matter entirely. I wanted to be on a ship sailing home to

England before their engagement was announced. Once we heard from Ivy, I would speak to Uncle Derrick about finding the most commodious berth on the most seaworthy vessel headed for home. I only hoped that Jack would find many interests to keep him in Barnstable or New Bedford and that good news would be coming soon from New York.

Uncle Derrick and I ate the cold collation Cook served for supper. Aunt Camellia remained in seclusion, resting.

"I don't believe in the practice of apologizing for the behavior of others, not even for my daughter's behavior," Uncle Derrick said. "But I am sorry that what she has done has so disrupted your life. I am particularly mindful of the role I played in encouraging you to accept Clive Brampton's marriage proposal. I do want you to know how much I—and Camellia, too—are distressed by the pain Ivy's actions have inflicted upon you."

"That is very kind of you, Uncle," I replied. "But, of course I know that neither you nor Aunt Camellia had any idea of Ivy's plans, any more than I did. And, of course, Clive Brampton must be assigned primary responsibility. As you might suspect, it is my pride, not my heart, that has been battered."

"What are you plans? You are certainly more than welcome to remain here with Camellia and me for as long as you like. I am sure that Camellia would appreciate your company."

"You know as well as I, Uncle, that as soon as news comes from New York confirming Ivy's safe arrival and marriage, Aunt Camellia will be planning a visit to the Brampton household. And I wouldn't be the least bit surprised if commercial opportunities open up for Fortesque Company in New York."

Uncle Derrick smiled a half smile, the first I had seen since the drama of the day began.

"I don't doubt the accuracy of both your predictions, my dear. I expect Camellia will be spending as much time in New York as she does in Boston." He looked wistful. "Camellia, better than anyone, knows the pain of separation from family after an elopement. She would never choose to inflict that on Ivy—or herself. So I shall be happy for her to see as much of Ivy as she wishes. But I am not inclined to move from Boston. I have become quite comfortable with the manner in which business is conducted here."

"I think it best if I leave at the earliest convenient time after we hear from Ivy," I said.

"Don't worry about a thing." Uncle Derrick kissed my cheek as he left the dining room. "I'll be on the lookout for the best accommodations for you."

If I had expected Aunt Camellia to remain entombed in her boudoir indefinitely, I was wrong. Twenty-four hours deprived of adequate staff was more than sufficient motivation for her to resume command of her household.

"I am dreadfully sorry for Ivy's thoughtlessness toward you, Drusilla, darling," Aunt Ivy said as she pulled on white kid gloves. "And I am deeply shocked by Ada's disloyalty and dishonesty. But her departure has made me realize that I never should have tried to manage with only one maid. I shouldn't wonder that Ada was perpetually glum with all of her tasks. I'm off to Mademoiselle's. She, alone, will know of a person capable of looking after my wardrobe. And I've asked Cook to find a housemaid for the rest of the chores."

By the next morning, Nadine, an inscrutable lady of uncertain age and little in the way of English vocabulary, had moved into an attic room and had taken charge of the maintenance of Aunt Camellia's wardrobe and belongings. Polly, a fresh-faced country cousin of the Joneses' maid, Josie, was tending to all of the other duties previously discharged by Ada.

So we had someone to answer the door when Susan Jones paid a call that afternoon. I was only surprised that she waited until Tuesday afternoon to discover why we were in need of a new maid. Josie would have shared the news on Monday when Cook asked for help.

Unlike Ada, Polly volunteered to bring tea and cakes after she announced Susan.

"I do apologize if I am intruding, but I wondered what became of Ada. Josie told me that Ada had left and you needed a new maid. Wasn't she with your aunt for years?" Susan said, settling her skirts about her.

How much should I reveal? How much did she suspect?

All of Boston would know soon enough. I might as well practice telling the embarrassing story. At least with Susan, I had a sympathetic audience.

I was given a few more minutes to collect my thoughts, because Polly appeared with a laden tea tray. Such efficiency was something of a shock after Ada's grudging service.

I took a sip of tea and fed Medora a nibble of cake. Heaven knew that I had no appetite for anything sweet.

"Ada accompanied Ivy to New York City," I said, finding guilty pleasure in the open-mouthed shock the announcement elicited on Susan's face. Tea sloshed as she hastily replaced her cup in its saucer and set it on the table next to her chair.

Having rendered my friend speechless, I continued.

"It is my understanding that Sir Clive and Ivy eloped in the early hours of Sunday morning—aboard *Flame Goddess*. Ada went with Ivy to serve, not only as her maid, but as chaperone. We are awaiting word that they have safely arrived and are wed."

"Oh, my dear Drusilla. I am so sorry! I don't know what to say," Susan whispered.

"There really is nothing that can be said. Sir Clive and I never pretended to be in love with each other." I began stoically. "But . . . but I *did* think I could trust him. . . ." I don't know whether I was more dismayed by what I had unthinkingly said or by the tears that began to run down my face.

Susan was by my side instantly, offering a clean handkerchief and urging me to drink a freshly poured cup of tea fortified with a double portion of sugar.

"Thank, you, thank you," I murmured, wiping my tears and trying to keep Medora from licking my face. "I believe I need a bit of fresh air."

Walking to the French doors and opening them gave me a chance to regain some composure.

"I really am all right," I assured Susan, "And I cannot tell you how relieved I am that you are the first person with whom I have discussed this matter. You are a true friend."

I settled back in my chair and took another sip of sweet tea and set it aside.

"I am dreadfully sorry, Drusilla. And shocked, too—at both Sir Clive's and Ivy's behavior. You can count on me to hold what you have confided in strictest confidence. But I fear the story will be all over Boston in short order. I haven't seen Douglas—Mr. Robertson—since Saturday evening. Of course his wharf would have been closed on Sunday, but the absence of *Flame Goddess* from the dock would have been noted as soon as the ship works opened yesterday morning. There must be speculation and rumors. . . . Douglas mentioned that he would stop by this evening. I will try to discover—subtly, of course—what he knows—or suspects."

"Thank you. I know it's not possible for me to stay hidden away here in the house until I leave for England. And I suppose it will be easier to face people if I have some idea of what they've heard."

"Must you leave, Drusilla? I shall miss you terribly. Can you at least stay for my wedding? We're thinking about September."

"I wish you all the happiness in the world, Susan, but I long for England and plan to return as soon as feasible. Just as soon as Uncle Derrick can arrange passage—after we receive word that Ivy is safe and sound."

Susan didn't stay long. She was too sensitive to my loss to speak further about her wedding plans. And I was too fragile to convincingly assure her that I wanted to dwell on any wedding plans—even those of a dear friend.

But the next morning she returned with news about her conversation with Douglas Robertson the previous evening.

"I didn't have to probe at all to encourage Douglas to talk about the disappearance of *Flame Goddess*," Susan said. "Of course, when they discovered Sir Clive's yacht had sailed, there were all sorts of conjectures. At first, most thought that he had taken it out for a brief excursion down Maine or to the Cape. When it didn't return yesterday, conjecture turned a little more jaded. Prevailing opinion is now that Sir Clive has bolted before his wedding. Ivy's role in the episode has not been discovered—at least among the workers at Robertson Ship Works."

"Thank you for letting me know what is being said," I responded to her news with genuine gratitude. "It will be easier to meet people, knowing what they must be thinking. And I'll have to brave the world outside this house sooner or later—if for nothing else, to walk Medora. She must be tiring of quick outings in the back garden and wondering what has become of her walks down the Mall."

The week dragged on. Mornings, Aunt Camellia took toast and tea in her room while Uncle Derrick and I ate in the breakfast room with little conversation. At least the ham wasn't burned and the porridge was hot—not that I had much appetite for either.

"You had better eat something, Drusilla, my dear," Uncle Derrick said. "You don't want to become gaunt."

Or else even the slim chance remaining that I might find a husband will disappear?

I refrained from uttering those words and smiled wanly.

"Sorry, Drusilla. You are no child to be cajoled, and you are entitled to do precisely as you wish." Uncle Derrick kissed the top of my head and left for India Wharf. I envied him the distraction of sorting through bills of lading and tide schedules.

Aunt Camellia scarcely emerged from her room before supper, which offered no more scintillating conversation than the breakfasts Uncle Derrick and I shared. But she sent out notes informing all who had been invited to my wedding that it had been canceled by "mutual consent."

Eventually, I mustered my courage and took Medora for walks. Indeed, the relief of actually moving was so great, I began much longer walks than I had previously indulged. I frequently had to pick up an exhausted Medora and carry her home. When I encountered friends and acquaintances, they murmured a brief "good day" and averted their glance. I almost felt sorry for them. What does one say to a jilted bride-to-be?

At last, on the morning of the day that would have been my wedding day, a rider, weary from having traveled at top speed from New York City, delivered two letters. One letter was from the "Reverend Mr. William Greene" verifying that he had united "Miss Ivy Fortesque and Mr. Clive Brampton in Holy Matrimony on July 10, 1818, in the city of New York."

The second letter was from Ivy to her parents. Aunt Camellia dabbed at her eyes as she read it. "I do not condone her actions, but I would be an unfeeling mother not to rejoice in her happiness. I *am* sorry for her thoughtlessness of you, though, Drusilla, my dear. I hope, someday, you can find it in you to forgive her."

I shrugged. Whom should I forgive? Ivy? Clive? Myself? "Please don't fret, Aunt Camellia," I said. "Perhaps she spared me more unhappiness in the future than she has caused me in the present."

Chapter Twenty

That evening, Uncle Derrick announced *Cerulean Wind* was bound for Bristol in two days' time and had excellent accommodations available, if I thought I could be ready for departure on such short notice.

Hez brought my trunk up from the cellar and placed it in the front parlor. It spared him the difficult task of negotiating another flight of stairs, and we did not expect guests.

I was relieved, finally, to be able to do something purposeful after days of waiting. Since the ship would be sailing on the tide Friday evening, I had little time to spare. I packed steadily all day Thursday. On Friday morning, I put a last few items in the trunk, setting aside my heaviest cloak, which I was certain I would need in the winds of the Atlantic.

As I packed, I kept telling myself that I was fortunate to be leaving Boston before Jack returned and his engagement to Beryl Corring became the preoccupation of society.

"Miss! I found this when I was cleaning in your room. It had fallen behind your dressing table. Didn't think you'd want to forget all these pictures you painted." Polly placed the folder of watercolors on the tea table and glanced around the room. "Looks like you're about ready for Hez to take your trunk down to the wharf. I'll let him know when he gets back from his errands for Cook."

There was a knock at the front door.

"Scuse me, miss." Polly hurried down to answer it.

"I do hope Miss Drusilla Fortesque is at home."

I wasn't alone in recognizing the voice. Medora, who had been sleeping, leaped from her chair and ran through the parlor door, yipping high barks of greeting as she raced down the stairs.

"If it isn't the living mop," I heard Jack say. "No need to announce me. I assume Miss Fortesque is in the front parlor."

Not even the conscientious Polly could resist Jack's casual presumption. He paused for a moment in the doorway, smiling his crooked smile, ignoring Medora, who was squirming in his arms, trying to lick his face. His shirt was rumpled and limp, his jacket was dusty, his breeches were wrinkled, and his jaw had not seen a razor within the past twenty-four hours.

I was so determined not to cry, I had forgotten to breathe.

"C . . . Cap . . . Captain Hatton," I managed before collapsing on the sofa. "Please do sit down."

Polly, who had followed Jack into the parlor, didn't bother hiding her curiosity and looked back and forth from Jack to me before saying, "I'll just fetch some refreshments."

Jack put Medora on the floor and sat in a chair across from me. He stretched out his legs, and looked at the open trunk.

"Bound for home, I see. And soon, by the looks of it."

I nodded, incapable of speech.

"When?" His eyebrows rose in question.

"This evening, about sunset, depending on the tide."

"Then it's lucky I caught you." He leaned forward, hands on his knees. "I had to . . . I wanted to see you before you left."

He's going to tell me of his plans to marry Beryl Corring. How can I bear it?

I pulled Medora onto my lap and patted her while I tried futilely to think of something to take the conversation in another direction.

Polly appeared with a tea tray. Jack sprang to his feet and said, "Here, let me help you with that."

I snatched the folder off the tea table and placed it on the sofa next to me while Jack lowered the heavily laden tray to the table.

The maid smiled up adoringly at him. "Oh thank you, sir!" Then dipped a curtsy, and departed.

"She's a great improvement over that other creature you had," Jack observed as he piled a plate high with offerings from the tray. Polly had seen to it that hearty beef and ham sandwiches were added to the usual selection of dainty cakes and biscuits. And a tankard of ale had been provided in addition to tea.

We sat in silence, I sipping tea and feeding Medora a biscuit. Jack, making short work of a sandwich between gulps of ale.

"You'll excuse me, I hope," Jack said, munching on his second sandwich. "Can't remember when I last ate. Smart lass, picking up on that."

"I take it that you rode straight through from the Cape—or from New Bedford."

"Didn't make it to New Bedford. Spent some time in Barnstable with Robertson's family and friends, and then headed for Provincetown." He took the last bite of sandwich, set the tankard on the tray, and wiped his mouth on a napkin. "I found the solitude quite . . . congenial. Amazing that Thornton was able to track me down."

"Benj . . . Benjamin Thornton?" I felt like a dullard. Why would Benjamin Thornton go searching for Jack?

Jack stood up and began to pace.

"Dash it, I'm sorry! Can't say where my wits are. But Thornton's reasons for searching me out are a bit complicated. For one thing, he wanted me to know that Brampton had taken off just days before your wedding. What a despicable wretch! But can't he be called on his perfidy? Your uncle, certainly he—"

"That might prove to be awkward," I said. "It seems that Clive Brampton did not leave alone. Ivy went with him. And earlier this week, we received news that they were married in New York City."

Jack stopped pacing, crossed his arms, and shook his head.

"No wonder you are in such a rush to return to England."

He ran a hand through his hair and sat down.

"And the other reason Benjamin Thornton went to such an effort to find you?" I could hear the tremor in my voice, but Jack didn't seem to notice.

"Ah yes. The *other* reason for Thornton's trip out to the Cape had to do with the rumor some busybody had been spreading around Boston. Evidently, there was a story that I had gone to find some opportunities in whaling so that when I asked for Beryl Corring's hand in marriage, I would have something to offer her—more than my own charming self and impressive lineage." Jack made a wry face.

"You weren't looking to invest in whaling?" My heart began to pound.

If he isn't planning to invest in whaling, then, perhaps the other part of Annette Ware's report is wrong, too. Perhaps he isn't planning to marry Beryl Corring.

For an instant, my spirits rose, before I reminded myself that one part of Annette's story could be true even if the other was not.

"Where would I find funds to invest in whaling? It would have been interesting to go to New Bedford and see firsthand how those Quakers ran their operation. No doubt my father would appreciate a report about it. But I can't imagine they would need or welcome my involvement in their enterprise." Jack shook his head.

"I suppose in many Bostonian's minds, the only reason to venture south is to look for commercial possibilities. Thornton certainly assumed that."

"Why . . .?"

"Sorry, I keep getting sidetracked. Thornton assumed that I wanted to marry Beryl Corring, at least in part, for her fortune. And he said he felt 'duty bound' to let me know that there *is* no fortune."

I took a sip of tea. It was cold, but I drained the cup.

Jack sat and crossed his arms. "It seems that Josiah Corring borrowed a considerable sum to build his new wharf. He wanted to put his personal stamp on Boston Harbor, and the man who lent him the money cared little for appearances, but much for control."

"Clive Brampton," I murmured.

Jack raised his eyebrows. "Perhaps you weren't as deceived about him as I have assumed you were."

His words stung. "I have come to learn a great deal in retrospect," I snapped.

"Sorry, sorry," Jack held up a hand. "That was uncalled for, and I apologize. Anyway, on the Friday before the Independence Day celebrations, Brampton visited Thornton at his bank and offered to sell him Corring's debt. Brampton explained that he was divesting himself of as much of his Boston interests as possible. Of course, Thornton had no idea that Brampton's removal from Boston was more imminent than anyone dreamed."

"So the Corrings . . .?"

"They aren't *ruined*, by any means. But there will be no dowry, no great inheritance for the beautiful Beryl. And from what Thornton says, it is all to the good that Ellsworth is marrying a fortune. Otherwise, his higher thinking might well lead to some very lean living."

"So Thornton was warning you, in effect . . . but I don't understand." I paused for a moment, trying to organize my thoughts. "Although, initially, I was not impressed with Benjamin Thornton's character, I had come to have a better opinion of him. However, I must admit, I find it extraordinary, to say the least, that he would disclose such sensitive financial information about Josiah Corring to you. I am trying not to be shocked, but . . ."

"A man in love is capable of doing rather shocking things, if he thinks he is about to lose his lady." Jack said. "And Josiah Corring's debts are not all Thornton is holding. He is also in possession of Corring's indiscreet letter to my father."

"How did he manage to come by *that*?" I asked.

"Remember your telling me about his prowling about his grandmother's drawing room that day you were having tea with her? It seems he made a habit of examining her treasures, and one day he discovered the letter Corring wrote to my father in a Chinese lacquered box on her desk. Straight away, he recognized its potential for danger to Corring, so he took it 'as a precaution' against its 'falling into the wrong hands,' as he told me on our ride back to Boston. When Mrs. Prudence later discovered it missing, she confronted Thornton. He was puzzled about her uncharacteristic agitation over the matter until she confessed that, in a fit of pique, she had written a threatening note to Corring. Evidently, Josiah's new wharf and the prospect of Edward Corring's becoming a member of Congress was too much for patriotic Mrs. Prudence to bear, in light of Josiah's disloyalty during the recent war."

Now I was *truly* shocked. "Is Thornton contemplating some sort of blackmail himself?"

Jack began to pace again.

"I don't believe that's his intention at all. Poor chap has been blindly in love with Beryl Corring since he can remember.

Always assumed they would marry. When he first started to take an interest in their families' partnership, he became aware of the blow the recent war had leveled on both families' fortunes, and he began to set himself up in private banking—to recoup both families' shipping losses during the war. He assumed that he was also providing for his future wife, Beryl Corring. But just as he was about to offer for her—and play the white knight—Beryl let it be known that Benjamin Thornton was not what she was looking for in a husband." Jack paused and smiled. "She seems to have followed her father's predilection for all things British."

I bit my lip to keep from crying. Benjamin Thornton had searched out Jack to warn him that Beryl Corring was not an heiress—hoping that Jack would abandon plans to marry Beryl. But Benjamin Thornton underestimated Jack. If Jack wanted to marry Beryl, he wouldn't let her lack of fortune stand in his way. Obviously, Jack had been building up to telling me that, and I had permitted him to string out his story, unable to hear the words he, so far, had been unable to say. But further delay served neither of us.

"Benjamin Thornton has played a brilliant, if devious, game," I began, my voice hoarse with emotion. "But he really doesn't know you if he thinks you would be deterred from marrying a lady just because she lacks a dowry."

"You have always understood me." Jack sounded wistful.

"I do wish you well with Miss Corring," I forced out each word.

"Miss Corring? Beryl Corring?" Jack looked mystified. My spirits soared so rapidly, I held on to the edge of the sofa, just to feel something solid.

Jack collapsed into his chair, shaking his head. "Lord, I've made a muddle of this. The thing is," he began and paused, rubbing his forehead. "The thing is that I made some important decisions while I was riding around those flatlands and bogs—reminded me a little of East Anglia in some places. And when I heard that you were, in all likelihood, not going to marry Brampton, I thought I wanted to tell you, to talk to you about what I had been thinking and I figured you might be planning to leave for England soon, so . . .”

Breathe, Drusilla. Breathe. Don't assume anything.

I concentrated on feeding Medora crumbs of biscuit.

Jack leaned forward, crossing his arms across his chest.

“I really have been drifting ever since I left the army. It may look as if I have some purpose in life, running hither and thither on secret missions for my father, letting people believe that I am rendering valuable service to the Crown.” He shrugged. “But every time I return to London, all I can see are former troopers, just like the men I used to command, ragged, hungry, begging on corners.”

What in heaven's name was Jack talking about? Why was he talking about destitute former troopers?

Medora nudged my hand, reminding me that I had neglected to deliver the next bite of biscuit in a timely manner.

Jack resumed pacing.

“I gave it a great deal of thought.” He paused and looked directly at me. “You know very well that the fourth son of an earl hasn't more than a ha'penny to give to one of those poor beggars. How, in heaven's name, could I be of any help to any of them? I asked myself what useful skills and knowledge I have.” He stopped pacing and looked at the hearth. “A humbling exercise, I assure you.”

He put his hands on his hips and let out a deep breath. “But I'll tell you one thing I know as well as any other living soul. I know horseflesh. I know horses. I understand horses. So *that's* what I'm going to do.”

“You're going to breed horses?” I was trying to make sense of Jack's sudden change of subject.

"Yes, yes. Isn't that what I said?" Jack began pacing again. "I reckon to find some place in the country—just think about it. A horse farm would provide all sorts of opportunities to employ old troopers. But it's not going to be a very fashionable sort of life. For one thing, I'll have to convince my father—and perhaps one or two of my brothers—to invest in the enterprise. And there won't be much time—or money—to spare for London seasons and . . ."

He sat back down and drummed his fingers on the arm of his chair.

"I think that sort of life might very well suit you," I began tentatively.

"But it's not the sort of life that particularly appeals to *you*, I fear. If I had only known before, before I made these plans and came to understand what I want to do with my life. It's difficult to explain. But now that I have committed to this course of action, I am not at all sure I can go back to a life centered on London society and its preoccupations. And I do understand how you would expect to be part of that world. If only Thornton had shown up and told me you weren't going to marry Brampton before I had sorted all of this out. . . . But try as I may, I just can't see how I could even begin to give you the life you were going to have with Brampton and not make you miserable with my own purposelessness. And you wouldn't even be addressed as 'Lady' in the way of compensation."

"I wouldn't have been addressed as 'Lady,' even if Clive Brampton had married me. Not long before the house party, Brampton was informed that he had lost his title. The wild cousin from whom he had inherited, apparently married a Spanish lady and sired a son before getting himself killed. That child has been declared the rightful baronet. You can imagine how shattered a man as proud as Clive Brampton was with that turn of events."

Jack looked at me in disbelief.

I focused my attention on the braid trim of the sofa arm, worrying it with an index finger. "That . . . that is why . . . I couldn't

. . . that afternoon in the library, I just could not bring myself to break off my engagement, because I believed Clive Brampton was depending upon me to see him through his public humiliation. I could not contemplate inflicting what I thought would be another devastating loss on him." I shrugged and tried to smile. "Now, I understand, he has declared that he is renouncing his title to become a citizen of the United States. Ivy is all admiration for his idealism."

Jack hung his head and covered his face with his hands. His voice was low and hoarse. "How I wronged you. How presumptuous." He looked over at the open trunk. "I hope you will find it in your heart—your very generous heart—to forgive me for the accusations I made that afternoon. But I'll spare you the presumption that you would be content to join me in a quiet life in the country."

We sat for a moment in silence: Jack looking wretched; I, unable to find the words to express my joy. Should I just blurt out that I loved him? That I would live with him anyplace? Go with him anywhere? Medora hopped down from my lap and I realized that tears had been streaming down my face, falling on her.

I picked up the folder next to me on the sofa. It wasn't difficult to find the only portrait among all the pictures of trees. I walked the three steps to Jack and handed it to him. He stood studying it for a moment.

"You painted this?"

I nodded.

"When?"

"Well before you arrived in Boston. Before I agreed to marry Brampton."

He tossed his portrait into the open trunk and pulled me into his arms.

"You'll marry me then?"

"Yes! Yes! A thousand times yes!"

Jack held me more closely and started humming a tune—the tune we had waltzed to the night before Constance's wedding. We danced slowly around Aunt Camellia's parlor, weaving around chairs, sofas, and tables.

"You know, I came to Boston only to ask you to marry me," Jack whispered. "Father was going to send someone else to sort out the Corring matter. I insisted only *I* could take care of it." Then, at last, he kissed me, and kissed me, and kissed me.

"Miss Fortesque! Are you all right? I've come for your trunk, but if you need assistance . . ." Jack released me and I turned to see Hez standing wide-eyed in the doorway.

"Congratulate me, my man," Jack said. "Miss Fortesque has just consented to marry me. And I don't believe she will be sailing for England this evening, so you might as well leave her trunk where it is—pending further instructions, of course."

He had the good grace to turn to me with a questioning lifted eyebrow.

"Captain Hatton is correct," I informed the astonished Hez. "Please do inform the master of the *Cerulean Wind* that I will not be sailing with them."

Hez shrugged and departed. No doubt his friends at the tavern he frequented would be hearing a fine tale of the goings-on in the Fortesque household.

July 27, 1818
Aboard Zephyr
The Atlantic

Jack and I were married in Boston one week ago today—just three days after I was to have sailed home alone on *Cerulean Wind*. And it is as well that we boarded our ship directly after our wedding, because I was floating—for sheer happiness.

When the astonished Hez had left us alone, all I wanted was for Jack to hold me, kiss me, and tell me how much he loved me. There was a good deal of that, but I also witnessed what he must have been like as a British officer who is accustomed to ordering, cajoling, and negotiating to reach a desired goal in the shortest amount of time. After having foraged for food and quarters for a ragtag company of troopers chasing Napoleon's army across war-ravaged Spain, acquiring a simple gold wedding ring, a qualified clergyman, and accommodations on a ship bound for England was child's play for him.

The crème silk shot with gold proved to be the perfect choice for a wedding gown—especially since I had finally made the perfect choice of a groom.

There was no time for the ritual of written invitations. We were married in Aunt Camellia's parlor, minus the taffeta bow. Susan Jones stood as my bridesmaid. Benjamin Thornton stood with Jack. Mrs. Prudence made herself the guest of honor, claiming that Jack and I owed our happiness to her anonymous note to Josiah Corring.

Uncle Derrick, of course, gave me away. Aunt Camellia fed a box of bonbons to Medora to keep her well behaved during the ceremony.

In all the flurry around our wedding and departure, I never did find the right moment to tell Jack about, much less show him, Clive Brampton's parting gift to me. I knew precisely what I wanted to do with all those rubies. But I felt the tiniest hesitation broaching the subject with Jack. The rubies represented two things that clearly bothered him: his lack of fortune and my engagement to Clive Brampton.

Then, on the third morning out from Boston, my moment of truth arrived. As Jack and I were having a light breakfast in the sitting area of our cabin, he began to talk of his plans to raise funds for a horse farm.

"Of course, I could always approach my father, but I would rather have an investor or two in hand before going to him—to demonstrate that other gentlemen think it's worth the risk."

"Actually," I hoped that Jack didn't detect the hesitancy I could hear in my voice. "I've been wanting to show you something that might go a long way toward funding a stud."

I reached into the small traveling valise where I had hidden the box containing the jewels and gave it to Jack. He opened it, and his face turned into a mask. My spirits sank.

"I don't have to ask you the source," he said.

"They were a parting gift that Brampton sent with his note of farewell," I explained.

He handed the open box back to me, each bloodred sphere reflecting back the pale morning light.

"I thought . . . just think . . . what they could purchase . . ."

"I want no part of them," Jack frowned. "They are yours to do with as you wish."

Tread carefully, Drusilla. What you say now could determine the happiness or misery of your marriage.

"Whatever I wish?" I said as brightly as I could manage. "Well. I believe I shall buy myself some horses. I imagine these baubles might buy several very pretty horses. I only lack an expert in horseflesh to advise me which horses would make the best investment."

Jack glared at me, but I kept the bright smile on my face.

At last he laughed and gathered me into his arms.

"Jack!" I said, my freshly coiffed hair tumbling around my shoulders. "It's ten o'clock in the morning!"

"Don't fret, my love," Jack whispered. "Medora will give us plenty of warning if anyone approaches our cabin door."

Author's Note

As readers of Georgette Heyer have guessed, the title, *Boston Tangle*, is inspired by *Bath Tangle*, Miss Heyer's tale of mismatched couples sorting themselves out. But let me assure you, the title is meant only as a tribute to Miss Heyer's masterpiece, not as a promise to match her level of artistry. Beyond the title and the general theme of unfortunate matches, no parallels with *Bath Tangle* are intended.

Contemporary Boston bears little resemblance to the Boston of 1818, but tantalizing fragments remain. Of Charles Bulfinch's many architectural contributions to early nineteenth century Boston, the State House, although modified over the years, is the most obvious survivor. The Colonnade, where the Fortesque family lived on what was then Common Street, and is now Tremont Street, was demolished in 1855.

In 1818, the Back Bay was, indeed, a bay. Roxbury and Dorchester were places of country retreat. Summer Street was a residential address. And although important houses were being built on Beacon Hill, Louisburg Square had not yet been created.

The bibliography is provided for anyone who shares my passion for the graciousness of cities past and my sorrow over the destruction of so many architectural gems.

About the Author

After career detours as a receptionist, social worker, psychotherapist, and English teacher, Judith Lown wrote her first traditional Regency, *A Match for Lady Constance* (Montlake Romance), which was set in the world of the London *ton*. Her second novel, *A Sensible Lady* (eFrog Press), took place in the Sussex countryside. *Boston Tangle*, Judith's third novel, is a sequel to *A Match for Lady Constance*, and includes a main character from *A Sensible Lady*. Judith welcomes your reviews of her novels.

Judith Lown lives in North San Diego County, California, with her husband, John, and two rescued dogs: Bingley, a retired racing Greyhound, and Magic, a Scottish Deerhound/Greyhound mix. Judith has always had dogs in her life and is active in Greyhound Rescue.

Bibliography

Andros, Howard S. *Buildings and Landmark of Old Boston: A guide to the Colonial, Provincial, Federal, and Greek Revival Periods, 1630-1850.* Hanover, NH: University Press of New England, 2001.

Bergen, Philip. *Old Boston in Early Photographs, 1850-1918: 174 Prints from the Collection of the Bostonian Society.* New York: Dover Publications, Inc.,1990.

Kirker, Harold. *The Architecture of Charles Bulfinch.* Cambridge, MA: Harvard University Press, 1969.

Kirker, Harold and James Kirker. *Bulfinch's Boston 1787-1817.* New York: Oxford University Press, 1964.

Krieger, Alex and David Cobb, eds., with Amy Turner. *Mapping Boston.* Cambridge, MA: The MIT Press, 2001.

Morison, Samuel Eliot. *The Maritime History of Massachusetts 1783-1860.* Boston: Houghton Mifflin Company, 1961.

Norton, Bettina A., ed. and Ruth Tucker, Patsy C. Boyce, Cynthia D. Fleming, Rebecca Karo, and Henry S. Miller, Jr. *Trinity Church: The Story of an Episcopal Parish in the City of Boston.* Boston: The Wardens & Vestry of Trinity Church of the City of Boston, 1978.

Sammarco, Anthony Mitchell and James Z. Kyprianos. *Then and Now: Downtown Boston.* Charleston, SC: Arcadia Publishing, 2002.

www.ingramcontent.com/pod-product-compliance
Lightning Source LLC
Chambersburg PA
CBHW021002120726
47905CB00009B/2819